Corrupted Temptation

Forbidden Dark Mafia Romance

Kiana Hettinger

By Kiana Hettinger

Corrupted Temptation is the second book in the Mafia Kings: Corrupted Series.

Mafia Kings: Corrupted Series
#0 Cruel Inception
#1 Corrupted Heir
#2 Corrupted Temptation
#3 Corrupted Protector

Your Exclusive Access

Thanks a million for being here. Your support means so much to me.

The best way to keep in touch with me is by signing up for my newsletter – sendfox.com/authorkianah (I promise I won't spam you!) and by joining my readers' group, Kiana's Kittens – facebook.com/groups/KianasKittens

You'll receive bonus chapters, inside scoop, discounts, first access to cover reveals and rough drafts, exclusive material, and so much more!

See you on the inside,
Kiana Hettinger

Author's Note

Nico and Raven's story is like Romeo and Juliet's—only theirs is darker. I learned a lot writing this angsty book. So this one's for everyone who's learning to embrace their dark side, to everyone who already has, and to everyone who's looking for the Romeo to their Juliet.

The brighter the light, the darker the night.

K

Table of Contents

Chapter One

Nico Costa

Isabella never turned her lights off.

Day and night, they always blazed like a beacon. And yet, every window in the three-story red brick house was dark, reflecting the glow of the streetlights outside while shrouding the interior in blackness.

I stared at the wide living room window, trying to see in through the darkness while a prickle of apprehension raised the hairs at the back of my neck.

Gabe stepped out of the car, oblivious to the darkness that was blaring just as bright as any beacon in my head.

"Go around back. I'll take the front," I told him, getting out of the Porsche and slipping the Glock 17 out of its holster beneath my jacket.

The carefree look on his face fell away, replaced by a furrow between his brows as he surveyed the property.

"What exactly am I looking for?" he asked, glancing around at the quiet scene.

Gabe would never question my orders, not out loud. But clearly, he didn't know Aunt Isabella like I did. After all, she never called him to fix the squeaky floorboards in the front foyer, or to do something about the leaky plumbing in the kitchen, or check her lawn for just *one last time* to make sure the racoon had left.

She'd had my number on speed dial since I was sixteen.

"I don't trust anyone else, Nico," she'd said then.

Just a paranoid old woman, I'd thought then.

"There's someone in there," I told Gabe as I scanned the darkness. There wasn't a doubt in my mind. A burglary in any other house was probably just that: a burglary. But not here. Not in a property that belonged to a Costa. Not even a dumbass punk kid would be stupid enough to set foot in here.

Gabe nodded, drawing his gun. He took a wide circle across the front lawn, slipping silently over the dark green grass and then the endless row of ornate stepping stones that led to the backyard.

I waited until he disappeared around the corner of the house before heading straight up the front walk to the double oak doors. They weren't locked. The handle turned easily in my grip.

I flexed the fingers in my free hand. It had been a while since I'd gotten down and dirty. The thought held a certain amount of appeal.

The door squeaked noisily on its hinges as I pushed it open, but the noise didn't bother me. I wasn't in the mood for a game of cat and mouse, so I'd rather the scumbags came right at me.

Inside, the house was quiet. I could hear the rustle of fabric scraping my skin lightly as I moved. The sound of my own careful breathing seemed to pound in my ears.

The back door swung open and then shut. It was Gabe. Right on time.

I flipped the light switch next to the front door, but it remained dark.

I clicked my tongue. They hadn't just turned off the lights. They'd cut the power.

This was no small-time hit.

The shattering of glass burst through the silence. The noise came from the second floor. I crossed the foyer in five steps, gun cocked and ready, watching for any sign of movement from the top of the spiral staircase. Heavy footsteps sounded from further down the hallway, getting louder with every step.

The thud of flesh against flesh. Then a deep, muffled scream. Even muffled, I recognized the voice.

Gabe stepped into the foyer as three dark figures appeared in the spill of moonlight at the top of the stairs. Two of the figures were unfamiliar. Tall and lanky, with the familiar blob-like outline of Matteo wedged between them, and two guns pointed at his meaty head.

"Put the gun down, Costa, or I'll kill him," one of the lanky men said, making Matteo whimper like a child.

I laughed. *"Perdonami, mi amico,* but you just picked the most worthless piece of shit for your shield."

Matteo was family—Aunt Isabella's grandson who spent his days doped and his nights jacking off to Maria Ozawa. No matter how tempting it was, I'd never deliberately get him killed, but relinquishing my gun wasn't an option.

Gabe and I would be dead before it hit the floor.

I raised my gun, taking aim at the guy on the left while Gabe followed my lead and pointed his gun at the guy on the right.

My bluff worked. They shoved Matteo down the stairs and turned to flee, but they were too late. I pulled the trigger and shot

11

my guy dead center in the back of the head. He dropped to the ground as Gabe's guy roared in pain but kept going.

"Get him," I barked.

Gabe went after him, taking the stairs three at a time while I turned my attention past the foyer.

Gabe had swept the house on his way in, but he'd missed something.

Isabella never slept on the second floor.

Dim light spilled in through the dining room window as I crept down the hall. Everything looked pristine. Chairs slotted in on each side of the table, not an inch off. The cream-colored curtains fell loosely from its bronze rod, the knob shaped into the head of a lion. Silver knives gleamed against the reflection of the parlor windows. Across the dining room, the parlor doors were closed—like always.

The parlor was where Isabella spent most of her time, knitting or reading her old smutty romance novels.

I pushed the door open, cursing the heavy curtains that blocked out every bit of light from outside. The room was black, but the coppery scent of blood filled the air.

A dark shadow from behind the door pounced at me, trying to wrestle the gun from my hand. I rolled my eyes inwardly at the poorly-thought strategy.

I kicked out, slamming my steel-toed boot into something bony. It didn't matter where I hit him, so long as it stunned him.

He screamed, and his grip on the gun loosened enough for me to yank it out of his grasp.

Using the sound of his voice as a guide, I spun him around and wrapped my arm around his neck, pressing down on his windpipe. I jammed the Glock into his back, right behind his liver. One wrong move, and the guy was dead no matter what.

"You really are one stupid motherfucker, aren't you?" I seethed while he struggled futilely. He was a big guy—but one whose access to oxygen had been cut off at the throat.

"Let me go," he croaked out, trying to pry my arm away.

I laughed drily. "Of course."

I released his neck, raised my gun above my head, and brought it down in a thudding blow to the back of his head.

He fell like a ton of bricks, hitting the ground with another sickening thud. I glanced at the motionless form in the dark—he'd be out cold for a while. I would have preferred to have done away with him, but I needed to know who ordered the hit. Extracting information, after all, just happened to be one of my areas of expertise.

I grabbed my phone out of my pocket and flipped on its flashlight. Aunt Isabella was sitting in her favorite paisley-printed chair with her knitting needles on her lap. The yellow light touched on her short white hair, the deep creases on her tanned face, and the wide bloom of black-red blood across the bodice of her high-necked gown.

I clenched my jaw and crossed the room to close Aunt Isabella's wide, open eyes. The deep brown of her irises stared back into my own as I scanned her face—the lightest splotch of pink remained on her cheeks, it would soon fade, the only color on her otherwise pallid skin. My eyes landed on the paler skin of the underside of her forearm.

It had been cut.

Mutilated.

Someone had taken a knife to Isabella's soft, wrinkled skin and carved a name into it. A name I knew very well. Everyone knew that name. But not in the way that my family did.

Luca.

Though crudely carved in bloodred scratch, the four letters were unmistakable.

Rage surged through my veins. I covered the marking with the first thing that I could grab—one of Isabella's knitting projects, a scarf. I was on my feet and back through the house in three seconds flat. They'd just declared war. But while they might have fired the first shot, there wasn't going to be a single Luca left standing by the time I was finished with them.

I stuttered to a stop in front of the oak door, slamming it shut. As I circled back, my heel balked mid-turn. Though I shook with anger, some small bit of sense had seeped through the haze. Sense enough to realize this made no sense.

What good did it do the Lucas to wage war on a family they were at peace with?

No territory wars. No battle over supplies. No tussles among men. Not so long ago, it had been Vincent and Lorenzo's most fervent wish to unite our families. I'd been seventeen years old when Lorenzo had tried to marry me off to a Luca. No wedding vows were sworn—the girl had died. I didn't know the kid, but I'm glad there isn't a marriage contract out there with my name on it.

So, if not the Lucas, who murdered and carved up Isabella? The reason, if I was right, was clear. They wanted me to find her, find the carving, and wage war on the Lucas. Though it was no simple task to determine who would benefit from that the most. The Nova family? I'd heard they'd had it out with the Lucas just the other night, though I hadn't bothered keeping tabs on the outcome.

Gabe marched down the stairs, stepping over Matteo's unconscious body. The wicked smile on his face was made all the more sinister-looking by the spray of blood that speckled his chest, neck, and face.

"Mission accomplished, *fratello*," he said.

"Isabella's dead." It wasn't that I wanted to bring down his high, but there was no sense in delaying it. "There's a guy out cold in the parlor. Put him in the trunk, then drag Matteo out and put him in the back seat, *per favore*," I said, then strode outside.

I turned to look back at the house where I'd spent almost every weekend as a kid. Aunt Isabella had been different then. Younger and more vibrant; she'd been devoted to the family and proud of it. Until the life we lived took her husband and her only son. She'd changed then, swearing off everything to do with the family. Everything but me.

I sighed heavily and tried to ignore the faint squeeze around my cold heart. It clearly attested to Aunt Isabella's feeble state of mind that the one Costa she'd kept close was the one the rest of the world was wise enough to fear. But whether she'd tried to distance herself from the family name or not, the Costas took care of their own, in life and in death.

I circled the yard to retrieve the large can of fuel from the garden shed. It was full; I'd been meaning to get around to mowing the lawn but hadn't made it over in a while. Lugging it back around and inside, I set it down next to Isabella's body.

She had her knitting needles with her, probably the most important of her grave goods. I grabbed a couple of the romance novels from the basket by the chair—the most creased ones—and then leaned down to kiss her on the cheek. Grave goods and a kiss of respect for the dead were old traditions. My family had practiced them for decades.

I uncapped the gas can and doused Isabella's frail body in the accelerant. She would never have wanted her body subjected to an autopsy, and not even Gabe could know about the name carved into her arm.

Not yet.

Not until I had answers.

I withdrew the lighter from my pocket, lit the bottom corner of her satin nightdress, and left without a backward glance. At the door, I could already hear the crackle of the flames, but the house was far enough outside the city; it would be some time before the smoke drew any attention.

Back at the car, Gabe stood outside the passenger door, staring at the house. I could see the orange flames reflected in his eyes.

"It's what she would have wanted," I told him before he could ask.

I swallowed down whatever scraps of human emotion Isabella's death had managed to muster up inside me. I couldn't afford to be human.

Not now.

I had a job to do. Soon, I'd have to report what I'd found to Lorenzo. If I couldn't managed to crack open the hostage in the trunk and pull out the truth of who'd sent him by then, what I had to report was going to mean war.

A war that was going to get bloody.

Chapter Two

Raven Ferrari

My muscles were burning.

My lungs were ready to explode.

Sweat dripped from my brow in rivulets.

A fist shot at me. I ducked to my left, ignoring the wave of dizziness that threatened to topple me over. There was no time for weakness. In a blink of an eye, I steadied myself and came back with an uppercut that grazed my attacker's jaw, but it wasn't a solid hit.

He came at me again, but I caught his intention by the direction of his eyes just as he pulled back his arm for the next blow.

This is my chance!

The tender flesh of his armpit was exposed. I ignored the blow coming at me and jabbed. He roared as his fist connected with my cheek, but his punch had lost its power thanks to the pain that now radiated down his side and up his arm. *Yes!*

With my attacker momentarily distracted, I took full advantage; a blow to his ribs, a hard punch to his jaw. His head shot back, throwing off his balance. I leaned away and drew up my leg, ready to send him careening backward.

I kicked, but I wasn't fast enough. He grabbed my ankle and yanked hard, pulling out my other leg from under me and sending me crashing to the ground.

"Damn it!" I roared.

"You're never going to beat me," Vito jeered, moving to stand over me with his arms crossed over his chest. The lights above gleamed off his bald head and cast shadows beneath his dark eyes.

I glared up at him, ignoring the sharp pain in my hip where I'd landed.

"Give up yet, *passerotta*?" he cajoled.

"I'm not your 'little sparrow' or any other freaking kind of bird," I spat.

And then as fast as a… okay, fine, as fast a bird, I shot my leg out, connecting with his ankle and knocking him off his feet. He landed with a hard thud that shook the ground beneath me.

"Ha!" I shot to my feet and turned around in a victory dance. "You're getting old, *caro zietto*."

"I'm not your 'dear uncle' or any other freaking kind of uncle," he said, mocking me with a sour look on his face as he climbed to his feet. But he couldn't fool me. He'd been training me for more than a decade, and all that training was finally starting to pay off. That was *pride* shining in his dark brown eyes.

"Face it, pretty soon you're not going to be able to keep up with me." I preened, tipping my nose in the air as I wiped the sweat from my brow.

"I hate to burst your bubble, *passerotta*, but I was going easy on you," he said, and I had to look closely to see whether he was telling the truth. After living with Vito Rossi for years, I knew when to question the straight face he wore too often.

It looked like he might have been telling the truth—a little bit. But in my defense, I was half his size and still managed to put him on the ground. Not bad, if I did say so myself—even if he had been going easy on me.

In all reality, what were the chances I'd ever need to know all the crap he'd taught me? I was in my third year of nursing college and had no intention of dropping out to join the military anytime soon.

I sighed, staring longingly at the door to the women's changeroom. All I wanted was a shower and some clean clothes, but we'd only been at it for an hour. It wasn't likely Vito would let me off the hook that easy.

"So, what do you say we ditch this joint and go find ourselves some pizza?"

He stared at me with his arms still crossed. I hadn't gotten quite good enough at reading him to know what was going on behind his eyes. So, when he dropped his arms and nodded, it caught me by surprise.

"Really?"

"Go," he said, pointing to the door of the changeroom, "before I change my mind."

I didn't need to be told twice. I hurried out of the room, grabbed a towel from the glass shelf, and stripped my way to the shower.

We had the place to ourselves—Vito paid handsomely, I bet, for his ongoing reservation; three times a week for the past decade—so I didn't have to worry about sharing the space.

Beneath the showerhead, the hot water sluiced away the sweat I'd worked up, soothing my aching muscles at the same time. I sighed in satisfaction.

If I took too long, Vito would be banging on the door and threatening to tear it down. He was a stickler for time—a real stickler. The only thing I could figure was he'd either been a soldier or an alarm clock in another life.

Regretfully, I shut off the taps, wrapped the towel around me, and padded over to the bench where I'd left my clothes. I kept my eyes on the news that was playing on the television on the changeroom wall. A dip in the Nasdaq today—not that it meant anything to me. A string of burglaries on the other side of town—not something I had to worry about with Vito around. No one would be stupid enough to break into the home of a guy who looked like he could bench-press a car.

The pretty reporter rattled off more headlines: a tsunami that had left hundreds of people homeless, a missing kid found safe after a weeks' long search, the death of the matriarch of a suspected New York crime boss, Maria Luca.

Maria Luca.

My mind spun the name around and around as the reporter's voice faded into the background. The lockers in front of me blurred. A numbness had crept its way up my fingertips.

Maria Luca was dead.

The words made no sense. Yet no matter how many times I tried to rearrange them and put them back together, they came out the same way.

Maria Luca, my mother, *was dead.*

I sat down hard on the wooden bench behind me. It should have been hard and cold beneath my skin.

It felt like nothing.

The numbness had crawled its way through my body.

"Raven," Vito's voice called from the changeroom door. It was muffled, just like the reporter's.

I couldn't answer him. I couldn't make my mouth move or find the words even if I could.

A picture flashed on the television screen—a beautiful woman who resembled my mother, just older. Then more pictures. A man who looked like an older version of my father. Three men who were no longer the teenagers from my hazy memory, from when I last saw them.

My breath was coming fast and shallow. I was going to hyperventilate, but I couldn't stop it any more than I could make my mouth move. The whole world was spinning wildly out of control. It had sucked me up in its chaos. Black spots flashed across my vision, speckling the picture on the glass screen.

I leaned in closer, trying to hear the reporter over my pounding heart. Something about a feud, or maybe he said "funeral."

"Raven, I'm coming in there," Vito said. He didn't sound angry, exactly, more like an annoying blaring alarm clock.

If he walked in here, though, and found me just sitting around, ignoring him, he'd kill me. Still, I couldn't muster the will to move. And besides, "dead" didn't seem to mean what it had five minutes ago.

"Dead" didn't mean dead at all, apparently.

The doorknob turned, jarring my spinning world to a stop and bringing my senses back to me.

My mother was dead.

My mother, who'd died eleven years ago, was dead.

My father and brothers, who'd died along with her, were alive and well.

And the person who'd told me they had died: *Vito Rossi.*

Chapter Three

Nico

The stonewalled room was humid, the air thick with the metallic tang of the blood that dripped from the spatter on the walls and ran in rivulets toward the drain on the floor.

Even though the room had been thoroughly scrubbed before, old rust-colored stains speckled the walls and floor beneath the fresh deluge. Layer upon layer, it spoke to the purpose of the room. It told the story of the vile things that had taken place here over and over again.

I dropped my serrated combat knife on the low metal table next to me and stripped off my shirt, using it to wipe the sweat from my brow like a blood-soaked rag. I chucked the rag on the table, the movement serving as a painful reminder that the hostage had gotten a good shot in, leaving a giant black-and-blue bruise across my ribs.

I operated on a principle of strength: I never tied my hostages to a chair. If he could go toe to toe with me, then maybe I wasn't the one who should have been doing the killing.

The guy had given me a name—just like I knew he would. Diego Berlusconi—the name of a middleman, maybe, but not one I'd ever heard linked to the Luca family. Or any other family.

This left me with a dilemma: *Hand over the truth of what I'd found at Aunt Isabella's house to Lorenzo or keep my mouth shut?*

I walked out of the room, leaving the door open behind me. It wasn't like the guy could escape now. Down the hall to the wall at the end, it didn't take me long to find the lever that opened the false wall.

The loud music from above thudded through the ceiling. It was barely after midnight, so it would be hours before Onyx shut down for the night. As much as I would rather have headed up the stairs and out the rear exit to the car waiting in the back parking lot, I turned instead into the second room on the left. I couldn't go wandering around the club floor shirtless and covered in blood. It might have aroused suspicions. I say "might" because a visit to this club had been known to leave more than the occasional cuts and bruises, lashes and rope burns. It all depended on what the club goer was interested in.

Inside the room, a spacious glass-walled shower stood against the opposite wall surrounded by plush sofas and chairs, all arranged for optimal viewing. Fortunately, the room was otherwise empty.

I stripped off the rest of my blood-spattered clothes, pressed the button to start the shower, and stepped beneath the hot spray. It burned like a thousand tiny flames. I welcomed the heat, gritting my teeth and taking it inside me like it could burn away every memory of the past hour, but it never did. No matter how many times I tried to burn or wash it away, the memories were still there.

The screams, the cries of agony, the blood, the torn flesh. Always there. Always threatening to burst free from the deep, dark vault I kept them locked in inside my mind.

And now we were poised for more bloodshed. A war, if I opted to tell my father about the name I found carved into Aunt Isabella's arm.

I was running out of time to make a decision.

Within minutes, all proof of the monster I was had washed away. I stepped out of the shower and wrapped a towel around my waist. I pulled out the spare change of clothing I kept buried in the back of the liquor cabinet against the far left wall. Pants, socks, and an Armani shirt, I'd only just finished getting dressed when my cell phone I'd left on the sofa started to ring. There was little chance anything but a headache waited on the other end of the line.

I glanced at my phone screen. *Lorenzo.*

Make no mistake; my father wasn't in the habit of making social calls. The only time the man ever called was when he wanted something. Still, I snatched up the phone and answered it to stop the ringing, feeling the weight of the decision I had to make like a boulder on my shoulders.

"What is it?" I said, a light pounding growing behind my eyes.

Everyone else cowered before the great Lorenzo Costa. But not me. Maybe that made me braver than most.

Or crazier.

"Maria Luca's dead," he said matter-of-factly. "Murdered in her home."

I paused.

Had my father somehow known about Isabella? Did he have the matriarch of the Luca family killed in retaliation?

"When?" I asked, squeezing my eyes shut against the pressure mounting behind them.

"Two days ago. Word is it was the Novas' doing."

25

My father was many things, but a liar wasn't one of them.

"That's terrible news," I said, keeping my tone neutral.

"The funeral is in two days. I'd like you to attend with the rest of the family."

"I don't see why that would be necessary."

I'd attended enough funerals to last a guy several lifetimes over. Why would I want to go play nice with a bunch of crying strangers? Strangers who I couldn't rule out had been inciting a war with my family.

My father cleared his throat—the first sign he was getting agitated. Lorenzo Costa did not like to be told no. "Vincent Luca was real sweet on his wife, son. He's going to be weak. Vulnerable. Now's the time to make our move."

This night just kept getting better and better. "So, you want me to play nice with the Lucas while we plot to take down their empire?"

Didn't we have enough on our plate at the moment? It wasn't that the families and cartels in the country had ever played nice, but there was less respect these days. Constant battles over territory. Families stabbing each other in the back. The Lucas were one of the few families that my family—if not trusted—then respected, which made it even stranger that the Lucas were behind Aunt Isabella's murder.

"We have always been interested in what the Lucas could offer us," my father prattled on. "You know that, Nico. If events had gone as planned—"

"I would have been hitched to some spoiled little bitch, and you would have had your hands deep in the Lucas' pockets," I finished for him. "I get it. But you're not talking about making deals with the Lucas; you're talking about stabbing them in the back."

It didn't escape my notice that if I was wrong about Aunt Isabella, that was precisely what the Lucas were doing to us.

"What. I'm. Talking. About"—There it was, stage two of Lorenzo Costa's descent into his infamous rage blackouts—"is the opportunity to ensure we stay on top. That is what we *all* want, isn't it, son?"

There was no sense in fighting it. What my father wanted, he got, one way or another.

"Fine, I'll be there with bells on."

"Bells or a noose, take your pick."

If it sounded like my father was kidding, he wasn't. Nobody defied Lorenzo Costa, though a noose wasn't really his style. Having his son tear a man apart, piece by piece... now, that was something Lorenzo enjoyed.

Chapter Four

Raven

It had taken me all of two minutes on our silent drive to my dorm from the gym last night to realize that whatever the truth was, Vito was no villain.

A person could only hide their true nature for so long. After more than a decade, I would have seen it.

He'd taken care of me. He'd sat through ballet lessons, art classes, and parent-teacher meetings. Even now that I was miles away in college, he called to check in with me every day. Those weren't the acts of an evil villain.

Yet I hadn't said a word to him about anything.

I'd sat quietly in the passenger seat of his SUV, dutifully munched on the pepperoni pizza he'd bought, then disappeared into the dorm building and into my room. Here, perched on my bed in front of my laptop, I thought I would find answers. The operative word here being *thought*.

A knock sounded on my door, and it flew open a moment later.

"Hey, Raven," Greta called before she walked right in.

She looked as refreshed as ever, even if we had just finished with a grueling week of midterm exams. But of course, she did. Greta subscribed more to the belief that college was a place to party and get laid rather than an academic institution. Since the woman could ace any test with her eyes closed, she had the luxury of subscribing to whatever belief she wanted.

"Hi, Greta," I glanced back at the news reports on the screen. The same news reports I'd been staring at for hours. My finger hovered over the small X button, but I couldn't force my fingers to click off the page.

"I was worried I'd find you here," Greta said as I stared at the news page on my screen, my pointer finger frozen on the trackpad.

The headline from September 17, 2016 flashed like a neon sign.

"Leovino Luca, Son of Suspected Mafia Boss, Vincent Luca, in Hospital Following Altercation."

"You do know exam week is over, right?" she teased as she leaned over behind me and propped her chin on the top of my head. She sighed while her long, blonde hair hung down like a curtain in front of my face.

"Friend of yours?" she teased, looking at the screen.

"No," I said.

"Well, then, is he single? Because he's—"

"He's my brother."

My breath hitched.

I wasn't thinking straight. Greta had been my best friend since I'd moved to California, but there were things she didn't know about me, like my real name, and who my real parents were, and that Vito wasn't really the head of some small-time security company.

"Umm, what's that now?" she asked, leaning away and plopping down next to me.

I swallowed hard, not quite ready to admit it. I'd read a quote once, *"Better terrible truths than kind lies."*

"They lied." I forced the words past my lips, then tried to blink back the tears welling in my eyes.

"Who lied, Raven?"

"Everyone," I said.

Greta looked at me like I'd lost my mind. Of course, I wasn't making a bit of sense, but instead of trying to explain it, I pulled up the other browser I had open. It was front and center on the page from the day following that horrid night.

Daughter of Suspected Mafia Head Dead After a Tragic House Fire.

"It's me, Greta," I said. I was the dead daughter.

"What are you talking about?"

It was difficult to hear her over the whooshing of blood past my ears. Speaking the words aloud made them real, like tangible things that now floated in the air between us and couldn't be unseen.

I opened my mouth, but no words came out. The reporter had gotten it all wrong. I wasn't even in the house that night. I should have been. I could remember it like it was yesterday.

"Good night, Bullet," I whispered in the dark.

I had just barely closed my eyes when I heard a soft click. The moonlight shone through the window, reflecting against my mother's dark eyes. At that moment, it looked like her irises were underwater, and I could see right through her soul.

"I have a surprise for you, stellina," she said in the dark.

Stellina *meant* little star.

She roused me out of bed, her hold gentle but firm. She drove us to Aunt Francesca's. The drive was quiet, the night was alive. It felt like it was just the three of us—me, my mother, and the moon.

"Ti voglio, tanto bene," she said, kissing the top of my head before leaving.

"I love you too, Mammina," I said.

Aunt Francesca lived alone in a grand, old house that always had fresh flowers around. And she loved to bake. We baked everything from biscotti to tiramisu that night. I watched the bread rise in the oven like I always did. I picked at the hot desserts and burned my finger. I fell asleep in the guest room. An ordinary night.

I shook my head, putting the memory back in its rightful place, at the dustiest corner of my mind. It was always lodged there, niggling at me day and night. It had been an ordinary night. No premonition warning me something was wrong. No prickle tingling down my spine.

I don't even think I thought of my mother that night after she left—all the while she and the rest of my family were dying, burning alive, a few miles away. I should have been there. With my family. Loyalty, in life and in death.

But they weren't dead. They weren't burned alive by a fire that devoured our family home. According to everyone else, I was the one who died. Burned alive.

For one strange ridiculous moment, I contemplated it—it made no less sense than anything else. So, was it possible? *Was I a ghost?* I've seen that movie where the guy didn't even realize he was a ghost. Was that me?

Then I shook my head again, pushed the impossible thought away, and stared at the screen. I was alive, and so was my family. Except for my mother, and I had no idea how to feel about that.

How did one mourn the loss of someone they've already lost?

I'd already grieved for all the moments I'd never have with my mother. Her hugs, her bedtime stories, the mother-daughter talks she and I would never have, the empty seat at my high school graduation. Each moment my mother and I had lost had been like a deep, gaping wound, but over time, those wounds had, if not healed, then patched themselves up. And yet, I could feel them opening up inside me, fresh and bleeding, like she'd kissed me goodbye in Aunt Francesca's foyer just yesterday.

"Raven, talk to me," Greta said, wringing her hands together. It was a testament to just how concerned she was because I'd never seen Greta anything but cool under pressure.

"It's all true," I said, wiping away tears I hadn't realized had escaped. "I lied to you." Maybe that made me no better than everyone else. I'd lied to Greta, just like Vito had lied to me.

"Are you telling me you're the dead daughter of some mafia boss?" There was a nervous edge to Greta's voice. Greta never sounded nervous.

I couldn't blame her, though. It sounded crazy.

"My real name is Sofia Luca," I confessed. "Vito and I moved here after my family died in a fire."

"*Whoever did this is dangerous, passerotta,*" Vito had told me as he bundled me into the back seat of his black SUV. "*And I promised your mother I would keep you safe no matter what.*" He'd then driven us across the country to California. Away from my home, away from the people who had been my whole world. My family, who had carried on without me. They'd kept up with business. Dominic had even gotten married—very recently, according to an announcement in a New York newspaper. Had he thought about me that day? I wondered.

I closed my laptop and stood up for the first time in too many hours. "I'm going to New York, Greta."

I had a father and three brothers who were alive and well. A father and three brothers who I'd thought had been dead all this time, and I wanted to know why.

Chapter Five

Nico

So, this was what hell looked like.

Two hundred weeping, sniffling, red-eyed faces—all Lucas—in the middle of an old cemetery. And here I stood, side by side, with my father, mother, and three younger brothers. We were an island of Costas amid an ocean of sharks—well, *potential* sharks.

Alessandro and Caio, my youngest brothers, whispered under their breath, reciting names and useless facts about everyone here like this was some study session instead of a funeral.

The two liked to pretend they were tough. Their shoulders were square, chins raised, like a man, but beads of sweat rolled down their foreheads. Every now and then, they'd glance to their right, where Lorenzo was. In the face of the almighty Lorenzo Costa, they were globs of modeling clay—malleable, pliant, ready to be molded into any shape or form as Lorenzo wished. I'd take a bullet for any of them, as any of us would. But only Gabe was on my speed-dial.

Lorenzo cleared his throat, and his two youngest sons fell silent.

I'd often wondered what I would do if it ever came to taking a bullet for Lorenzo. Would I do it? The man had been valuable to the Costa family, so the right answer was obvious. But the truth was the man had been a monster who'd beaten his wife and kids every chance he got. One day, shortly after I'd turned fifteen, I'd stepped between him and my mother. I pointed a gun in his face, finger on the trigger.

His face had contorted in rage, just like I'd expected, but then something changed. A light in his eyes that slowly transformed the rest of his face until he looked like a kid in a candy store.

"If you can kill your own father so easily, Nico, I think you're ready," he'd said. "Do well, and I'll never lay a hand on your mother again. Do we have a deal?"

"You keep your hands off all of them, and I'll do whatever you want," I'd bargained instead of pulling the trigger like I should have done.

We'd both held up our ends of the deal, but I couldn't wait to see Lorenzo wiped off the face of the earth.

For now, I stood solemnly with my hands behind my back while the casket that held the Luca family matriarch's body was lowered into the ground. Vincent Luca's face was soaked in tears, and even his second-in-command, Dominic Luca, had a tear streaking down his cheek. The pretty blonde woman next to him held his hand tight, though her eyes were just as watery as everyone else's. Maria Luca was well-loved. That much was obvious.

I wondered how many tears would be shed at Lorenzo's funeral—not many if I had to guess. And my own? Maybe even less. Aunt Isabella would have cried for me, if for no other reason than she'd have had no one left to do her bidding and listen to her prattle on about the "good ol' days." But Aunt Isabella was dead, and even though she deserved a better burial than I'd given her, there would be few tears shed over her passing either.

It wasn't the Costa way. We didn't cry. We didn't weep. Cold, hard, unyielding; those were the traits Lorenzo had instilled in his family.

As the casket reached the bottom, the mourners stepped forward, one by one, with a single long-stemmed rose to drop in the hole. There were so many flowers, there'd be no room for dirt pretty soon. It didn't escape my notice that instead of roses, Vincent Luca, his sons, and the blonde woman had tossed lilies onto the casket.

The Lucas remained there until the roses had been tossed, and the mourners had begun to venture away from the grave site. Only then did Lorenzo step forward, making his way to Vincent Luca. It was the first time I noticed my father's posture wasn't quite what it used to be. The tone of his skin wasn't quite right. *Sallow* was the best way to describe it.

I turned my attention to the brood of Lucas as we approached, watching for subtle shifts in body language, anything that would give them away.

"My deepest condolences, Vincent," Lorenzo said, holding out his hand, then clasping Vincent's hand between his, firm but no warmth.

Lorenzo did not care that Maria Luca was dead. In his defense, though, he wouldn't have given a damn no matter who it was sealed in that casket.

"Thank you, Lorenzo," Vincent replied with a slight catch in his throat. The mildly irritated look in his eyes said he wasn't buying my father's bullshit either, but he conducted himself well.

"If there's anything at all I can do, don't hesitate to ask. And my boys are always here to lend a helping hand," Lorenzo said, motioning to me and then my brothers, ignoring my mother completely. "Old families like ours are a dying breed, Vincent."

"I appreciate the offer, but Dominic has things well under control, don't you, son?" Vincent said, turning kind eyes to his eldest.

Dominic nodded. For the first time in the dozen times I'd met him, he looked anything but under control. It wasn't the hard lines of grief that etched his face that caught my attention. It was the look in his eyes. He looked like his mind was running calculations.

"*Signor* Costa," Dominic addressed my father, eyeing him closely, "do you by any chance have a son named Vito?"

Dominic knew the name of every son, soldier, and associate of the Costa family. So, what was this really about? I kept my gaze on him, trying to read through the storm in his gray eyes.

"No, I don't, son," Lorenzo replied, looking at Dominic like he'd lost a small piece of his mind to his grief.

"A relative, then?" Dominic persisted, drawing a questioning look from even his own father.

An odd line of questioning… unless someone had been murdering his relatives and carving names into their arms too. *Vito Costa?* Would so many letters, crudely etched, fit on a forearm? And why lead the Lucas to a man who didn't exist?

"No relative that I'm aware of, and since nothing happens in my family without my being aware of it, I guarantee you that no such man exists," Lorenzo answered. I could detect the thrum of irritation underneath his words.

"Come," Vincent spoke up, motioning to all the Costas around him. "The repast will be held in my home, and you and your family are welcome, Lorenzo."

Lorenzo nodded and fell into step beside Vincent, leaving the rest of us to follow behind.

A meal at the Luca estate? Could this situation possibly get any more fucked up?

Chapter Six

Raven

The tantalizing aromas of basil, rosemary, and oregano wafted from the door of *Via Carota*. Even standing outside, amid the damp subway and burnt street meat odors of New York, it was enough to make my mouth water. My stomach rumbled quietly in agreement.

"When you said you were going to New York, this wasn't really what I thought you had in mind," Greta said, standing next to me while we peered across the street at *Via Carota* as surreptitiously as possible.

It wasn't really what I had in mind at the time either. "You don't have to be here, Greta. Go back to the hotel room and chill. I'll catch up with you in a bit."

"What? Leave now, and miss out on spying on the real-life cast of *The Godfather* until they catch us and kill us before you have a chance to explain you're really their dead daughter? Pfft," she said, waving her hand in dismissal. "How could I pass that up?"

Maybe she had a point. Spying on the mafia—even if they were my family—wasn't the smartest plan I'd ever concocted. But this wasn't espionage. I just wanted to *see* them.

I'd stood outside the big iron gates to my family's estate for two hours the day we arrived in New York. I couldn't do it. I couldn't walk through the gates, not knowing what I'd find on the other side. So, here I was, trying to scope them out like I was Nancy Drew.

Via Carota was a long shot. It was the same restaurant my parents had taken us to every week for as far back as I could remember. It was the only place I could think to look for them where I could see them all together from a distance.

I glanced at my watch. "Fifteen more minutes and then we'll leave. Deal?"

It was a stupid plan anyway. What were the chances—

Two black SUVs pulled into the restaurant parking lot, and a big guy in a nice suit stepped out from the front passenger seat of each car and opened the rear passenger door.

I was holding my breath. It came out in a whoosh as my father stood up, brushing an errant piece of fluff from his jacket's sleeve. For one brief moment, I saw the gray in his hair, along with the lines etched across his face, that hadn't been there before. Then they disappeared, and all I could see were his warm gray eyes, the strong, confident line of his jaw, the wide chest I'd cuddled against for more hours than I could count. All that I had seen in him as a child.

"Greta," I whispered, though it came out as an unintelligible croak.

I wanted to launch myself across the street and into my father's arms. My father. He was *alive*, right in front of me. Tears stung my eyes, and the lump at the back of my throat made it hard to swallow.

Leo stepped out of the second SUV, and my eyes gobbled up the sight of him until Dominic made his way next to my father. He looked different, but so much the same, and yet, I'd never seen him smile like that. He looked *happy*.

A blonde woman got out of the car next, standing between my father and Dominic. She was pretty—that's what struck me first. And then my father smiled at her. It lit his whole face up, just like it did when he used to smile at me, eyes warm, face aglow with affection.

Something inside my chest broke. I could feel it, like a sharp, clean snap where my heart should have been.

The last thing I saw was Dante standing next to Leo.

I clenched my hands into fists so hard my nails were digging into the palms of my hands.

They were all smiling—even Dante. It didn't look at all like something was missing from their lives.

"I need to leave," I whispered to Greta past the lump in my throat.

"But…" She waved in the direction of my family, but hot tears trickled down my cheeks, and she nodded. "You got it, hon. Let's go."

She turned back the way we'd come, and I tried to follow her, but I couldn't make my feet move. The people who had been my whole world were right there, so close, I would have sworn I could smell the sandalwood top notes of Dominic's cologne.

But I wasn't part of their world anymore. They'd moved on. They'd forgotten about me. They'd replaced me.

The blonde, I knew who she was. I recognized her from the wedding announcement I'd found in the paper. Fallon Douglas; now Fallon Luca, Dom's wife. Sister-in-law to Dante and Leo, and daughter-in-law to my father. Daughter-in-law, but there had been more than polite affection in the way he'd smiled at her. He cared for her. He… loved her? Like his own daughter? Like he had once loved me?

I forced my legs to move, putting one foot in front of the other. Away from here. Away from the place I should never have returned to. I felt like a ghost, returned after so many years dead to find the wounds my absence had caused were long-healed.

People brushed past me, but I kept going. I had no destination in mind. Maybe back to California? I should never have come.

"Raven, talk to me, hon," Greta said, grabbing hold of my forearm to slow my steps.

"How long?" I gasped.

"How long… What?"

"How long do you think it took them to get over me? Or…" I slammed my lips shut.

There was another possibility I hadn't considered.

I stopped in the middle of the sidewalk, then immediately regretted it when the herd of human bodies behind me kept moving. I sidestepped as quickly as I could onto the narrow strip of green space next to the sidewalk.

"They had to have known, Greta."

"Known that you were here?" She looked back like she expected to see the dark heads of my father and brothers amid the crowd of bodies.

I shook my head. "They had to know I was alive."

With every passing second, it made more sense, no matter how much the little girl I'd been screamed in objection. But even if I thought Vito capable of kidnapping—which I didn't—my father would have found me. He had the resources to tear the whole country apart, searching for his missing daughter. But he hadn't

42

found me because he hadn't searched for me… because I was never missing.

My chest hurt so much, it curled me over. I braced my hands on my knees while I fought to draw a full breath.

"They did this," I said when I could force the words out. "They sent me away and made me believe they were dead."

It explained how Vito had taken me but not kidnapped me. He'd only been following orders.

Maybe they'd had a good reason. But it wasn't good enough. No reason was good enough. Not to me. If they'd just sent me away, I could have believed it was to protect me. But to let me believe my whole family had died was reprehensible.

Greta's silence spoke volumes. The look of horror on her face told me all I needed to know.

I wasn't crazy; I was right.

And I was going to be sick.

I looked left and right, my eyes quickly scanning my surroundings. I dashed toward the closest thing to privacy I could find—a narrow alley a few yards away. Garbage bags were stacked up a few feet in, but I wasn't going to make it that far. I dropped to my knees just inside and vomited up everything I'd eaten in the past twenty-four hours.

I could feel Greta behind me. She stood there, blocking me from the view of passersby while she held my hair back from my face.

When my stomach finally relented, I leaned back and wiped the sweat from my brow.

"Raven?" Greta said quietly.

She squatted down next to me and brushed back the wisps of hair that clung to my damp brow.

"I used to wake up screaming, Greta—I still do sometimes. Images of Dominic, and Dante, and Leo engulfed in flames playing behind my eyes. The sounds of my parents screaming in agony ringing in my ears. How could they do that? How could they let me believe that had happened to them, and then tell the whole world I was dead?"

Greta pressed her lips together, her eyes caught up in thought. I prayed she had an answer. Some way to make sense of what they'd done. But she shook her head. "I don't know, hon. I wish I could tell you why, but I don't know."

I didn't know either. But I was darn sure going to find out.

Chapter Seven

Raven

"All right, we're going out," Greta said, throwing a silky black dress at me. It landed on my laptop, covering up the screen.

"Out?" I said, blinking my dry, bloodshot eyes.

"Yes, you know, out the door, beyond the four walls of this hotel room. You've been cooped up in here for the past four days, and as your best friend, it's my job to make sure you don't turn into some housecoat-wearing cat-loving recluse."

"I'm allergic to cats, remember?"

"Ha-ha, very funny. Go get your butt in the shower." She pointed down the short hall to the bathroom. "Onyx. It's a top-notch nightclub five minutes away. We are going there to let sexy men buy us drinks and dance until you're either too drunk or too tired to think."

Onyx? The name tickled my memory. Not that it mattered. "You know I don't drink, Greta. Vito would—"

"You're twenty-one, Raven, and if you haven't noticed, Vito isn't here at the moment," she said, looking around exaggeratedly.

"But—"

She held up her hand and shook her head. "I know you don't drink or date or screw, hon, but you need to do something to blow off steam. I can't fix this," she said, waving at the laptop. "I wish I could, but I can't. But what I can do is help make sure you don't burn out." Greta crossed her arms over her chest.

I had a feeling I wasn't winning this argument no matter how much I persisted. I nodded and uncrossed my legs. My feet tingled after spending so much time in one place, and my brain had taken on a strange, fuzzy quality after four days of searching for answers in front of my laptop screen.

Wait—that's where I'd seen the name "Onyx." It didn't belong to the Lucas—we or *they* were outside their territory—but to another New York family. But I couldn't recall which.

I sighed and wriggled my tingling toes. "I haven't come up with a single thing. No old family feuds that could have put me in jeopardy. No newspaper articles about vendettas against the Lucas."

"The answer's not in there, hon," she said, nodding to the laptop. "I don't know why your family did what they did, and unless you confront them, I doubt you'll ever know. But in the meantime…" She pointed toward the bathroom and cocked a brow.

"You're right."

I hated it when Greta was right. I didn't want to confront them, but I was going to have to talk to somebody if I wanted answers.

And as if the universe was in agreement, my phone rang from the bed next to my laptop. He'd called seventeen times in the past twenty-four hours, so it was really no surprise he was calling now. I didn't silence the ringer this time.

I grit my jaw, steeled my shoulders, and answered the phone. Greta nodded like she avidly approved.

"*Ciao, zietto.*"

"*Dio*, Raven, why haven't you been answering your phone?" Vito barked, though I could hear the tightness in his throat.

I swallowed hard. "I know the truth, *zietto*. I saw the news about *Mammina's*... about Maria Luca's death. The rest of my family is alive."

Vito sighed. "I know, *passerotta*. I'm sorry I couldn't tell you."

"Then tell me now, *per favore*. Help me understand what possible reason they had for convincing their ten-year-old daughter her whole family was dead?" I may have sounded angry, but really, I was begging him. Pleading with him to throw me a lifeline because it felt like I was sinking, a little more every day.

"I can't do that."

A knot formed in the pit of my stomach, and my heart pumped harder. "Can't? Or won't?" Because I couldn't imagine that Vito had been kept entirely in the dark. He must have known *something*.

"You need to stay away from your family, Raven."

But what about me? Didn't I matter in this equation? He had to have some inkling of what this was doing to me.

"They *can't* know about you," he said, his voice thick with sympathy. But I didn't want his pity.

"You're afraid I'm going to waltz up to them and ruin their lie?" I spat.

"That's not—"

"Let me put your worries to rest," I said, throwing my free arm wide. "I promise I will not show up at my family's door. They can keep right on going like I never existed."

It was mostly true. I had no intention of showing up at their door, but somehow, they were going to know I existed. They couldn't just sweep me under a rug and forget me.

"That's not what they wanted, Raven."

"No? What is it they wanted?"

Silence.

"*Arrivederci, zietto*," I said then hung up the phone.

I regretted it right away. Vito wasn't just some stranger who'd whisked me away from my home. He was the man who'd made me spaghetti and meatballs for every birthday. The man who'd kept the bathroom cabinet stocked with tampons and took me shopping for my first bra. The man who used to hound me about homework and then cheered at the top of his lungs the day I graduated. Vito had done everything a father was supposed to do. He was my father. He *is* my father.

I wanted to collapse back on the bed, curl up under the covers—maybe forever—but at the same time, my heart was still pumping hard.

My whole body seemed to vibrate with the need to move, to fight, to do *something*.

"I'm sorry, Raven," Greta said.

I shook my head, trying to shrug it off, but the movement *and* the adrenaline seemed to jar my brain into action.

"The Costa family—they own Onyx, don't they?" It had been in some news headline somewhere.

"I don't really know," she said slowly, her jaw clenching, eyes darting left and right. "Why?"

"An alliance with the Costas was important to my family. I don't know why, but I remember my father talking about it." I'd been instrumental to that somehow, though apparently, not enough to bother keeping around.

"Is that so?" She spoke lightly enough, but there was a furrow between her brow now.

I nodded. "But there's no overlap between them. No appearances at the same places, no border blurring, no joint ventures. Nothing."

"And?"

"And that means they never got their alliance, right?"

"Okay, hon, you've got a look in your eyes that's telling me you're thinking of doing something crazy. And since you never do 'crazy,' it's kind of scaring the crap out of me."

I laughed. It felt good. It was the first time I'd laughed in too long. "I could do it, Greta."

"Do what?"

"Form an alliance—become part of them somehow. Find some way to become valuable to them." I was already running the plan through my head.

"And how exactly do you plan to weasel your way into the Costa family?"

I shrugged. "I'll do whatever it takes."

The details could come later.

I shut my laptop and made my way to the short hall.

"I'll be ready in thirty minutes," I called back over my shoulder.

If Onyx was owned by the Costas, it was entirely possible there were Costas there. Right now. And somehow, one of them was going to help me show my family just how useful Sofia Luca could have been.

Chapter Eight

Nico

Harry Belemonte was the slimiest piece of shit to ever walk the earth.

He'd stab a guy in the back as easily as look at him. More than once, he'd been known to play both sides of the fence.

I held out for months as the grueling search was giving us a whopping amount of nothing for answers. Needless to say, turning to Belemonte left a more than sour taste in my mouth. We didn't have any territory issues with the man, but that wouldn't have stopped him from trying to pit one family against another just for kicks.

I'd walked into the Mirage three minutes ago, and already, I could see half a dozen men, each with a hand in their jacket, moving closer, like hawks circling their prey. They probably thought they were being stealthy about it. I clicked my tongue. I had no patience for incompetence.

The guy behind the bar poured me a scotch while two of Belemonte's whores sidled up closer on the barstools on either side of me. I kept my gaze straight ahead.

"Shoo," Belemonte said, waving at his girls and taking the newly-vacated seat himself. He'd been hovering inside the office door across the club for the past two minutes—he probably thought I hadn't noticed that either. "And Edoardo, what are you doing pouring my friend here the usual stuff? Only top-shelf for *Signor* Costa," he admonished, then waited while the bartender reached for a bottle of top-shelf scotch, poured out two glasses, and placed them in front of Belemonte and me.

"To what do I owe the pleasure… What shall I call you? *Signor* Costa seems so formal, does it not?"

"Nico is fine," I said, gripping hands with Belemonte. It was hard to ignore the slimy feeling he left in my palms. "I'm just looking for some information."

He tipped back the scotch then smiled. "What kind of information, Nico?" He cocked an eyebrow while doing a piss-poor job of signaling surreptitiously to his men to stay put. They'd crept closer since Belemonte sat down, now forming a rough semicircle around the bar.

"There's been a death in the family," I said, gauging his response.

He'd heard about Aunt Isabella's death, no doubt. What I wanted to know was how he'd respond when confronted with it. Would he flinch? Would his shoulders stiffen? Would something dark and sinister pass through those beady eyes? Snakes communicated via their body language after all.

"I did hear about that," he said smoothly. "Two deaths, if I heard correctly."

I shrugged. "Some deaths matter more than others."

In truth, Matteo wasn't dead. Though he was a waste of space as far as I was concerned, he was still family. He was under lock and key at the moment, just in case whoever had called for the hit wanted to finish the job.

Belemonte laughed. "It would be so much easier if we could choose our relations, wouldn't it?" he mused while he held up his hand for another round. "But I'm afraid I didn't know either of the deceased, so I'm not sure what information I can give you."

"You're a man with plenty of ears to the ground, Belemonte. I was hoping you'd caught wind of any chatter about the person responsible."

I would never trust any information that came from him. All I was looking to do was ascertain what role he'd played—if any. If he did anything to hint in the direction of the Lucas, that would put him at the top of my list.

"No chatter, I'm afraid. And I can't think of anyone who would go to the trouble of murdering an old woman in her own home," he said with a shake of his head and a frown that I would've loved to punch off his face.

You would, you son of a bitch. Everyone knew it. Belemonte would have his own mother murdered in her bed if it served his purposes. But nothing about his demeanor said he was lying when it came to Aunt Isabella. Too bad, really. Just looking at the guy made me want to bury a knife hilt-deep in his gut. Worse than a useless waste of space, Belemonte wreaked havoc everywhere he went. I was looking forward to an excuse to put him in the ground.

I nodded, flipped some bills on the bar for the drinks, and stood up.

"There is one thing I can do for you, Nico. Just a small show of how useful a relationship between us could be," he said, snapping his fingers.

One of his goons appeared at his side and handed me an envelope.

"You'll have to come back and visit me," Belemonte said, climbing to his feet. "I never got to know your father as well as I would have liked. With him getting on in years, I wouldn't want to make that same mistake with his son."

I tried to hide my grimace as I shook his hand and left the Mirage, the envelope shoved inside my coat pocket.

It took the entire drive across town, to a club that wasn't filled with ten-dollar hookers, to shake off Belemonte's stink. I exhaled loudly, the stench filling my nose. Save for crossing Belemonte off my list of suspects, I was no further ahead than before I'd walked in the Mirage.

Inside the club, the music blared while throngs of bodies gyrated beneath strobe lights to the techno-beat. The tables scattered around the edges of the floor were littered with more bodies, some of them watching with drinks in hand, others engaged in intimate conversation. Most of the girls who worked out of the club weren't on the floor, which meant they'd already found their Johns for the night. Our girls, unlike Belemonte's, were well-cared for and paid well. In return, they offered their patrons top-notch service. We had girls to cater to every whim, from the mundane to the extreme, and seldom had there been an unsatisfied customer.

As I glanced around, Caio shot his hand in the air from a table across the floor, flagging me down. All three of my brothers sat around the table with empty shot glasses in front of them. Sandro and Caio were laughing, but the look on Gabe's face was grim. Whatever had my two younger brothers in good spirits, Gabe was not sharing in their mirth.

The urge to leave Gabe to his misery was potent, but I ignored the fresh pounding in my head that had picked up the beat of the music and strode across the floor to their table.

"Sit down, Nico. We've got news," Caio said before I could open my mouth while he rubbed his hands together in anticipation.

Gabe rolled his eyes and signaled to Tommaso to bring a fresh round.

It only took Tommaso one look to know what right drink to serve. The outdated suits and slicked-back hair made him look like an accountant, but he was a mind reader if I ever saw one.

"So, what's the news?" I asked, taking a seat in one of the hard-backed chairs.

Sandro's eyes lit up like he'd found the Holy Grail. Maybe I'd misjudged him. He wasn't a blob of modeling clay; he was more like an excitable Chihuahua.

"We've got news on the Lucas," Caio said, dropping a thin file folder down on the table. "They got approval for a casino a couple months ago."

It was a little late in the game to be moving into the casino business. The Costas already had three casinos in full operation, but it was still a smart move for the Lucas. I cocked an eyebrow, waiting for either Caio or the Chihuahua to go on.

They both looked at me with wide, expectant eyes. Caio was starting to look like a beagle.

Gabe sighed. "They've gotten approval for the casino, but with Maria Luca's death, they've just started moving on getting the building underway," he explained in a tone that said he wasn't any more impressed by the find than me.

"So, that means we can block them," Sandro said. "Dad's got dirt on every government official within a three-hundred-mile radius. He calls in a favor, and the Lucas are neck-deep in sorting out paperwork for the next three months."

"And?" I crossed my arms over my chest.

"And… what?" Caio said, exchanging confused glances with Sandro. "While they're distracted, we slip in and scoop up whatever they don't have eyes on."

"If you try to block them after they've already gotten approval, don't you think they're going to wonder who was responsible for it?" I sighed, trying to rub out the pounding ache in my temples. "And even if they were too stupid to question that, it would be their lawyers tied up in paperwork for three months. Not Vincent Luca. Not Dominic or his other sons. And not the hundreds of men who might notice when you waltz in and try to lift their product or steal their business."

Caio's face fell. "But—"

"But nothing. It's a dumbass plan."

No need to mention I wasn't taking part in it even if it hadn't been. I'd yet to find who'd put out the hit on Aunt Isabella, and my gut told me it was not the Lucas.

"*Grazie, fratello,*" Gabe said, running his fingers through his shaggy, dark hair. "That's what I've been trying to tell them for the past half hour."

The table grew quiet as Tommaso set four drinks down in front of us—a whiskey, neat for me. *Perfetto.* We nodded our thanks, and Tommaso returned to the bar.

"So, there's no way we can use this?" Sandro looked at the folder on the table and then at me like I'd told him I just killed his dog—

which Sandro didn't have. No animals growing up because Lorenzo had no use for them.

It was at times like this that I almost felt something akin to guilt for the way I thought about him and Caio. Neither of them were even old enough to legally drink, and here they were, trying to figure out how to take down an empire, all to impress our un-impressable father. They should have been chasing tail and getting drunk at frat parties, or whatever the hell it was normal nineteen-year-olds did.

"No," I said, sweeping the file folder off the table and flagging down a waitress to throw it out.

"So, what now?" Sandro asked with his arms crossed over his chest and a scowl on his face, but there was a nervous glint in his eyes. Yet another failed attempt to impress Lorenzo Costa.

"Go on, get out of here," I said to the three of them together. "I'm working an angle, and I'll let you know if it pans out."

I needed to buy more time, and my brothers needed a night off from worrying about impressing Lorenzo.

Gabe got to his feet and headed for the door. Without question, Caio and Sandro tailed behind him.

We were not stealing business from a grieving widower. Not until I'd gotten to the bottom of Isabella's murder. If I was wrong about the Lucas, then the man was fair game.

I signaled Tommaso for another drink and leaned back in my chair as the three made their way through the crowd.

A distraction was what I needed. Something to take the edge off after dealing with Belemonte and my brothers' *proposal.* I glanced around the room, taking in the usual sort of women who frequented the club. I spotted a group of three whose brand-new purses looked freshly bought with Daddy's Credit Card. If they knew what went on downstairs, they wouldn't touch this place with a ten-foot bedazzled pole.

I considered the women who worked downstairs. They did the job well; clean, easy, and simple. Exactly what I needed right now.

And then I saw *her*.

A dark-haired beauty who stood alone across the floor in a dress that skimmed all of her curves. Her lips were painted in bloodred. Her ebony hair fell loose in waves down her back. Her sapphire eyes blazed even from afar.

She looked left and right, tucking a wayward strand of hair behind her ear every now and then. She shifted the weight of her legs from one foot to the other.

A kitten in a den of lions.

Her eyes roamed over the crowd, like she was searching for someone. Maybe a friend she was meeting? Her eyes met mine. A split between a second. Her lips parted just a little. I could imagine the tiny gasp that she let slip.

I stood up and crossed the floor of gyrating bodies toward her. She didn't look away, but she looked more like a deer caught in strobe lights than anything. A small smile touched my lips. As I came closer, something seemed to tick at me. *I feel like I've seen her before.* My memory was reliable because I needed it to be, but I couldn't place her anywhere. It was strange. A man just didn't forget this kind of beauty.

When there was only a finger's difference between us, she flashed me a smile that made the hardness growing in the middle of my legs harder to ignore.

Chapter Nine

Raven

He was like a jungle cat with its eyes on its prey, stalking forward with jaws wide open. At least, that's what it felt like. In reality, the man coming toward me was the most handsome man I'd ever seen. Tall, broad-shouldered. Even dressed in a suit, it was clear he was all chiseled planes underneath. He had short, dark hair with just enough length to it to look perfectly styled. His emerald eyes somehow seemed to be penetrating through me.

And he was heading straight for me. Maybe it would have been less intimidating if he'd actually been a jungle cat. I'd feel no less urge to turn around and run, but at least I wouldn't have felt like a fool for doing it.

I had no doubt this was not a good idea. In fact, it was the worst idea. About as good an idea as hopping into a shark tank with bloody fish tied around my neck. Nico Costa. A knife was his weapon of choice. He'd used it to carve up dozens of men, maybe hundreds.

He stopped right in front of me, not so close he was touching me, but close enough I could feel the heat radiating from his body. It should have repulsed me. It should have scared the heck out of me. It should *not* have been sending a strange tingling sensation through my body.

"You look lost, *signorina*," he said, throwing me for a loop.

"I'm exactly where I want to be," I crooned then cringed inwardly. Maybe I was pulling up my inner Greta better than I'd thought.

He flashed me a grin that made my insides clench. "I'm glad to hear it," he said. "I'm Nico."

"I'm Raven," I told him, ignoring the strange breathiness in my tone.

He smiled a lopsided grin that would have had Greta dropping her panties. Then he nodded toward the bar and started in its direction.

Was I supposed to follow like a dog behind him? I wondered incredulously. I glanced around, trying to find Greta, and there she was across the room, giving me the thumbs-up as a tall, sandy blond pulled her onto the dance floor.

Nico flagged down the bartender and signaled for the man to bring us two drinks. Greta had said it was douchey for a guy to order for his date, but was I supposed to object? Insist on ordering my own drink? Then again, what was I supposed to order? *Piña colada, virgin. Like me.*

The bartender returned with a whiskey glass half-full of amber liquid for Nico and a wide-brimmed stemmed glass full of orangish liquid that he placed in front of me.

"It's a sidecar," the bartender explained before I could open my mouth to ask. "An excellent cocktail for newcomers to darker alcohol," he added matter-of-factly.

"Tommaso here is a bit of a genius when it comes to drinks," Nico explained with a grin. "Hasn't gotten one wrong yet."

Praising the bartender? That didn't sound much like a murder-y thing to do.

"Thank you, Tommaso." I smiled at the too-intuitive bartender then took a sip of the strange drink. A very good drink, in fact. Orange and lemon flavors with a faintly floral undercurrent.

Nico took a sip of the amber liquid in his glass, but I could feel his eyes on me. His gaze was so hot, it prickled my skin and sent tingling sensations down my spine. *Holy crap*. This guy was way out of my league. I needed an easygoing—less lethal—Costa to pull off my charade.

The problem was, I didn't want to leave. I'd never been in a nightclub with the sexiest man alive sitting next to me, looking at me like I was exactly what he wanted.

"You're not from here, Raven," he observed while desire pulsed hot and heavy through my veins.

"No, I'm not," I answered.

It scared me a little—feeling attracted to this man. I'd always kept guys at arm's length before because of Vito. And I had a feeling Nico was exactly who Vito was warning me about.

"Does that mean you're here for business or pleasure?" The way his lips wrapped around that last word sent a fresh rush of arousal through me.

I gulped back the rest of the fruity orange drink.

"For pleasure, of course."

A complete and total brain meltdown, maybe.

He smiled like the devil himself, but then it vanished.

"Where is it you're from?" he asked, calm, cool, and collected like there weren't sparks snapping in the air between us.

"California," I replied, a little dazed.

The smile peeked through again, but disappeared just as quickly. "And what is it you do in California?"

"I'm going to school to become a nurse."

His eyes grazed over me, and the smile made a reappearance. "I imagine you'd make one hell of a nurse."

If he was trying to keep me off-balance… Wait, that was exactly what he was doing. Sex personified one second, and the next, chatting me up with boring questions. But why?

"Why are you doing that?"

The words slipped out of their own volition, but it was too late to take them back. Worst case scenario, he left and I went back to looking for the Costa I was supposed to find here.

Or he gets mad and cuts you up into tiny pieces, a voice whispered from the back of my mind, sending a cold shiver down my spine.

He smiled. Not the devilish smile, but one that actually held a modicum of respect. "You're not like other women, are you, Raven?" he seemed to muse aloud.

"I don't know," I confessed. Was that a stupid thing to say to a dangerous man?

But instead of watching the fire in his eyes fizzle out, it seemed to burn brighter.

He opened his mouth and shut it as he turned his head toward the right. Something had caught his attention out of the corner of his eye.

I turned my head to see whatever gorgeous blonde he was checking out—a wave of relief should have washed over me, not a flood of disappointment.

Then I froze.

A lone man stood across the floor, almost exactly where I'd been just a few moments before. Not just any man.

My brother.

Dominic Luca.

Chapter Ten

Nico

Dominic Luca. At the Onyx. What the *fuck?*

What I wanted to do was grab Raven's hand and lead her to one of the empty suites downstairs where lavish four-poster beds and Persian rugs awaited.

"I'll be right back," I told her instead. *Merde.*

I knew it was a long shot that I'd get anything useful out of Dominic. Still, this wasn't an opportunity I could pass up. Not even for the dark-haired beauty who had the zipper of my jeans bursting at the seams.

She nodded, freeing the dark lock of hair that she kept tucking behind her ear. It had quickly become my favorite lock of hair ever— if such a thing were possible. Long and silky, with absolutely no intention of ever being tamed.

Dominic spotted me the moment I stood up, but he stayed where he was.

I never mixed business with pleasure.

I watched him as I crossed the floor. His spine was straight, shoulders back, but the even jut of his chin told me he wasn't looking for trouble.

"It seems you've wandered awfully far from home," I said with a wry grin, motioning for him to take a seat at the empty table next to where he stood. I sat down but didn't bother signaling for Tommaso to bring a round of drinks. Dominic Luca wouldn't be staying long.

"I have," he said matter-of-factly, taking a seat. "From one wolf's den to another, it seems." He returned the wry grin, but then his face settled into the unreadable mask we all wore so well. "I came to ask you a question."

"Ask away," I said.

"At my mother's funeral, I asked your father about someone—"

"Vito Costa," I filled in.

"Yes." He had a grim smile on his face as he spoke. "Your father said no one by that name existed." He said it more like a question than anything.

"But you were hoping I might know someone he didn't? Or were you hoping he was lying, and I'd offer up the information you wanted on a silver platter?" I offered.

He scoffed. "When you put it that way, it doesn't sound very good, does it?"

I eyed Dominic closely, his gray eyes met mine—the storm brewing beneath them was not difficult to see.

"Look, it's important, Nico. I wouldn't be asking if it wasn't. And if it's of any assurance, I don't think it has anything to do with your family. But with mine."

I cocked an eyebrow.

64

"My mother said the name just before she died. I was hoping…" He trailed off, looking more defeated than I'd thought a Luca could look.

I could string him along. I could use his desperation a hundred different ways. It's what Lorenzo would do.

"I'd never heard the name before, so I looked into it after your mother's funeral. There's no record of a Vito Costa in our family," I said.

"Thanks, I appreciate it," Dominic replied, a note of sincerity in his voice.

The gratitude was earnest, but so was the look of hopelessness in his eyes—which told me all I needed to know.

The Lucas had played no part in Isabella's murder. Even if he'd had the balls to walk in here, plotting behind my back, there would have been no gratitude. Dominic would be just as busy reading me as I was reading him.

"I'm sorry I couldn't be more helpful, *amico*," I said, getting to my feet to put an end to the conversation.

"I appreciate you taking the time, nonetheless," he said, standing up and extending his hand.

I shook it then waited for a moment while he headed for the door. Then I turned my heel and headed back to my original seat.

Raven still sat at the bar, with her long legs crossed and her back to me, sending blood pumping all the way down. The dress had been a painful tease—it was open all the way to her tailbone in the back, driving my imagination wild.

When I slid back onto my barstool, something about her was different. She was paler than she'd been, like she'd seen a ghost. She stared down unseeing into the empty glass she held clutched between both hands. Slim, innocent-looking hands, somehow. No rings, no color on her nails.

The wayward lock of hair had escaped its confines, but she made no effort to tuck it behind her ear. My fingers itched to do it for her.

"You're nervous," I noted, tucking the wayward strand back.

Raven did not strike me as the kind of girl who made a habit of prowling for men in nightclubs. Is that what had her on edge?

"Yes," she admitted, sending a fresh onslaught of electricity through my veins.

"Why are you nervous?" I asked, putting my hand on her thigh, just above her knee.

Her aquamarine eyes shot up to meet mine, but she made no move to swipe my hand away. Instead, her breath came faster and her pupils dilated.

"Because of you," she confessed, though her eyes widened just enough to tell me she hadn't meant to be honest.

"I make you nervous?" I inched my hand higher, sliding beneath the hem of her dress; her satin skin seemed to sizzle under my touch.

She looked down at her thigh and nodded, making my cock throb harder.

"Does it make you nervous to know that I'm going to have you on my bed, on your knees, before the night's over?" I inched my thumb higher, grazing her inner thigh.

Her gaze shot up to mine once again while two pink splashes of color appeared across her cheeks, instantly becoming my favorite color. Nervous or not, everything in her eyes was screaming yes.

"Nico—"

I put a finger to her lips then leaned in until my lips brushed her ear. "The next words out of your mouth had better be, 'I want you to fuck me,'" I whispered, feeling the way her body began to tremble.

She nodded, then swallowed hard. "I want that," she whispered, barely audible above the music.

I shook my head and stilled my hand against her thigh. "That's not what I said."

The pink splashes across her cheeks darkened more, but I could feel the energy leaping off her skin like sparks.

"I want you to fuck me, Nico," she said, meeting my gaze dead-on. Her pupils were dilated, narrowing the bands of pale blue that seemed to stand out in even starker contrast to the dark centers.

I stood up and took Raven's hand to pull her to her feet.

"Your place or mine?" I asked, pulling her close so I could feel the soft curves of her body.

"Mine," she said with no hesitation.

"Then lead the way, *signorina*," I said, hanging back just a little to watch the sway of her hips as she walked. This girl was going to be one hell of a ride.

Chapter Eleven

Raven

Nico, then Dominic. This night was *not* going as planned.

Nico Costa wasn't supposed to swoop in. My brother wasn't supposed to waltz into the club. And I sure as heck wasn't supposed to be bringing one of the deadliest men in the country back to my hotel room.

"*Whatever it takes,*" I told Greta, but suddenly that phrase had taken on new meaning. Was I prepared to offer myself up to the man sitting next to me in the driver's seat of his shiny black car? For a brief moment tonight, after seeing Dom, all I'd wanted to do was run to him and wrap my arms around him. But then he'd looked at me. Not a real look, just a passing glance, really.

If he recognized me, if there'd been the slightest glimmer of recognition in his gray eyes, I would have done it. I'd always had a weak spot when it came to Dom. It seemed even after more than a decade, that hadn't changed.

But his eyes never swiveled back. Nothing about me had struck a familiar chord. Even Dominic had forgotten me. The truth hurt, but not for long. I'd let the anger consume it, swallow it up, and turn it into something harder.

Then Nico had returned, and he'd ignited a different fire inside me, a fire that was far scarier than the heat of the rage I nurtured in the center of me. This man was like a wildfire, consuming everything in his path.

But every inch of my body was screaming yes. When he touched me, when he whispered in my ear, it sent arousal coursing through my veins like nothing I'd ever experienced. Even now, the air between us snapped with tension. So much so I was afraid if I lit a match, the whole car would combust.

He slowed the car as we approached the parking lot of the Hilton hotel. There were only five miles between the club and the hotel, but had we traveled so far already?

He slipped into an empty parking space and turned off the engine.

It was silent. No purr of the engine. No horns or sirens in the distance. Just the sound of our breathing. His was slow and steady. Mine was not. My breathing was coming a little shallower than usual, making me feel a bit light-headed.

But in the end, it wasn't Nico who broke the silence.

"Come up?" I asked him. The words came out thick and sultry; I barely recognized my own voice.

Heat flashed in his eyes. He nodded, climbing out of the car and coming around to open my door. My hands were shaking so much I probably couldn't have opened the door. And just to make sure there was no way to keep my nervousness to myself, he took my trembling hand in his and led the way to the hotel's entrance.

Inside, he headed straight for the elevator and pressed the button. There was no one around but a receptionist behind the main desk, but I kept my eyes glued to the floor. She had to know what we were doing, standing hand in hand, waiting for the elevator at two in the morning.

The moment the elevator door opened, I fled inside, still hand in hand with Nico beside me, and pressed the button for my floor, trying to escape the woman's knowing stare. But if I'd hoped to find a reprieve inside the four gleaming mahogany walls of the elevator, I was wrong.

The moment the door closed, he lunged. His free hand was on my hip in a flash, holding me still for him. He slammed the hand he still held over my head and pressed my back hard against the wall with the weight of his body.

He took my lips hard and fast. Not gentle. No beseeching me to open. His kiss demanded my lips part for him, and they obeyed. But instead of delving in, he traced my parted lips with the tip of his tongue, and my body jolted in response. He was doing it again, one moment forceful, the next teasing.

He pressed his body harder against mine, molding my softer frame to his hard planes. I could feel the thick, hard length of him against my abdomen, making my insides clench while warning signals went off in my head. I had no real-life gauge by which to judge, but he was big enough it made me more than a little worried.

He gave me no time to flesh out my apprehensions when all of a sudden, he delved between my parted lips, sliding his tongue along mine. He tasted like whiskey, and it went straight to my head.

He stretched my hand up higher above my head, making me arch into him, pressing harder against him as his tongue glided in and out of my mouth. My breasts felt heavier, and my nipples sent tiny shockwaves of electricity down a line that seemed to travel straight to the apex of my thighs.

His wildfire was consuming me.

It scared me because I'd never felt so out of control. His body, his lips, even the way he held my hand pinned above me; he was the one in control here. He was bigger than me, stronger than me. He could do anything he wanted to me, and that sent a shiver of fear down my spine. What was worse than the fear, though, was that I was quite sure that nothing had ever excited me more.

Without warning, he pulled away, tearing his lips from mine, though he remained so close I could feel the warmth of his breath against my cheek.

"You don't have to be nervous, Raven. I don't bite," he said, meeting my eyes dead-on.

I swallowed hard as he leaned in closer until his lips were right next to my ear.

"Not unless you ask me very, very nicely," he whispered.

My whole body jolted from the shock of his words, from the brush of his lips against my ear, from the image his words conjured in my head.

The elevator stopped.

The door slid open.

He took a step back, leaving my body cold and bereft of the hard planes that had pressed against it. He let our hands fall between us as he stepped off the elevator and pulled me out with him. I stared at the big hand enveloping mine as we walked down the long hall to the door at the end.

The moment I stopped in front of my hotel room door, he dropped my hand and reached for my hips. Instead of pulling me to him, he pushed me back up against the door, crushing me with the weight of his body until I could feel every groove of the grain in the wood behind me.

"Nico," I breathed.

His lips captured mine, demanding obedience once again. When I parted for him, there was no teasing this time. His tongue met mine, sliding in and out like a promise or a warning of things to come.

I reached for him as that thought sent a fresh tidal wave of arousal coursing through my veins. I grabbed onto his shoulders like I could use him to hold me upright even though he pressed his body so hard against mine, I couldn't have wriggled out if I'd wanted to. The muscles of his shoulders flexed and bunched beneath my grasp, hinting at the hard planes and rippling muscle I'd find beneath his clothes.

He tore his lips away and lunged for my neck, forcing my head back and leaving my throat exposed for his onslaught. He kissed his way down my neck as I explored every inch of his arms and back I could reach. Every so often, I could feel the slight nip of his teeth against my flesh, and I had to squeeze my thighs against the throbbing arousal that had already left me soaking wet.

"I want to hear you screaming my name, Raven, not whispering it," he said against my skin then continued his path down lower to where the neckline of my dress exposed just the upper swells of my breasts.

I held my breath, silently hoping he'd move lower. The backless dress didn't allow for a bra, so the only thing between his mouth and my bare flesh was a thin layer of fabric. But just when I'd thought he might, he leaned away, just enough to meet my eyes.

"I want you n—"

Ring. Ring.

"Fuck," he cursed.

He kept his body pressed against mine as he retrieved his phone from inside his jacket.

"What?" he snapped, then continued to run his lips along my flesh in a teasing trail across the neckline of my dress.

I couldn't make out more than a faint murmur from the voice on the other end of the line. After a moment, Nico shut his phone off and groaned against my skin.

My whole body sagged with disappointment because I knew what was coming.

"I have to go," Nico said, kissing a fast trail up my neck and then settling his lips over mine one last time.

I'd expected a brief parting kiss, but once again, he threw me off-balance when he wound his fingers in the hair at the nape of my neck, holding me still while his tongue explored every inch of my mouth.

Then he released me without a word, turned, and strode away, back toward the elevator. But instead of pressing the button to call it up, he bypassed it and threw open the door to the stairs next to it. And then he was gone.

Only then did I notice the middle-aged couple standing outside their door at the opposite end of the hall. Their hands were twined together while they stood there staring at me.

My cheeks grew hot as flames as I scooped up my purse I'd dropped on the floor at some point. With shaking fingers, I dug out the key card to my room and disappeared inside, slamming the door shut behind me.

I sagged against the door, hoping it would help to cool my overheated body. But the wood grain against my skin reminded me too much of the way Nico had me pressed up against it on the other side. I pushed away from the door, when I realized what an absolute idiot I'd been.

I dropped my purse onto the coffee table then padded down the hall to the bedroom and flopped back on the bed, most definitely not thinking about what could have happened right here. I was the one who was supposed to have been doing the seducing. I was supposed to be the one getting a Costa wrapped around my finger. And the Costa wasn't supposed to be Nico Costa.

I squeezed my eyes shut and proceeded to beat myself up over my stupidity for the next twenty minutes. Eventually, the truth slipped through. Nothing had happened, not really. I'd made a mistake. It wasn't like I was the first woman to fall victim to Nico's appeal; I was sure of it. All I had to do now was learn from my mistake and not let it happen again.

I couldn't help but wonder how the night would have gone if that phone didn't ring.

Chapter Twelve

Nico

I was going to murder everyone—the guy who called me and the guy who murdered Abruzzo. The guy who sold him his gun. Hell, the guy who worked in the factory that had made the gun. *Everybody.*

I was so *close*; every thrum of the throbbing in the middle of my pants was a reminder of where it wanted to be instead. Yet here I was, driving away in the opposite direction because some son of a bitch had to murder some guy's family then burn his house to the ground. The meathead couldn't have done it the other day, or even waited until tomorrow.

Someone was going to pay for this.

I pulled up behind the club, parked right outside the exit, and stormed in through the back door. Gabe paced back and forth behind the wall, looking more frazzled than I'd ever seen him.

"It was the Lucas," he spat the second I pulled the false wall closed.

"What are you talking about?" I hissed, glancing around to see if we had company. Fortunately, it was just the two of us, aside from the unconscious man tied to a chair who looked like he'd been beaten by a mob of *Twilight* fans.

"It was right there on the fucking front lawn, Nico. A goddamned blazing *L* right there. What the hell else could it mean?"

If there was ever a man I could trust, it was Gabe. If Gabe knew the truth, he'd be forced to choose between his loyalty to our father and me.

"Calm down, Gabe," I said, as my mind searched for a way to neutralize what had just become a very volatile situation.

"What do you mean, 'calm down,' Nico?" he said, waving a hand in exasperation. "You know what this means, don't you? Dad was right. We should have been going after them all along. Hell, we should have put a bullet in every one of their foreheads."

If there was one thing I wasn't willing to do, it was to admit that Lorenzo Costa had been right about anything.

"Gabe, just take a breath," I said, scrubbing my hands through my hair.

It was clear that I only had two options left. *Come clean, or go to war.*

My mind flashed back to the look on Dominic's face tonight.

"What the hell is wrong with you, Nico? Don't you want to make those bastards pay?" Gabe asked, throwing his arms wide.

I sighed. "*Sì*, I do. I want to make the bastards pay. But I want to make the *right* bastards pay."

Gabe stared at me wide-eyed, trying to make sense of my words.

"It wasn't the Lucas," I supplied.

"What do you mean, it wasn't them? Of course, it was. I saw it, Nico."

"It wasn't them. Just like it wasn't them who carved their name into Isabella's arm either." I confessed what I'd been keeping to myself for months.

76

Gabe's eyes bulged. "You said Aunt Isabella had been shot. You never said anything about the Lucas carving their name into the poor woman's arm."

"Because they didn't," I ground out between gritted teeth, remembering Isabella's bloody, lifeless body and the crudely-etched name in her arm.

"How do you know that? What proof do you have?"

"None," I said, meeting Gabe's gaze dead-on.

"Oh fuck, Nico," he breathed, gripping both sides of his head like he was trying to keep his brain from bursting out of his skull. "If Dad finds out about this—"

"He'll probably kill me if he finds out what I've been keeping from him, I know. And I can't make any promises about what he'll do if he discovers that you kept your mouth shut because I asked. All I can tell you is I'm good at what I do—you know that. I'm good because I learned to listen to my instincts. And my instincts are telling me there is no way the Lucas are in this."

Gabe squeezed his eyes shut and turned his head up to the ceiling. It looked like a war was going on inside his head, a war I could well understand. It wasn't every day a guy's brother asked him to pick sides. If there were any way around it, I would have done it. Any way other than burning an innocent family to the ground.

"I know I'm asking a lot, *fratello*, but I need you to keep this to yourself. Lorenzo can't find out about any of this until I've figured out who is really responsible. Those are the fuckers that need to die."

Gabe was silent for a long time. So long, I contemplated calling our father and offering up the truth just to get this over with.

"All right, Nico. I'll keep your secret," he conceded, leaning back against the cold stone wall. "I know what you've done for us—for Sandro, Caio, and me. For *Mamma*." He looked at me pointedly.

I didn't think Gabe knew about the deal.

"You don't owe me anything, Gabe. Not like that," I said, leveling my gaze with him.

"No? I think you're wrong. You let him turn you into a monster to keep the rest of us safe."

The word had always been there in my mind, lurking beneath the surface, bubbling up every once in a while. But I'd always justified it. I had no choice, I told myself over and over. I had to keep my family safe—even from our own father. It had been for them. For Gabe. For the very person looking at me with eyes that knew the truth.

And the truth was that I liked it.

I liked the adrenaline that coursed through my veins. The challenge. The conquest. As much as it made the blood in my veins boil, Lorenzo had created a perfect replica of himself.

A perfect monster.

"This," I said, encircling the dank bloodstained room, "is who I am, Gabe."

"Nico, that's not what I meant—"

I held up a hand. "I want you to keep the information about the murders to yourself because you trust that I know what I'm doing. Not because you owe me."

He nodded. "You know I trust you."

"*Grazie, fratello*," I said, wrapping an arm around his shoulders. "Now, go on and let me get to work. One way or another, we'll have answers soon."

"I could help," Gabe said, nodding at the unconscious man.

"No." That was where I drew the line. "I've got this."

I wanted to believe the need to protect my brother had me ushering him out of the room. But maybe the truth was the monster in me just didn't like to share.

***

The man was covered in blood. A gash to his abdomen. A bone-deep slice to his left arm. A stab wound to his right thigh that had just missed his femoral artery.

"You give me a name, and this ends," I told him, circling his swaying form. He had snagged a knife from the neat row of weapons on the cold steel table, but he'd yet to manage to get in a shot of his own.

"You're... *crazy*," he hissed, stumbling back before he caught himself.

"So I've been told." I stood there, giving him the chance to recover enough to make another move.

I could still remember my first time in this room, the day after I made the deal with Lorenzo. He didn't believe in giving a man a fighting chance. Russo had been tied to a chair, and I watched as my father carved him up until he was unrecognizable. For an hour and a half, Russo screamed and begged for his life. It didn't stop after that. My father just cut out his tongue, which put an end to Russo's begging.

"I tell you nothing." The bleeding man in front of me seethed as his grip tightened around the Bowie knife in his hand.

Lorenzo's Bowie knife. The same one he used to cut out Russo's tongue. It was always here. Always serving as a reminder of the man who put me here and the reason I never walked away.

"You *will* tell me everything," I said with a shrug. "What do you think is going to happen when you can no longer stand?"

I gave him a moment to picture what I could do to him when he lost the ability to sidestep me. The possibilities were endless.

"If I tell you, what do you think they're going to do to me, huh? I'm no better off." He tried to reason with me, but his logic was flawed.

"They're not going to do anything to you, *amico*. You die today, one way or another. It's up to you how long it takes you to get there. That's the only choice you have left here. Make the right choice," I cautioned him.

"You're crazy," he shouted, and then his arm shot forward, grazing my forearm just enough to make it sting.

I had to hand it to the guy; he was fast. The momentum combined with the blood loss left him unbalanced though, so he tumbled to the ground at my feet while the stench of defeat began to radiate from him.

Not much longer now. Soon, he wouldn't be able to get back up.

I put my knife down on the table, leaned down, and grabbed him by his collar to drag him to his feet. He dropped the knife when he fell, but it wasn't my fault he couldn't keep a grip on his only lifeline.

He gasped as I shoved him back against the stone wall, but it had been less to intimidate him and more to give him something to keep him upright.

"Okay, I tell you. I'll tell you," he said, holding his hands out in front of him in supplication.

"Good. Now you're making smart choices, *amico*." I released him and took a step back.

I picked up my knife. It was saturated in his blood.

"I was hired to kill them—Abruzzo and all his family," he confessed, staring at the knife.

"No shit." I cocked an eyebrow.

"It was the Lucas. It was them. They hired me. They hired me to kill them, burn the house, and draw the letter on the grass. I was just doing what he told me to do."

I shook my head. Looking in his eyes, I saw no deception there. But that just couldn't be the truth.

"Which Luca hired you?"

Maybe the young one had gone rogue, or some pissed-off relative was out for revenge.

He looked at me like I'd lost my mind. "I'm a nobody. I didn't talk to any Luca. Diego Berlusconi hired me. He said the Lucas wanted the job done. I owe him a debt. I have no choice."

I spent three months looking into it, but no man by that name existed. It was just an alias.

"Berlusconi isn't a Luca. Who the hell is he?"

"I don't know. He works for them. He said he works for them. That's all I know." Again, I could detect no deception in either his tone or his eyes.

Ignoring the unsatiated itch that crept to my fingertips, I straightened my spine and squared my shoulders. I pretended that I needed to prepare myself for what I was about to do, but I was ready.

I was always ready.

"You let him turn you into a monster…"

Gabe's words played through my mind as I buried my blade to the hilt, straight through the man's heart.

"This is who I am."

My father would have been so proud.

Chapter Thirteen

Raven

Greta sat cross-legged on my hotel room bed, staring at me while I turned back and forth in front of the mirror.

"Are you sure about this?" I asked her, trying to hike up the low neckline of the tight red dress. Half an inch lower, this dress would be illegal.

"You've got to play to your audience, hon. The Costas like their women sexy and sophisticated. From what I heard, the guy you're going to see today likes them just plain trashy."

I laughed, but there was no humor in it. Between the slutty dress and the overdone makeup, "trashy" aptly described the woman who stared back at me in the mirror. It was good to know, though, that if I couldn't hack it as a nurse, I could fall back on a career as a hooker.

"You still haven't told me how it went last night?" Greta probed, eyeing me while she leaned forward and pulled out the cherry-red nail polish from her giant Tackle Box of cosmetic goodies.

I'd gone to bed before she got back last night, and I'd been delaying the inevitable ever since I woke up. It seemed my time was up.

"It didn't go... exactly as planned," I hedged. I'd hooked the Costa that should have come with warning bells. And yet I couldn't quite stop the smile that kept trying to tug up the corners of my cherry-red lips.

"Oh?" She cocked an eyebrow. "Because that smile tells me it didn't exactly go badly." She flipped her legs out from under her, held the nail polish bottle between her thighs, and unscrewed the top. "Sit," she said, nodding at the space next to her. "The guy next to you at the bar looked like an awfully good plan to me from behind. And you look way too happy for a girl who struck out, hon."

I sat down and held out my unpainted fingertips. "I guess that's because I didn't totally strike out." The smile was back. *Stupid smile.*

"All right, spill."

I held my breath for a moment before speaking. "His name was Nico. Nico Costa."

Her hand paused, leaving a blob of nail polish on the middle of my thumbnail. "You're not serious?"

"Um, serious as a heart attack?"

She scoffed. "Yeah, right. Heart attacks aren't really that guy's style, are they?"

"I didn't plan it. It just sort of… *happened*." I shrugged with one shoulder while she went back to smoothing out the blob.

"Raven, that guy is trouble. A random hottie was one thing, but Nico Costa? That's just a bad idea, and you know it."

"It isn't like anything is going to come of it. He's not the kind of guy who keeps coming back for more, so it's done. It's no big deal."

It wasn't entirely the truth. Part of me very much wished he was the kind of guy who came back for more, but he was notorious for more than his murder-y side. The guy was never seen with the same woman twice, but it didn't matter because Nico Costa wasn't the objective here.

She slipped the nail polish brush back into the bottle and looked at me. "You're sure about that?" she asked. "I get the appeal. He's like a roller coaster you want to ride again and again, but even if he wasn't a psychopath, he's a one-time use only kind of guy. He's not going to let you ride him until you get bored and want off. I don't want to see you get hurt—or dead."

"Well, I have no intention of going on that ride. I don't like roller coasters, and I'm kind of attached to breathing."

She eyed me for a minute, but then her lips quirked up in a smile. "Nico freaking Costa, huh? You've got to tell me how you managed that one."

I smiled. "A girl's got to have her secrets. Besides," I said, glancing at the clock on the wall, "it's time to get my slutty butt moving." I glanced at the mirror once more, trying not to cringe.

If Vito could see me now, he'd lock up my barely-covered butt indefinitely.

***

I slid out of the cab onto my three-inch stiletto heels and clicked and clacked my way across the pavement to The Coliseum's front door—it was a wonder I didn't fall flat on my face.

A man in a faded pair of jeans and an old black T-shirt opened the door for me. I could feel his dark eyes grazing over me from head to toe, leaving a slimy feeling all over my body. I paused just inside the door, though I took a step to the right to escape the slimy guy's line of sight.

The Coliseum wasn't like Onyx, which looked like the local nightlife hangout for the rich and famous. This club looked more like a hangout for Wall Street's rejects. Men in wrinkled suits with their hair mussed and their ties undone. The few women I saw didn't look like they spent much time in the financial district, though. They looked like me, with clothes too tight and makeup overdone—which was fine. I wasn't judging. It just made me wonder how the heck I was going to stand out among the crowd of them.

Steeling my shoulders, I tucked my purse beneath my arm, made my way across the room to the bar, and sat down a few stools away from the Wall Street rejects. The bartender was tall, dark, and handsome, but there was nothing intuitive in his gaze, nothing like the bartender at Onyx. This guy's gaze was just slimy. It seemed to be the overarching theme here.

"What can I get for you, *signorina*?" he asked.

"A—"

"Top-shelf scotch for the lady, Edoardo," a man's voice spoke from behind me.

I hadn't even heard him approach.

I turned around to find out which one of the Wall Street rejects was trying to buy me a drink. But this was no reject. Well-dressed, relatively muscular. The lines etched around his eyes and mouth were deeper than they'd appeared in pictures.

"*Buongiorno, signorina,*" he greeted me, sliding onto the stool next to me.

"*Buongiorno,*" I replied, desperately trying to call up my inner-Greta, but she wasn't answering the call today.

My dress felt like it was clinging to my skin uncomfortably, the interior fabric a matted mess from my body sweat.

Edoardo placed two glasses down in front of us, each filled a third-full of amber liquid. I nodded graciously and took a sip, but I had a feeling hard liquor wasn't going to help me here. I steeled my shoulders and cleared my mind. *This* was the man Greta had heard knew all that went on in the state. She'd also heard he was as wily as a fox.

"What brings you to my little club?" he asked after taking a healthy swig of his own drink.

It was showtime.

"*You* did, *Signor* Belemonte," I crooned, hoping it didn't come out as awkward as it felt.

"Oh?" he said, quirking his brows. His eyes darted down to my breasts, which were nearly overflowing the dress. "I can't say I'm disappointed to hear that. What is it I can do for you?"

I turned to face him, letting my bare knee brush against his outer thigh. "I hear you're an important man. Nothing happens in New York without you knowing about it," I said, stroking his ego. "I'm hoping you might have some information for me."

"Oh, well, now I'm disappointed," he said, but the spark of interest in his eyes hadn't dulled any. "Information pales in comparison to what I could offer you, *signorina*."

"I'm sure it does, but I assure you I would be most appreciative," I said, batting my eyelashes while I slipped my hand into the purse on my lap and withdrew the thick stack of bills. It wasn't much in Harry Belemonte's world, but it was every penny I could get in loans and cash advances from my credit cards. All my savings were being used up on plane tickets and hotel rooms.

I dropped my purse on the counter but kept the stack in my hand beneath the bar, letting his gaze linger at where it sat on top of my thighs.

"It seems this information is rather valuable to you." He reached out and thumbed through the stack of bills, grazing my thigh in the process.

I resisted the urge to recoil from his touch. "Very valuable," I said.

Five thousand dollars in value, actually. If I'd had more, I would have paid that too.

He thumbed through the stack again, then withdrew, grazing his fingers along my thigh to my knee as he went. If I'd thought slimy was bad, this was worse. It was like someone had injected live worms beneath my skin. I fought the urge to bat his hand away, focusing on the reason I was here. The satisfaction that would come when I pulled this off.

"All right, *signorina*. If you'll tell me what information you're seeking, I'll consider your offer."

"I'm curious about any recent aspirations of people like the Morettis, the Lucianos, the Lucas, or the Costas." At least this way, it sounded like I was listing off families at random. But if I was going to make myself useful to the Costas, I needed to have some idea of what they valued.

"Aspirations?" he asked without missing a beat.

I'd really hoped to offer up as few details as possible. The less anyone knew about what I was planning, the better.

"Any aspiration in which they may benefit from outside help, or perhaps an aspiration in which more than one family has shown interest?" I treaded.

Technically, if I could help the Costas snag something away from the Lucas, that would prove the bigger victory. I didn't want to hurt my family, but a part of me wanted to make them feel *something*.

Belemonte's brow furrowed, and for the first time, his thoughts seemed to turn inward. I could almost see the calculations going on inside his head. Almost, but not quite. What was he thinking about?

I forced myself to take slow, even breaths, clenching the stack of money tight in my hand and hoping I wasn't soaking it in sweat.

Eventually, he pursed his lips and let out a long, slow breath. "That would be very dangerous information to have, wouldn't it?"

It seemed more like an observation than a question, but the expectant way he was looking at me said he was waiting for a response.

"It would be *useful* information, *Signor* Belemonte."

It was the only answer I could come up with.

"True," he acknowledged. "But even if I had information for you—which I don't—I don't think it would be in your best interest to have it."

I raised an eyebrow. "I'm a big girl, *Signor.*"

"Indeed, you are. In all the right ways," he said as his gaze settled on my breasts once again. "But there is no information to give you, not that I've heard. And as you said, nothing happens in New York without me hearing about it."

"Thank you, *Signor* Belemonte. I appreciate your time." I pursed my lips, trying to hide my disappointment.

I grabbed my purse to slip the money back in, but he put his hand over mine. I paused.

"I'm not generally the magnanimous type, but I feel compelled to warn you that whatever game you're playing is far more dangerous than you realize. Walk away, *signorina.* It would be a shame to find your delectable body at the bottom of the Long Island Sound."

He withdrew his hand, and I stuffed the money into my purse and slid off the stool, trying to hide the cold shiver that rippled down my spine. I hadn't fully considered the ramifications of what would happen if I got caught. Even Greta's countless warnings had never really sunk in with me. But thanks to Harry Belemonte, I was now having second thoughts. I'd wanted to prove my worth. I'd wanted my family to regret abandoning me. I did not want to end up dead.

"Heed my warning, *signorina*. It isn't often I give one for free."

I nodded, knowing my voice would never make it out past the lump of fear lodged in my throat.

He stared at me for a moment longer. His gaze raked over my scantily-clad body one last time.

"*Arrivederci*," he said, then got up and strode past me, headed straight for a slim brunette in a black sequined dress that was even shorter than mine.

I stood there for a moment, trying to remember how to put one foot in front of the other. It came back to me eventually, and I was only too happy to hightail my butt out of there.

Heck, I was tempted to hightail my butt all the way back to California.

Chapter Fourteen

Nico

I stood in the middle of suburbia, staring at the tidy row of two-story cookie-cutter houses in front of me. Every one of them was surrounded by the iconic white picket fence. I could imagine the minivans tucked away in the garages, ready for the next soccer practice or ballet lesson. It was enough to make me gag.

Inside the unimaginative vinyl-clad house in front of me sat the kind of scum that made me sicker than just about anything else. This particular garage was empty—the wife and twin seven-year-old girls were out with the minivan for the next hour, leaving more than enough time for what I'd come to do.

"Go ahead, Cesare," I said to the tall, gangly man on my left.

Cesare didn't look like much, but the guy had broken more than his fair share of bones since coming to work for us, and he was loyal to a fault.

He nodded and took off around the house just in case the scum inside tried to make a hasty exit.

Gabe and Salvatore followed me up the front walk, which was lined with actual *daisies*. At the front door, Gabe worked his magic. My brother could crack any lock and disarm any security system in

91

thirty seconds flat. If the mafia life didn't work out for him, he could make a killing as a bank robber.

Inside, the house was just as unimaginative as the exterior. Wall-to-wall carpeting, beige walls, and white wainscoting. The fridge on my left was peppered with cheesy hand-drawn pictures. Just a typical family from suburbia. At least, it looked that way. The man of the house, who I could hear rummaging through papers somewhere further inside, was not the typical suburban family man.

I nodded, and Salvatore strode ahead, past the dining room on the right, and they disappeared around the corner.

The meaty thud of flesh against flesh followed a second later, then the shatter of glass.

"What the—" a gruff voice shouted, cut off by another meaty thud.

By the time Gabe and I rounded the corner, Cesare was coming in through the back door and Salvatore had Mr. Suburbia facedown against his walnut desk with his arms bent up behind him.

"Thank you, Salvatore," I said, moving around the room to take the seat behind the desk. I waved a hand, and Salvatore released him.

"Have a seat, Gino." I motioned to the vacant chair on the opposite side of the desk.

Gino took a cautious step back, but then paused. His gaze flashed to the men around him but kept coming back to me. He was a smart man, I realized. Instead of panicking, I could see his mind working in overdrive, trying to calculate the outcomes of every possible move. Too bad there was only one outcome for Mr. Pisano today.

Maybe coming to the inevitable conclusion that he had no other move to play at the moment, he perched himself on the edge of the chair, loosening his tie like it had begun to strangle him.

"It seems you didn't heed my warning, Gino, and you know what that means."

In the movies, this was the part where the mafia guy gave the long, drawn-out "'I'm disappointed in you'" speech, and then the guy begged and begged, building tension until the inevitable end.

I wasn't much for speeches.

"Whatever you think I did, I didn't do it, *Signor* Costa," he said, meeting my eyes with a level stare.

"Save it, Pisano," I said, then nodded to Salvatore, who then dropped an envelope into Gino's lap. The envelope Belemonte had given me.

His steady gaze faltered, and he reached into the envelope with shaking hands. The photo he withdrew was all the proof I needed.

"I warned you what would happen if I caught you recruiting kids again. You do recall that conversation, don't you?"

It was the kind of conversation that involved broken bones, so I imagined it would be difficult to forget.

"You don't understand, *Signor* Costa. I needed the money."

"I don't care what you needed."

Gino's gambling addiction wasn't my problem.

"And the kids, they were just teenage shitbags. They would have been high on something whether I gave it to them or not."

"And you thought my orders were open to interpretation? Gabe," I said, turning to my brother. "Do I look like the kind of man who lets others decide what I really mean?"

Gabe laughed. "About as much as I look like the Queen of England. I could pull off the crown though, don't you think?"

Gabe and Cesare sniggered.

"How many, Gino? How many children did you get hooked on my product?" I asked.

"Just them. Just those two kids in the picture, I swear."

I nodded to Salvatore, and he slammed the guy's head into the desk.

"Let's try this again," I said while a bloody goose egg formed on Gino's brow. "How many?"

"All right, there were more. But it doesn't matter," he whined.

I nodded to Salvatore once again, but Gino threw up his hands.

"Wait. Please, let me explain."

I crossed my arms over my chest and nodded to Gino.

"Those kids, I didn't recruit them to sell your product, *Signor* Costa. I swear," he sputtered out.

I glanced pointedly at the photo in his lap.

"I mean, I recruited them, *si*, but not for you. I needed the money, but I know you don't like selling to kids, *Signor* Costa... but there's others... other people who don't have a problem with it."

"In my territory?"

The guy was still going to die, but now he was going to die slowly and painfully.

"But it isn't your market, *Signor* Costa, so I figured what would you care?" Gino's eyes looked wild, as he scrambled for an excuse.

Gino had figured wrong.

"Whose product was it?" I asked.

"I don't know, I swear. Some guy—Berlusconi—just gave me the stuff and said I could keep thirty percent. He never told me who

94

the stuff belonged to, and I didn't ask. It was a lot of money. I needed the money, *Signor* Costa. My kids—"

"Don't make excuses, Gino. Your children didn't gamble away the money I've given you."

I took note that Gino mentioned Berlusconi, too.

"But I was going to lose my home—"

"And now you're going to lose your life."

Gino had no more information he could give me. I nodded to Salvatore and Cesare, and they yanked him up out of his seat.

"How you finish him off is up to you," I told them. "Be sure to get creative." Salvatore had a real flair when it came to stopping a heart. "But don't make a mess in his wife's home," I reminded.

"We'll take him for a ride, boss," Salvatore said, then clocked the guy on the back of the head with the butt of his gun.

I sat there for a moment longer as Salvatore heaved an unconscious Gino over his shoulder and carried him out of the room. I slipped a thick envelope out of my jacket and laid it down on the walnut desk.

Gabe cocked an inquiring brow.

I shrugged. "The guy's got two kids."

The money in the envelope wouldn't last them a lifetime, but it would put the kids through college and leave a nice little nest egg besides. It wasn't the kids' fault their father was a gambling child-recruiting scumbag.

***

"So, what's next on the agenda, *fratello*?" Gabe asked from the passenger seat of my Porsche as he typed away on his phone, letting Lorenzo know the task was done.

I knew exactly what I wanted to do next. It was the same thing I'd been wanting to do since I spied the dark-haired beauty in Onyx last night. For some reason, I couldn't get the girl out of my head. Maybe it had been the interruption that was doing strange things to me. It wasn't often I was deprived of what I wanted.

My phone rang. I pulled it out of my jacket, hoping like hell something hadn't gone wrong with Pisano. But the number didn't belong to any of our men. I squeezed the steering wheel tighter and held the phone up to my ear.

"*Buongiorno*, Belemonte." The guy had his uses, but that didn't mean I enjoyed talking to him.

"*Buongiorno*, Nico. I hope my information proved useful to you."

"It did. *Grazie*," I said, trying to keep the revulsion out of my voice.

"I'm glad. Truly. I had the most scintillating visit today, and I thought it might interest you."

Dealing with Belemonte did not "interest" me, but if he had information about who was killing Costas—who also seemed to be the same guy who was trying to infringe on our territory—I was willing to play along.

"I appreciate the call. What can you tell me?"

"Someone is very interested in finding areas of contention between families like the Lucas, the Lucianos... the Costas. When she mentioned your family, it seemed pertinent to share that information with you."

It wasn't like Belemonte to hand over information with no strings.

"What is it you want, Belemonte?"

"Only to prove how useful I can be, Nico. I told you, I regret not getting to know your father better. I wouldn't want to make that mistake twice."

He was hoping to benefit from a long-term relationship with the Costas. It wasn't something I could rule out if I was looking out for the well-being of the family. Even snakes had their uses.

"What can you tell me about the woman making inquiries?"

"I didn't get her name, I'm afraid, but she was quite memorable. Very young. Long, dark hair, blue eyes, and a body that was hand-sculpted by the gods."

My knuckles turned white around the steering wheel.

Long, dark hair.

Vivid blue eyes.

A face that no man could forget.

I had no doubt that there was more than one blue-eyed brunette in New York. But something had struck me about Raven last night. Perhaps this was why. She hadn't been at Onyx for a night out—she was there to sink her claws into the Costas.

"Anything else?" I asked, not sure if I was looking for something to confirm or to negate my suspicion.

Belemonte sighed. "I'm at an impasse, Nico. I fear the information I have will lead to harm to the girl. That really would be a waste."

Belemonte concerned about the girl's well-being? I scoffed inwardly. "What is it you want?"

"Nothing much, really. If you decide to… do away with the girl, give her to me instead. I think, when presented with the choice between death and working for me, she'll come to my way of thinking."

"I'll consider it."

It was up to the Costas how we dealt with our business. Belemonte should have known that.

"Fair enough. I had one of my men follow the young lady. She took a cab straight to a hotel—the Hilton Hotel."

Fuck.

And then it hit me. That's why Raven had looked familiar. I couldn't put a name to her, because maybe I'd never met her before in my life, but her features were one hundred percent Luciano. High cheekbones, pale blue eyes. A slightly stubborn chin. A small, slightly upturned nose. Raven was a Luciano, just like Maria Luca had been before marrying Vincent Luca.

Were the Lucianos trying to pit one family against another? And if so, what was Raven's role in it?

"Thank you, Belemonte. I appreciate the information. I won't forget it."

I hung up the phone, trying to ignore the grimy feeling of being indebted to the man. A snake might have its uses, but it was still a snake.

"Problem?" Gabe asked, eyeing my white-knuckled grip on the wheel.

"The Lucianos are up to something," I said, pushing down on the accelerator and veering across traffic, which elicited angry beeps from the cars behind me—not that I cared.

A plan had already begun to take shape in my mind.

98

"How do you know?"

"Because a woman showed up at the club last night. A Luciano woman—who was also looking for information from Belemonte. She mentioned the Costas."

She'd looked so innocent. She'd seemed so honest. How had I missed what had really been going on?

"Does this mean they're working with the Lucas?" he asked, though I could hear the real question he was too good of a brother to ask: *Did the Lucas and Lucianos murder Aunt Isabella and Abruzzo?*

The Lucianos? Maybe. There could have been a parting of ways between the families. A long shot, perhaps, but it was more plausible in my head than laying the blame on the Lucas. It just didn't sit right.

"Okay. Then what do we do now?" Gabe asked.

"I need you to look into who's been trying to scoop up our territory, Gabe. If we could find this Berlusconi guy, then maybe we could figure out who he was working for."

The Lucianos? Or was the sly kitten up to something else?

Gabe nodded. "What is it you're going to do?"

"I'm going to look into our Luciano problem."

I still needed to figure out Raven's game.

Was it her job to get me distracted? To collect intel?

Either way, I was onto her. I held all the cards. I could use her to steer the Lucianos in the wrong direction. Everything was fair game now that they'd made the first move.

And the idea of playing with Raven while I used her as a pawn? Well, it might just turn out to be the best game I'd ever play.

Chapter Fifteen

Nico

I dropped Gabe off at Onyx and drove the few short miles to the Hilton. I had no doubt she'd still be at the hotel. It didn't do the Luciano family any good for their little seductress to disappear. But what to do with her? Wining and dining her at some fancy-ass restaurant left her with too much comfort, too many ways the Lucianos could be keeping an eye on her. There was only one place I could think of that would knock her right out of her comfort zone.

I typed in the phone number for the caterer my family had used often in the past and grit my teeth through the ringing, trying to focus on how the benefits of my plan outweighed the drawbacks.

My home was a private retreat from the horrors of the rest of the world. I'd never allowed another living soul to set foot in it. But now, if I wanted to throw Raven off her game, I'd have to let the enemy walk right in. It was a calculated move, I reasoned. No one was forcing me to do it.

I wanted Raven out of her element and one hundred percent at my mercy.

"*Ciao*," a rough and tired-sounding Italian voice greeted from the other end of the line. Mario, if my memory served correctly—and it always did.

"This is Nico," I said.

"Oh, *si, Signor Costa*," Mario said with a higher, more accommodating inflection in his tone now. "What can I do for you, *Signor Costa?*"

"I need a dinner for two catered in my home." My throat tried to close around the last word, but I forced it out. "I need it ready and waiting for me this evening, eight o'clock. No waitstaff will be required."

"*Si, Signor.* I can do that. And the menu?"

"Whatever you think, Mario, will be fine."

"*Buono, Signor Costa.* I'll take care of the details."

"*Grazie*, Mario," I said, then forced my address out through gritted teeth and hung up the phone. It was a good idea, but it still pissed me off to let strangers into my home.

But when I thought about the lovely, deceptive Raven in my home, and on my table, and on the rug in the living room, and in my bed, it helped to take the edge off the sense of intrusion. Before it could lose its dulling effect, I got out of the car and walked into the hotel. The moment she opened the hotel room door, though, my plan took a back seat to the arousal pounding through my veins.

Raven stared up at me wide-eyed with that same deer-caught-in-the-headlights look she'd had last night. But that was where the similarities ended.

This was Raven. Not some dolled-up siren. Not a heavily made-up vixen looking for attention. No stiletto shoes or flashy jewelry. Just one hundred percent Raven.

Her hair was wet, and the thin, black dressing gown she wore clung to her damp body. And while her pale blue eyes had looked incredible last night, without makeup today, they looked real, lightly fringed by her long, dark lashes. How it was possible she looked even sexier now, I had no idea, but I liked her this way. I liked her this way so much I almost missed the movement of her lips and the words spilling from them.

"What are you doing here?" she asked.

She didn't sound angry, more like she thought I must have taken a wrong turn somewhere and wound up at her hotel room door by accident.

"We were interrupted last night," I said with a careless shrug of my shoulders.

She opened her mouth, parting lips that I'd already imagined doing a thousand different things. The image was even more vivid now with her right in front of me. Before she'd made a sound, though, she closed them again and started worrying her bottom lip with her teeth.

Why I liked her like this—nervous and guileless—I couldn't say. I wanted to rattle her just to see every honest response that came from it. Too bad it was just an act, but I had to hand it to her; it was one hell of an act.

"You look different," I said bluntly, curious whether she'd take it as the compliment it was or assume something less flattering.

Though her cheeks turned the pink that had become my favorite color, she looked at me curiously like she was waiting for me to explain before rendering judgment, though her teeth bit harder at the inside of her lip.

"I like you like this," I told her, doing nothing to hide the thick arousal in my voice.

She swallowed hard, making the muscles of her throat work the same way they had when I'd had my lips and teeth on that smooth column last night.

The wayward lock of her hair had worked its way free. I reached up to tuck it behind her ear, and she swayed toward me. Just a little. Just enough to tell me she wanted this even if she did have ulterior motives.

I stepped inside the room, closing the door behind me, watching her closely. It wasn't part of the plan, but a few minutes of indulging couldn't hurt.

She moved in tandem with my steps, keeping her gaze locked on mine.

"Are you nervous, Raven?" I asked as I put one hand on her hip to maneuver her up against the closed door.

I didn't need to ask. It was just as clear in her eyes as the arousal that leapt in them like pale blue flames. But I wanted to hear her say it.

"Yes," she admitted quietly, sending a white-hot jolt of heat through me.

"Why are you nervous?" I pressed my body against hers while I kissed my way along her jaw.

She smelled like jasmine, and she shivered at the same time her lips parted on a quiet sigh.

"You make me nervous," she said, moving her hands to my shoulders.

I liked the way her fingers pressed just hard enough to feel me through the fabric of my suit like she was tentatively trying to explore what lay beneath.

"Tell me why," I persisted, trailing lower, kissing a path down the soft skin of her throat. I wanted to catch her flesh between my teeth, but I resisted the urge. For now.

"Because you're dangerous."

Of course, it was because I was dangerous. Everyone who'd ever heard of me knew it, and in her precarious position as enemy, she knew it more than most. I scared her. That's why she was nervous. Why that disappointed me, I wasn't sure.

"You make it so I can't think straight, Nico, and that scares me," she said, meeting my gaze despite the effort I could see it was costing her to be honest.

But that was what she meant? It wasn't because she was afraid of me? Why that pleased me was even more of a mystery.

"Then don't think, Raven. Just feel."

I moved lower, grazing across the deep V neckline of her dressing gown with my lips.

Her fingers dug into my shoulders as she dropped her head back against the door and closed her eyes. I headed lower, kissing along the upper swells of her breasts through the silk fabric. I wanted it off, but I liked teasing her like this too. And ultimately, no matter how much I wanted to forget about it at the moment, I had a more important goal here.

She dug her fingers in deeper as she whispered, "You have to leave."

I wondered if she could hear the lack of conviction in her own tone.

"Why?" I asked, pausing with my lips hovering a hair's breadth from her taut fabric-covered nipple.

"I have plans," she said.

It was a lie if ever I'd heard one.

"Then cancel them."

I swirled my tongue around her nipple. Her whole body jolted against me, and when I suckled her nipple into my mouth, fabric and all, the moan that slipped out of her lips shot right through me. If I'd had any blood left pumping through my veins, that quiet sound sent every last drop to my cock, making it throb harder than possibly ever before.

"I can't. I can't do that," she said, but instead of pushing me away, she pulled me closer.

I was happy to oblige, taking her nipple between my teeth this time and grazing gently.

"Yes, you can."

I moved to her other nipple and gave it the same treatment.

This time, her moan was louder and her hips writhed. I could smell her arousal and it was making it difficult to focus. It would be so easy to take her now. To lift her up, wrap her legs around me, and bury myself deep in her. But I didn't want her hard and fast against the wall. Well, I did. But not yet.

Stick to the plan.

I leaned away and stood up straight.

"Put your hands above your head, Raven," I told her, anxious to see if she'd comply like I thought she would.

Her eyes, clouded with arousal, met mine, and slowly, she raised her arms, clasping her hands together high above her head.

"That's perfect."

I held her gaze while I reached for the thin sash that held her robe closed. With two quick flicks of my fingers, the sash gave way, and the dressing gown gaped open, revealing a body even more toned than I'd expected, perfect breasts, and a smooth, bare pussy. I'd barely had time to look over her when she unclasped her hands.

"Don't move," I commanded in a voice that brooked no refusal.

I didn't miss the way she squeezed her thighs shut against a fresh rush of arousal. The bright pink slashes across her cheeks spoke of her discomfort, but she obeyed, keeping still while I looked my fill, taking note of the gentle flare of her hips, the definition of muscle across her abdomen, and the wetness on her inner thighs.

"You're beautiful," I said.

I clasped my hand over her wrists, keeping them pinned against the wall as I leaned in to claim her lips.

Knock. Knock. Knock.

Her whole body jolted, and her eyes widened. She yanked her hands out of my grip as the pink blush across her cheeks traveled all the way down to the upper swells of her breasts.

"Raven, I forgot my stupid card thingy," a woman's voice called from the other side of the door while Raven covered up and secured the sash around her waist with short, jerky movements.

"Crap, you shouldn't be here," she whispered as her eyes glanced wildly around the room, then settled on the window for just a little too long.

"I'm not going out the window if that's what you're thinking." I laughed.

She eyed the window longingly for one more second, then nodded. "Okay, I guess you should probably go."

Not a good time for jokes then.

"Raven?" the voice called through the door.

"I'll go for now," I said, leaning back in to leave a trail of featherlight kisses along her jaw. "But I'll be back. Be ready at seven-thirty."

I opened the door without waiting for a reply. A pretty blonde stood there with her hand raised, ready to knock.

"Whoa," she said, dropping her hand as her eyes grazed over me from head to toe. This woman was certainly bolder than Raven. Surprisingly, even with a raging hard-on, that didn't impress me.

I smiled at her, nonetheless.

She laughed. "You shouldn't flash that thing in public. You'll end up getting arrested for causing a riot."

Me, arrested? I almost barked out a chuckle.

"I wouldn't worry about that, *signorina*, but I appreciate your concern." I flashed her another grin.

I turned back to Raven, leaning in close enough to whisper against her ear. "I'll see you this evening," I said, then left the room without a backward glance.

Chapter Sixteen

Raven

Greta stood in front of the door with her hands crossed over her chest. She was trying to give me the evil eye but couldn't quite get her lips to cooperate. They kept tugging up at the corners.

I waited patiently. At least, I hoped it looked like I was waiting patiently for the tongue-lashing she was trying to muster up. In truth, I needed a minute to collect myself. To get my heartbeat to resemble something normal and to stop breathing like I'd just jogged a mile.

I'd never dreamt Nico freaking Costa would show up at my hotel room door. Maybe if it hadn't been for his darn lips and his hands and the heat in his eyes, I would have been able to figure out some way to use it to my advantage. But my brain took a back seat to my body when the guy came around. That was going to have to change.

Fast.

I had until seven-thirty to figure out how to make Nico Costa the perfect conduit for my plan. It was just too good of an opportunity to pass up. The fact that I'd rather have been thinking about all the things he could do with his lips and hands than what he could do to help me prove myself to my family meant nothing at all.

Absolutely nothing.

"Are you still going to tell me last night was no big deal?" Greta piped up when she'd managed to get control of her lips. "Nothing was going to come of it?" She might have been able to keep the smile off her face, but it was there in her eyes. She was good at getting me to "spill," but she was lousy at serious lectures.

"I didn't think anything was going to come of it. Now, I just need to figure out what to do with it," I said, silently rubbing my hands together now that the tidal wave of hormones he'd drenched me in had begun to ebb.

That's all it was. *Hormones.* Just chemicals in my brain, thanks to the stimulus he provided. It wasn't like I'd never been attracted to a man before, though admittedly, this kind of felt like attraction on steroids.

"What do you mean, you just need to figure out what to do with it?" Greta's voice rose higher with every word. "Nothing—that's what you do with Nico Costa. Nothing, Raven. You go to bed tonight, close your eyes, and get off on the wildest fantasies of him your sweet little mind can conjure. And that's it."

I shook my head. "I've got a Costa right in front of me. I can't just walk away."

She threw out her arms in exasperation. "Coming here to confront your family was one thing, Raven. Nico Costa is a whole different ball game—a game that ends with knives and a pair of concrete shoes if he figures out what you're up to."

"He's not going to find out. It's not like I'm going to come out and tell him." I was going to do whatever it took to make it believable. *Whatever* it took.

"Even if he doesn't figure it out, what if it equals nothing? What if you do what I think you're planning to do with him, and it doesn't bring you any closer to what you want?"

"Then I'm no further behind, am I?" I said with a shrug. "I'm prepared to do this." And a bit crazy scared too, but Greta didn't need to know that.

She sighed. "I've created a monster," she said with a quick quirk of her lips.

I laughed and flopped back on the sofa, still hyperaware of the brush of my dressing gown against my skin. It seemed the hormones hadn't ebbed completely.

Greta plopped down next to me and put her hand on my arm. "I'm here for you—you know that—but you haven't even figured out how you want to use the Costas to—"

"I've been thinking about that." I sat up straight. "I was hoping Harry Belemonte could have confirmed it for me, but I think the casinos are the way to go. The Lucas must have dumped a fortune into getting one established—it's still in the construction phase. It would be stupid of me to try to stop it, and besides, I don't want to cripple my family. I just need to find a way to keep the Costas' casinos on top, even if it means sabotaging my family's casino a little bit."

Greta cocked an eyebrow, waiting for me to continue.

"For the Costas, it would be a smart move. Even in a different territory, the Lucas' casino is going to be drawing some of the business away from the Costas' casinos."

"Maybe," Greta said, but the look on her face was pained. "But territory is a big thing with mafia families, right? If you get the Costas to sabotage a casino on Luca territory, you might unwittingly incite a war, Raven. A war, you know? Where things get real bloody and people get really dead."

My shoulders sagged, and my stomach turned a little. I'd been looking at moves and countermoves from a strategical standpoint, not a human one. Trying to prove myself useful to the Costas was one thing, but starting a war where people died because of me was something else entirely. I couldn't do it. I wouldn't. But that left me back at the drawing board.

I slumped back against the sofa, defeated for the moment, but even more than that, a bit disgusted with myself. I wanted to be a nurse—someone who helped people—and yet, I'd been completely ignorant of the harm I could have caused.

"There's something else," Greta said, flinging an arm over my shoulder and pulling me a little closer. "You know I love you, and I hate that you're hurting, but are you sure about this?"

"No, you're right about the casino. I can't risk doing something that ends up really hurting people. I wouldn't be able to live with myself."

"I don't mean the casino. I mean, what happens if you succeed, hon? Do you really think it's going to make you feel better? That it'll undo what they did to you?"

"No, nothing could undo that. But I have to do this," I said, willing her to understand but knowing she couldn't. Not really.

Greta didn't understand what my family had stolen from me or how they'd torn me apart with their lies. It made no sense to her that I had to do this because the only way I could show myself to my family was to be the success they'd never given me the chance to be.

Still, I leaned closer against her. The truth was, I had no idea how to make it happen.

She dropped her head on mine. "Then of course, I'm here for you. But you have to promise me you'll be smart, and that means no Nico—"

"I'm going tonight, Greta. I won't do anything stupid, but I can't throw this away. Next to Lorenzo Costa, Nico is the most influential man in his family."

What I couldn't admit aloud was that it wasn't entirely for the plan that I was going. Right or wrong, I wanted Nico.

She sighed. "All right, then I suppose as your best friend, I'm supposed to help get you ready."

I shook my head, remembering the way he'd looked at me when I'd opened the hotel room door.

"No?"

"If I keep trying to be whoever that girl was last night, he's going to figure it out. That wasn't me." In truth, it was just a cookie-cutter copy of the women Nico had every night. "If I want any hope of pulling this off, I've got to be as real as I can be."

"Eighty percent truth, twenty percent lie?" she asked with a wicked little grin.

"Exactly."

And the way he'd looked at me like he wanted to devour me had nothing to do with it. Absolutely nothing.

Chapter Seventeen

Nico

At precisely seven-thirty, I slid the Porsche into park in front of the hotel where I'd left Raven just a few hours earlier and stepped out. I had no doubt she'd be there, waiting in the hotel lobby. She had to be, if the Luciano family wanted her to keep me distracted or garner intel, or whatever it was they were after.

But I wasn't prepared for the woman who walked out of the glass doors.

I'd expected makeup, and jewelry, and five-inch heels. This Raven was the one I'd seen earlier today. Her dress, the color reminded me of human bones, showed off her bare shoulders. On her feet were a pair of sandals. I could spot the pink on her toenails from a mile away. It was the same pink her cheeks turned when she was flustered. The same pink that had become my favorite color.

The woman knew what she was doing. It pissed me off to know she had taken what I'd told her earlier about liking her this way and used it to her advantage—which was ridiculous since I was playing her just as much as she was playing me.

"Hi," she said, meeting my gaze and then glancing down at her toes, making the wayward lock slip free of its restraint. The blue in her eyes were a little darker than before; I didn't miss the note of sadness in it.

"Hi, Raven," I said, ignoring the rush of arousal that was coursing through my veins. Tonight was about knocking her off-balance, which meant no getting sidetracked by silky hair, or pink toenails, or sad eyes, or anything else she was going to try to throw at me.

I opened the passenger side door for her and waited for her to slip inside, taking absolutely no notice of how her painted fingernails matched her toenails. Then again, maybe it was not such a bad idea to notice. Maybe once I'd gotten her worked up tonight, I'd have her use those fingers on her own body.

She was quiet as we began the long drive outside the city limits. When I glanced over, her whole countenance seemed to scream of sadness. The slump of her shoulders, the dejected tilt of her chin. This was obviously part of the act, so maybe it was time I made her think I was taking the bait.

"Why are you doing this?" she blurted out, throwing me a curveball before I could open my mouth.

"What do you mean?" I asked slowly.

"I mean…" She pressed her lips together and turned inward like she was searching for words. "I mean, why did you want to see me again?"

The guileless act again? She played it so well it took effort to remember it was all an act.

"Because I liked what I saw the last time," I said easily because it was the truth. Or at least, part of the truth.

Her cheeks pinkened, but she forged ahead. Her determination would have been impressive had it been real. "But I know who you are, Nico. I know what all the tabloids say about you."

"And what is it they say?" I wasn't really a tabloid guy, so I was actually kind of curious.

"They say you've never been seen with the same woman twice, that a one-night stand pushes your average relationship length to its limits."

Well, the tabloids got something right.

"So, you can understand why I'm a little baffled?" she said.

Fuck. If she were the honest, guileless girl I'd foolishly thought she was, I might have been tempted to tell her that I didn't know quite what it was about her that had me coming back for more. It could have been that we'd been interrupted, but in truth, that would have just pissed me off with any other woman. I would have been onto something new in three seconds flat. But even if I could explain it, I still wasn't telling the conniving, manipulating woman sitting next to me anything she didn't need to know.

"What can I say, Raven? You amuse me, and I like to be amused."

I probably should have come up with something more flattering if I wanted to keep stringing her along, but she'd made a fool out of me. She deserved it.

"So, I'm like a shiny, new toy you haven't tired of yet," she said, though it came across more as an observation than a question.

"Does that bother you?" I sat up a little straighter in my seat as I waited for her response, my ears almost pricked up in anticipation.

She was silent for a moment like she was putting a great deal of thought into the question.

"No," she said eventually with a slight shake of her head. "The moment I saw you, I knew who you were. It wouldn't be fair of me to expect you to be something different."

A woman who didn't want to mold me into something different? That was new. But then, it wasn't real. Raven was just playing a role. How she knew how to play it so perfectly, I had no idea.

"Where are we?" she asked as I turned into the long drive that led to my house.

"This is my home," I told her with a casual shrug as the wood and stone structure came into view.

My sanctuary. My private retreat. And I was about to let her walk right in.

Chapter Eighteen

Raven

It was like something out of a woodland fairy tale. A foundation of stone held up two stories of rich cedarwood walls. There were windows everywhere. Stone columns supported a wraparound balcony that overlooked forest as far as I could see. I could hear the trickling of water nearby. A stream, maybe, and I could so easily picture it winding through this peaceful place.

"This is beautiful," I said, still looking around in awe.

"Thanks," Nico said, but the jut of his chin and the pride shining in his eyes said this was more than just a house he'd purchased.

"You designed it, didn't you?"

His eyes widened just a little and then narrowed. "How did you know that?"

I shrugged. "You don't just seem happy when you look at it. You look proud. You created this."

"Yes, I did," he said, then motioned for me to accompany him up the stone steps to the dark double door entryway at the top.

I wanted to ask him more about the house and find out his inspirations behind the design. But the odd tension in the air told me to drop it.

He pressed his large hand flat against a screen on the wall next to the door, which made a quiet click a moment later, and he pushed one of the doors wide open.

"After you," he said, gesturing for me to go ahead.

Inside, the house was no less impressive than the exterior. The wide plank wood floors throughout the open concept main floor were dark, but everything else was light. Off-white walls, cream-colored rugs, light sage sofas in the living room, pale wood furniture in the dining room. There were no curtains or blinds on any windows, leaving an unobstructed view of the forest surrounding the house. I could imagine the interior on a bright, sunny day filled with so much light it would warm the coldest soul right through.

I noticed Nico watching me as I gazed around this tranquil oasis. It must have been a trick of the light, though, because the way he was looking at me, it was like he was gauging my response, trying to decipher what I thought of his home.

"It's incredible," I said, just in case.

He nodded then led me through the house without another word.

Every piece of furniture and every piece of artwork on the walls looked like they belonged here, like they'd been handcrafted for this very home. A pale wood coffee table that matched the dining table. An abstract woodland painting done in soft, earthy pastels. The only thing that didn't blend perfectly with the décor was the scent.

I imagined this place would have smelled like pine forest and rich earth on any other day. Today, the savory scent of roasted garlic and the camphoric aroma of oregano wafted from the kitchen at the far left end of the open floor.

Nico made a straight line for the wall oven in the corner, opened it up, and slipped on an oven mitt to withdraw the dishes warming inside. One by one, he placed them down on the pale beige granite counter beside the oven: pasta dishes, potatoes, fresh breads, vegetables baked to golden perfection.

"Did you make all this?" I asked, trying not to sound surprised but failing miserably.

"No." He barked out a laugh as he transferred the uncovered dishes to a side table next to the pretty bistro table already set ten steps away. "The kitchen was my mother's domain growing up, mainly because my father didn't venture in there too often."

He flinched the moment the words were out. I didn't have to wonder why. That was an awfully personal piece of information he'd let slip, and I imagined he didn't make mistakes like that very often.

"I can make a mean French toast," I offered. "I can't explain it. I've been told I must have been born without a cooking gene."

It wasn't as personal as the bit of information he'd offered up accidentally, but it was a piece of me, nonetheless. It had frustrated me to no end all the times Greta had pulled together an eggs Florentine breakfast or an eggplant parmesan dinner effortlessly while I struggled not to screw up heating soup from a can.

"I suppose that's why God created caterers," he said, like it was normal to hire someone else to cook meals every day.

I scoffed. "Yeah, right. Try paying for a caterer and a full-time college education," I said but then immediately felt stupid.

Nico Costa was next in line in Lorenzo Costa's empire. He would know nothing about juggling bills. As the dead not-dead daughter of Vincent Luca, I should have never known what it was like either. Vito had offered countless times to pay for my college education, but I refused every time. I did not want to give him that burden. And maybe, deep down, I wanted to do something on my own. So, I had worked hard, gotten every scholarship I could, and worked and saved up every summer to pay for what I could.

Nico looked at me strangely then pulled out a chair for me without saying a word. I sat down, and his fingers at the back of the chair brushed across my back, sending shivers through my whole body. He remained still for a moment, and I thought—or maybe hoped—he was going to touch me again, but he didn't. Instead, he took the seat across from me while I tried to ignore the wave of heaviness that weighted down my chest.

"You said you were going to school to become a nurse."

I wasn't sure if it was a statement or a question, so I nodded.

"What made you decide to do that?" he asked, cocking an eyebrow like he was daring me to answer.

I wasn't sure I wanted to share such a personal story with a man I likely wouldn't see again after tonight. But my mouth opened, and the words spilled out of their own volition.

"I guess you could say I had troubles when I was a kid. For quite a long time, I was always sure I could smell smoke or that something was going to light on fire at any second. Or if one of the kids in my class didn't show up to school one day, I was convinced they'd died, and the teacher just wouldn't tell me." I paused, laughing self-consciously.

Why was I telling him this? But maybe it made sense. When this was over, he'd forget about me. I could tell him anything, and he'd never reveal my secrets. That was the great thing about being me, it seemed. I was disposable. Easily forgettable.

Nico poured two glasses of wine and handed me one. "Go on," he said, looking at me like he was interested, not like he thought I was batshit crazy.

"One day, Greta didn't show up to school—I guess she was home, sick—but I was certain she was dead. My best friend was dead," I choked out, remembering how I'd felt even if it had all been in my head. "I freaked out so much, I hyperventilated, and I guess I passed out. I woke up in the nurse's office, and the nurse was just... there, stroking my hair back and telling me everything was going to be okay. When she learned why I was upset, she got Greta's parents on the phone and let me talk to Greta. And then, the nurse arranged for me to get some really good therapy."

It had seemed harmless to tell him, but I felt exposed the moment the words were out. *Why did I tell him that story?*

"And that made you want to become a nurse?" he asked with a slight furrow between his eyebrows.

"But that wasn't all she did," I added. It sounded like I'd decided to become a nurse because some lady had been nice to me for five minutes. "For years after, even when I was no longer convinced the whole world was going up in flames, she checked on me all the time. She pulled me out of class, and I got to hang out with her in the nurse's office. And she just let me talk, I guess. She didn't have to do any of those things, you know? It wasn't part of her job, and eventually, I figured I wanted to be just like her. Not just doing my job, but actually helping people."

"You're saying you lost people you cared about in a fire," he said. There was a hard edge in his tone.

I'd thought I had, but those wounds were too fresh to talk about.

"No," I said instead. "I never lost anyone in a fire."

121

He looked at me for a moment, like he was trying to see behind my eyes. His piercing stare made me feel like he might have just been able to do it.

I glanced away, turning my attention to the wine in front of me and the food on the side table. I hadn't eaten all day, I realized, as I filled my plate. I'd sat in the living room of my hotel room, telling myself I was going to dinner with Nico because it could help with my stupid plan. I wanted to ignore how much I craved the way I couldn't focus on anything but him when he was around. The vetiver and clean scent of him. The hard, muscular body concealed beneath his crisp navy-blue suit. The heated look in his eyes whenever he looked at me. The charged energy in the air between us.

"So, what is it you do all day when you're not seducing women at nightclubs?" I asked, trying to drag my mind away from the only direction it wanted to go.

It came out sounding kind of lame, but I had no idea how dinner-date conversation was supposed to go with a dangerous killer. It was insane that even that thought sent a hot-cold shiver down my spine.

"I work," he said with a casual shrug of his shoulders. "Business has been busy lately, so it occupies most of my time."

"Busy?" I asked.

Did he mean he was busy arranging shipments and overseeing production all the time? Or was it the other part of the business that kept him occupied? The part where he'd built an infamous reputation torturing and killing people?

A flicker of a knowing smile crossed his expression, but he took a sip of wine, and it was gone. "We have new warehouses we've recently acquired. They're not manned with as much security as they should be, so there's a push to move production along faster than some of our men are accustomed to," he said with another casual shrug.

I didn't really understand what that meant, but I smiled anyway.

The room was silent as we delved into our food. I could hear too much. The too-fast thud of my heartbeat. The inhale and exhale of our breathing, mine coming twice as fast as his. Even the quiet rustle of fabric as I uncrossed then crossed my legs beneath the table. It was like my senses were working overtime.

I could see every muscle working in his throat when he swallowed. His scent carried over the top of the spicy aroma of the pasta. My dress felt heavier against my skin. Though it was made of silk, it felt cloying and uncomfortable, and I just wanted it off.

I couldn't say how much time had passed when he swallowed back the last drops of wine from his glass and stood.

"It seems you're not very hungry," he said with a knowing grin.

I glanced down at my barely-touched plate and empty wineglass. The food was excellent, but I still had no appetite. I'd worked my way through two glasses of wine, though, and I could feel the effects tingling through my extremities, making them feel just a little heavier than usual.

Searching for some sort of apology, I opened my mouth, but he shook his head.

"I'm not hungry either, Raven. Not for food, anyway."

Leaving our plates on the table, he held out his hand. The moment I took it, the sparks in the air ignited, zapping the oxygen from the room and heating me from the inside out.

He led me back through the house to the living room, and I tried to hide my quiet sigh of disappointment. I'd kind of been hoping he would have led me straight to his bedroom. This was not my main purpose in coming here, but I wanted it more than I ever thought possible. Nico made it so tempting to forget about my real life and bury myself in experiences I've never had. To overwhelm my senses so much that everything else disappeared—even if only for a little while.

"Something wrong?" he asked with a quirk of his brow.

"No," I lied.

Having sex for the first time with a veritable stranger was one thing. I was fine with it not being all about roses and candlelight. I didn't really believe in all that love and romance nonsense anyway. But begging this man for sex seemed like something else entirely.

"Good," he said, then he pulled me close with one quick tug of his hand.

Chapter Nineteen

Raven

His lips swooped in, capturing mine while his hands settled low on my hips. *Yes,* my mind screamed.

There was something different about his kiss this time, like it was more restrained than before. It seemed to have no less effect, though. Sensation rippled throughout my whole body, feeding a fire that had already begun to burn low in my abdomen. By the time he pulled away, I was breathless and trembling.

My mind was one hundred percent consumed with the man in front of me. Just like I wanted. Even if I shouldn't.

He took a step back and flashed me a smile that read more like a warning. "Take off your clothes, Raven. I want to see *you*," he said, his words seeming to echo after that last word. His deep guttural voice vibrated within me, lingering low in my core.

He took another step back, settled in the middle of the light sage-green sofa behind him, and held me in place with his gaze. It had been one thing to stand there and let him undress me. Heat climbed up my neck, no doubt staining my cheeks. I felt like a stripper at a private club. Ice ran through my fingertips.

Then I looked at him. The heat in his eyes as he grazed over my body left me feeling so warm my clothes felt even heavier. They clung to my skin uncomfortably. What would his eyes look like if I did what he asked? I remembered the fire in them when he'd untied my sash and my dressing gown had fallen open. I *longed* to feel the scorch of his gaze on every mound, inch, part of my body.

With fingers that I wished had been steadier, I reached for the buttons that ran down the front of my cream sundress between my breasts. His eyes followed my movement, and it excited me to watch his gaze travel lower with every button I unfastened.

I'd nearly reached my waist before the sides of the fabric parted and my naked breasts spilled out. Nico groaned quietly, sitting up straighter on the sofa.

"Keep going," he said in that tone that brooked no refusal.

My fingers obeyed, continuing down the column of buttons until I'd flicked open the last one.

Three.

Two.

One.

"Stop," he said as I moved my arms to let the dress slip to the floor. He stood up and closed the distance between us. "Turn around," he whispered against my ear.

I complied. Now I couldn't see him. I couldn't see the look in his eyes as his fingers slipped the dress down my arms, and it pooled at my feet. I was completely naked. I'd even forgone panties in anticipation of this moment. But now I was holding my breath, waiting for him to say something. To do something.

"What are you thinking?" I asked when the silence had stretched like an elastic inside me, ready to snap.

"I'm thinking that you look incredible, Raven. The most perfect, fuckable thing I've ever seen."

His words raced through my veins like a drug, dangerous and addictive.

He grabbed hold of my hips, and I nearly jolted at the contact. He pressed his body against me from behind. The firm planes of his chest, the hard length of his erection, but it was all muffled by the clothing he still wore.

I wanted him naked, like me. I wanted to feel every groove and contour of his body against mine. When I tried to spin around, his hands held my hips still.

"Not yet. Just stay still like a good girl." His breath whispered against the back of my neck as he spoke, making me shiver.

The warmth of his breath turned into the softness of his lips pressing down the back of my neck. His teeth nipping at my shoulder. His tongue blazing a fiery trail down my spine.

"Lie down," he said as my body strove headlong toward combustion.

So caught up in the fire burning inside me, I had to process what he was saying, but the moment his words registered, the fire blazed like an inferno.

This was it.

I'd never done this before, and while butterflies on steroids still fluttered in my stomach, I had to have been more ready than any woman had ever been in history. I wanted this. Him. Nico.

He released my hips, and I spun around to comply, lying back on the plush cream-colored rug. I kept my legs together. A little foolish, and a little late in the game.

"Open your legs, Raven. I want to see you," he instructed as he slipped off his jacket and began to unbutton his shirt.

He stared at me, waiting expectantly while I watched, mesmerized, as every button he unfastened revealed more of him. My fingers itched to touch him, my lips tingled, anxious to taste all that hard flesh.

And then the thought struck me. I had no idea why it had never hit me before. I supposed I'd just had no reason to consider it until now. Growing up with Greta, who had to be one of the most comfortable people on the planet when it came to sex, I'd heard her talk plenty about the importance of seeking out my pleasure. Ways to enhance sex for me. Ways to make my orgasms better. I only knew about the secret pleasures of a pulsating showerhead because of Greta.

But what about Nico? He was used to worldly women. Experienced women. *Women who'd had sex with something other than a showerhead!* That meant he was used to women who knew a whole lot more about how to make sex pleasurable for *him*.

I hadn't thought it was important to tell him. After all, it was me having sex for the first time, not him. But maybe I was wrong. At least if I told him, he wouldn't be surprised when I had no idea what I was doing.

"Open your legs now," he demanded with a quiet growl in his voice.

I wondered if anyone had ever defied one of his commands. Probably not. Because despite what I'd been thinking seconds ago, I drew up my knees a little and opened my legs for him, watching him as the heat in his eyes blazed hotter. Despite the pants he still had on, I could see his cock jerking against its restraints. My mouth watered, and my pussy clenched like my body couldn't quite decide which part of me wanted to take him first.

"*Perfetto*," he said, but again, there was a hard edge in his tone.

Instead of stripping down further, he knelt over me, pressing his lips against mine for just a moment before he began to travel lower. I grazed my hands across his naked back, feeling the flex and bunch of muscles beneath my fingers as he moved. His arms supported him on either side of me, and I could see the veins in his biceps that stood out from the muscle. I'd never thought veins could fascinate me before, but I'd been wrong—I could get off with this alone.

Down my neck he traveled, kissing and nipping in a way that did strange things to my insides. The pinch of his teeth stung, but that sting traveled down the line connected to my pussy, and somewhere along the way, the message changed, transforming into something dark and pleasurable.

He kept going, wandering a zigzag line to the upper swells of my breasts. His lips, tongue, and teeth continued lower, kissing and nipping until he reached my nipple. His tongue swirled around the taut flesh, and then he suckled my nipple into his mouth. I could feel his teeth grazing me, just lightly at first, but then harder. And harder. The sensation shot down the line, eliciting a quiet squeak from me, but at the same time, my back arched off the rug, pushing my breast harder against him.

He chuckled against me, but then his tongue bathed my nipple, soothing and stimulating at the same time before he turned his attention to the other, suckling and then biting down until I was a hot, wet mess. It was like sensation overload, but instead of pulling away, it made me want to cling tighter, digging my fingers into the muscles in his shoulders.

Lower and lower, he kept going. Down my abdomen, branching out to kiss and nip my hips, then back down my center, over my bare mound. My breath came hard and fast. He was right there. His lips were just a hair's breadth from where I needed him most.

He leaned away, sitting back on his heels, staring down at my needy flesh.

"Open your legs wider," he said, not taking his eyes off my pussy.

I complied, watching his lips, trying to compel them back where I needed them. But he didn't move.

"Give me your hand," he said, holding out his own to take mine.

Confused and more than a little flustered, I did as he asked.

He moved my hand between my thighs, then took two of my fingers and placed them on my clit. My body jolted at the contact, clouding whatever embarrassment I should have been feeling.

"Show me," he instructed.

My fingers remained frozen.

"Show me how you like it, Raven. Let me see your fingers work."

Swallowing hard, I squeezed my eyes shut and nodded, moving my fingers in slow, languid circles.

"No," he said, holding my fingers still. "Open your eyes, and look at me."

I could only imagine how my cheeks would flame afterward, remembering what I'd done, but I forced my eyes open and met his gaze.

"Good girl," he crooned.

He released my fingers.

I began to move, circling my clit while his eyes flickered back and forth between my pussy and my eyes. I wasn't sure which one was sending me higher: my fingers or him watching me.

I moved faster, not bothering to try to stop the quiet moans that slipped from my lips. Faster still, I could feel the coil already begin to wind up tight inside me.

I couldn't believe I was doing this. All my life, pleasuring myself was something I'd done in private, usually beneath the covers with the lights off. But now, I was going to come right in front of this man with only my own fingers on my body.

The coil wound up tighter, and my moans grew louder. I wanted to squeeze my eyes shut like I usually did when I was by myself.

I kept them open, watching him watch me.

"Stop," he said.

If it had been anyone else, I couldn't have stopped. I would have kept going, careening right over the edge. But I stopped, stilling my fingers on my engorged clit.

It only took *one* word.

The corners of his lips turned up in a wicked grin. He knew how close I'd been. He grazed a finger along my wet pussy, and my lips parted easily for him. Again and again, but never penetrating me.

"Nico, please," I breathed, pleading with him.

"Do you want to be fucked?" he asked.

I nodded eagerly.

"Then go ahead," he said, taking my hand and guiding it lower.

A slight curl furrowed between my brows.

"Finger yourself, Raven. I want to see those pretty fingers disappear," he said, his voice thick as he pressed my finger against my opening.

Shamelessly, I delved in, realizing that with every command he gave, it drove me higher.

The moment I had my finger buried inside me, he lunged like a man starving. His tongue lapped at my clit, over and over again. He suckled me into his mouth, threatening to drive me over the brink.

I felt his teeth, just the light scrape as he grazed me gently. But it was enough. Or just right. Or so much more than I could bear.

My back arched clear off the rug, and I could feel the walls of my pussy clench tight around my finger as shockwaves of pleasure rippled out from my core.

Before I came back down, Nico was on his feet. He stripped off his pants in a flash, unleashing his massive erection. He grabbed a condom out of his pocket, sheathed himself.

He was back before I'd taken two breaths.

He yanked my finger away, slamming my hand down on the rug above my head. And then the head of his cock was pressing against my wet slit. Without a moment's pause, he plunged forward with one hard thrust of his hips.

I screamed as pain tore right through my body.

He went still.

He was frozen hilt-deep inside me while the burning pain slowly began to ebb.

"What the hell, Raven?" he ground out between clenched teeth. "Why would you let me…" His voice trailed off as he squeezed his eyes shut and sunk in just a little deeper with a strangled groan.

A seed of panic blossomed in my chest. I'd never thought it would bother him. It was my virginity. Not his. Mine to choose what I did with it. Mine to give or to keep. But then, I hadn't thought about whether it could have caused him pain. *Did it hurt to tear through a hymen?* I'd never thought to Google it.

"I'm sorry—"

132

"You're sorry?"

He still hadn't moved. He didn't look shocked, yet it didn't seem like he was in pain either. I could tell it was taking him a tremendous amount of effort to remain still. His arms were shaking, and it was a wonder he didn't break his teeth with how hard he was gritting his jaw.

"If I hurt you, I mean..." I tried to explain.

He scoffed, pressing his forehead against mine. "No, you didn't hurt me."

"Then why are you angry?" I asked because it was the only emotion I could equate with the look on his face.

"I'm not angry, Raven. Fuck, do you have any idea what it's doing to me to know I'm the first man who's ever been with you?"

"*Oh.*"

I'd heard some men had a particular taste for virgins, but I'd just assumed that Nico wasn't one of them given his constant, ready supply of women. All the ones I'd seen plastered on the Internet had struck me as experienced. If he wanted virgins, he probably could have ordered them up on a silver platter.

"Do you still hurt?" he asked while the muscles spasmed in his jaw.

"No, not really."

It had come on strong, but it was nearly gone now. I felt stretched to the max, but it wasn't painful exactly.

"Good," he growled.

Some of the tension in him eased as he withdrew until only the tip of him remained inside me.

I almost whimpered, but he thrust back in, slower this time, making the coil inside me begin to wind. Again and again, and

133

eventually, the stretched feeling began to ease like my body was changing to accommodate him, to fit him inside me perfectly. I'd always imagined sex to be an intrusive feeling, like an invasion of sorts. But it felt like he was filling me. Like there was a part of me that was previously empty, a part of me that I had no idea existed before.

He still held one of my arms above my head, but I reached for him with my free hand. I wanted to feel him; the hard planes of his body, the bunch and flex of muscle. My fingers traveled lower, down his back and then his ass where every new inch I covered was just as firm as the last.

The coil wound up tighter. I wrapped my legs around his waist. It was only then I realized he'd been holding back. With my hips tilted, he plunged in deeper, hitting the top of my cervix.

I cried out, the pain twisted as it traveled down the line and sent the coil spinning out of control.

Harder, faster. I squeezed my eyes shut against the onslaught of pleasure that was coming too fast. Too potent. No matter how I tried, I couldn't slow it down.

Greta had said that orgasms during sex were rare for women, but I was on a fast climb. Moans tumbled out, one on top of the other. I couldn't stop them any more than I could slow the building orgasm.

"You feel fucking incredible, Raven. So tight, so warm," he ground out, thrusting faster.

I wanted to say something. I wanted to tell him that I'd never imagined sex could feel so good, but all that came out was a scream as I reached the top of my climb, and a kaleidoscope of sensation exploded inside me. His lips took mine as he picked up his pace, his teeth crimping my lower lip in between.

He groaned like I was hurting him, but the expression on his face wasn't pained. His jaw was still clenched tight, but the look in his eyes mirrored the pleasure that coursed through my own body.

"So. Fucking. Tight," he growled as my pussy spasmed around him. And then he thrust in once more, stilling deep inside me as he groaned through his own release.

He remained there for one blissful moment, but then he slipped out, and the emptiness I hadn't realized I'd felt before came rushing back.

I recognized it now, and all I wanted was to feel it again.

He collapsed onto his back next to me and pulled me against him.

"You're very unique, Raven Ferrari," he said as I nestled in the crook of his arm.

A smile tugged at the corner of my lips, and I didn't miss the single drop of blood that seeped into my mouth.

Chapter Twenty

Nico

Virgins were messy.

They were emotional, and clingy, and were generally not happy with being shoved out the door afterward. At least, that's what I heard.

I had no idea what I was missing. I thrust right through the thin barrier I had no idea would be there. The rush that had followed had been like nothing I'd ever experienced in my life. Just thinking about how I was the only man who'd ever been with her was already draining the blood back to my cock.

I wanted her again. Now. But that was a bad idea.

Raven's chest rose and fell against me, the cadence growing steadier by the moment, but she wasn't asleep. I could almost feel the breeze from the thought cyclone whirling around in her head.

"What are you thinking about?"

There's a first time for everything. Today, conversation after sex. Tomorrow, movie date with Lorenzo.

She laughed. "Did you know the human body burns about five calories a minute during sex?"

"I didn't know that."

"And it's been proven that sex can boost recall skills and activate the part of the brain that's associated with learning."

"Are you trying to find reasons to not regret sleeping with me?" I played it out as a light joke, but I waited to hear what she would say.

"No." She laughed. "I always thought people kind of just fell asleep, exhausted, after sex, but I'm not tired. My brain feels like it's going a hundred miles a minute, but all it can come up with is useless sex facts."

A grin quirked my mouth upward. "Did you know the combined scents of lavender and pumpkin pie are a major aphrodisiac for men?"

"Seriously?" she asked, drawing circles down my pecs with one finger.

"*Cosmo* said it, so it must be true, right?"

Her finger paused. "You read *Cosmo*?"

I could imagine the incredulous look on her face.

"Not exactly."

I had an eye for detail. There was a *Cosmo* magazine on Pisano's desk, and it had Gino Pisano's name on the mailing label. How many men subscribed to women's magazines?

"I read that women prefer men who wear red," she said and then yawned, fitting her body closer against me.

"And what are your thoughts on the matter?"

She shook her head sluggishly against me. "You look amazing in blue."

"Then I guess it's like I said, you're *not* like most women."

"I hope not," she said, but her words came out slow and quiet.

I stayed still for a minute, listening as her breathing settled into the even rhythm of sleep. It would be quite a while before my high started to wane. I was so hopped up, hooked, *addicted* I might never be able to sleep again.

I waited another minute, then shifted out from under her as carefully as I could and stood up, tearing my gaze away from Raven nestled peacefully on my Mahal rug. If I glanced at her, that would be it. I'd be hilt-deep inside her in two seconds flat.

I threw on my pants and left the room. I made my way across the house to the open doorway that led to the basement and the gym I had set up there. It wasn't often I had this much pent-up energy after sex.

Down the winding maple wood staircase, I crossed the black mat-covered floor to the punching bag suspended from the ceiling on the other side of the room and started my session. I focused on the windup, the bunch of muscles across my back, and threw everything I had into each punch, slamming my fist into the stiff leather.

What had Raven been thinking? Her virginity had been a high price to pay in whatever game she was playing. Was this an angle I couldn't calculate?

I cocked back and threw my fist into the bag again, and then again.

It made absolutely no sense. If she'd heard about me in the tabloids, then she was aware of my reputation. The minute I'd fucked her, I'd be done with her. I did not come back for seconds. *What am I missing?*

My muscles started to burn as I pounded the bag relentlessly. Every punch traveled up my fist and shot through my arm like a jolt

138

of electricity. Sweat trickled down my nape, slipping down the damp flesh of my back.

She had an angle only she was seeing—and I needed to be in on it. A Luciano turning up now cannot be a coincidence. I considered sending Raven on her way and going after them head-on.

Then my swing froze mid-air as the thought brought a heavy feeling in my chest, draining everything inside out.

No matter how much my muscles burned, it did nothing to stop the high. She was a drug, and I was already jonesing for another hit. I wanted to explore every inch of her body. I wanted her in every way imaginable so that when this was over, there'd be nothing any man could do to her that I hadn't already done. No pleasure he could give her that I hadn't given her first. Nothing he could teach her that I hadn't already taught her.

I landed one last punch, my rhythm already off. I thought of the useless sex facts she'd been spouting earlier and how I secretly filed away every single one in my head.

If Raven's job was to mess with my head, then she deserved a gold star from the Luciano family council. All the reward I needed was having her body as my playground for a while. I'd explore every mile, mound, plane of her until no part of her remained untouched by me. My heart rattled in its cage, cold and long untouched.

As I headed for the shower, I realized that this was a whole new ball game now. It had just turned into a race: *How much time do I have to enjoy myself before the Lucianos walked right into my trap?*

I set the dial on the shower, stripped off my pants, and stepped beneath the hot spray just long enough to get clean. Now that I had a plan in mind, I was anxious to get started.

As I shut off the water and wrapped a towel around my hips, an image of Raven's lips parted in ecstasy sprung to mind, along with an idea for the perfect starting point.

It was time to teach her how to her lips to good use.

***

Raven was still asleep in the living room. Lying on her back, she had her arms stretched up above her head with her legs just slightly parted. My fingers itched to force her thighs open wide as they would go, stretching her joints to the max to keep her strung taut while I buried my tongue deep inside her. I shook my head, ignoring for now the hardness that came almost at once. Some part of this plan had to go as I intended after all.

"Wake up, Raven," I whispered and then watched as her body came awake.

Her toes flexed, her arms reached higher above her, thrusting out her breasts. Her eyes moved behind her eyelids, and she let out a quiet sigh of contentment that shot straight through me.

Her eyes opened slowly at first, but they flew open wide the second she spotted me. It took her a moment to get her bearings, but then the wild, sleepy look in them vanished, replaced by something hot and liquid as her eyes grazed over my towel-clad body. Lower and lower, until her gaze settled on the jut of my cock that tented the towel. Her tongue darted out to lick her lips.

"I like your thinking," I said, then reached out a hand to pull her to her feet.

The splotches of color across her cheeks had returned, stroking my cock some more. I liked her nervous and a little uncomfortable, but it wasn't enough to deter her, and that pleased me even more.

"I was dreaming about you," she said, not quite meeting my eyes.

"What about me?"

"I never got a chance to…" She bit down on the inside of her bottom lip, but instead of saying more, she raised her hands to my shoulders and grazed downward over my pecs and abdomen. When she reached the towel slung low around my hips, she hesitated.

"Do you want to see more, Raven?"

"Yes," she said, running her fingers across my abdomen, just above the edge of the towel.

"Then go ahead," I said, giving her permission.

I wondered if she'd be as uncomfortable as when she'd stripped for me. It was the best strip tease I'd ever seen though. Nothing contrived, no choreography, no jazz. Just one hundred percent Raven. That's the way it had seemed anyway. If it was all part of her act, then give the girl her Oscar.

Her fingers hesitated for a moment, but then she untucked the towel.

It dropped to the floor.

She let out a small gasp, her eyes like blue flames ready to combust at any moment. My cock jerked. Her lips slightly parted, I couldn't help but imagine them wrapped around my throbbing shaft. I placed my hands on her shoulders.

"On your knees, Raven," I told her and pressed down gently.

Her eyes shot up to meet mine as she dropped to her knees at my feet. *No resistance.* My member seemed to come to life as it throbbed, veins pulsating on the surface.

141

She reached up to my hips and trailed her fingers down the front of my thighs. The tips of her thumbs just grazed my balls, but it sent a sizzle of electricity to the base of my spine.

"Open your mouth," I told her, taking hold of my cock and pressing the tip to her lips.

She obeyed, leaning forward to take the head of my shaft into her mouth while her tongue grazed along the sensitive ridge. Her tongue slowly ate me up, working me further into the wet heat of her mouth until she'd taken all she could.

I wanted to press further, to thrust my hips and feel the sweet clench of her throat muscles, but I withdrew instead until I'd all but slipped out before letting her work me back in. Over and over again. One of her hands settled on my hip to hold herself steady while her other hand moved to my balls, rolling them between her fingers, tender but nimble. Her gaze fixed into mine, her lashes seemed to curtain a gale of fervor and uncertainty.

"*Perfetto*, Raven. That's what you are," I said in an answer to the question that whirled behind her eyes.

Not even in my fantasy had I imagined her looking like this with her lips stretched taut around me. It was like she'd been made just for this, just for me.

I buried my hand in her hair at the nape of her neck and held her still while I picked up the pace, fucking her mouth faster.

Her throat spasmed around the tip of my cock, sending jolts of pleasure through my body. I pulled out and dragged her up to her feet. I'd intended to fuck her mouth until she'd swallowed every drop of my come, but I wanted to bury myself in her pussy. I wanted to feel her come around my cock while her spasms milked me dry.

Once she was on her feet, I sheathed my cock and lifted her. She wrapped her legs around me. I planned to move us to the bedroom but at this rate, I wasn't making it that far. I pressed her up against the living room wall, lined myself up, and drove in, using every ounce of strength I could muster to keep some semblance of control.

She was new at this. I had no idea if there was some sort of adjustment period for her body to get used to being fucked. But she was wet and so tight, and it was doing crazy things to my head to know that sucking my cock had aroused her so much. Crazy, wonderful things that had me striving headlong for the brink.

Keeping an arm beneath her for support, I slipped a hand between us and settled two fingers on her engorged clit.

"Oh god, Nico," she moaned as I started to rub.

Between her wet pussy and all the noise she was making, I didn't think I was going to last much longer.

I picked up my pace on her clit, making her moan louder while her fingers dug into my back. I'd have plenty of bloody scratches by the time we were finished—not that I minded.

She dug in deeper and slammed her head back against the wall, leaving the smooth column of her throat exposed like an invitation. I took full advantage, kissing and suckling until I couldn't resist any longer. I caught her flesh between my teeth and bit down, not enough to break skin, just enough to leave my mark on her.

She jolted against me, but at the same time, moans tumbled from her lips, growing louder with every passing second.

I fucked her as shallowly as I could, but her pussy was like a magnet, drawing me deeper until I couldn't resist the urge to ram in, filling her up, forcing every inch of my cock inside her.

She cried out, but she wrapped her legs tighter around me.

"Don't stop," she cried breathlessly. "Nico, don't ever stop."

"Never," I lied.

Not even I could go forever, but I sure as hell never wanted to stop.

Her fingernails dug in deep, drawing blood and sparking up my brain. Faster still, I lost all rhythm, driving into her like a man possessed until her moans turned to screams, and her pussy began to spasm around my shaft.

I didn't fight it when my balls drew up tight, and the tingling at the base of my spine transformed into live current that shot through every fiber in my body while I emptied my cock deep inside her.

"Ow," she said.

I froze. I wanted to use her. Pain held a certain appeal, but only when it was measured and deliberate, not when I'd hurt her unintentionally.

I leaned away to look at her, and there was a languid smile on her face.

"I think you broke me," she said, then dropped her head against my shoulder and giggled, a sound that made my heart twitch and jerk, as if it could be revived.

I left her wet heat reluctantly and lowered her feet to the floor.

"You don't look broken to me," I said, grazing over her naked body that was flush from her orgasm. "You look like an advertisement for all things *sin*."

I turned her face up and kissed her lips.

It was getting late, I realized, catching sight of the microwave clock in the kitchen. Work had been keeping me busy lately, even if the new warehouses I told Raven about were actually already up and running with a full-staff count. I was counting on her to relay news about the Costas' under-protected warehouses to the Lucianos. It was the perfect trap, even if I was currently regretting setting it up quite so quickly.

If she left soon, she'd have plenty of time to share the news with her underhanded comrades. If I kept her here, she wouldn't be able to relay the message, which guaranteed me more time.

The battle waged in my head. Ultimately, the plan had to win out. As much as I wanted to cuff Raven to my bed and never let her leave, I was trying to stop a war and protect my family.

Without a word, I went and retrieved her dress from the floor and handed it to her.

"I'll be right back," I said, then darted up to the bedroom for a fresh change of clothes.

She was dressed when I returned, standing with her hands clasped in front of her. She was looking around at the different art prints on the walls.

"I don't know how this works..." she said, trailing off. "I mean, when you have other women here. I can call a cab..."

"I've never had another woman here, Raven."

I tried not to regret the words the moment they were out.

Regardless of what game she was playing, she paid a high price tonight. For some reason, I wanted to offer her something in return. "You're the first woman to ever set foot in my home."

She looked at me with a slight furrow creasing her brow, and I felt compelled to offer more.

"I guess you could say this is my escape from reality," I said with a shrug that I hoped minimized the enormity of what it meant that I invited her here.

It was a calculated move. But I couldn't help but wonder if I would have made the same move had it been any other woman.

"I'll drive you back to the hotel," I said before she could say anything.

She nodded and followed me through the house to the Porsche waiting outside. I opened the passenger door for her, and she slipped inside.

All the while, I was cursing my plan. I'd never admit it aloud, but part of me was secretly hoping the damn thing would fail. Just for now. Just until I'd gotten my fill of her and had no reservations about burning her family to the ground.

Chapter Twenty-One

Nico

No nibbles.

No bites.

Raven had not taken the bait I set up so freely in the open.

What was worse was that I couldn't stop thinking about her even when I needed to get my head in the game.

The club was pretty busy considering it was only six. Every stool at the bar was occupied, the dance floor was writhing with bodies, and only two of the tables that surrounded the floor were vacant.

I was proud of Onyx. I'd taken it from the shady club it had been under my father's care to what it was today. It was the kind of the place that appealed to everyone, from average Joes who needed to let off some steam after a week working at a cubicle to the upper crusts who knew that what couldn't be found on the dance floor was readily available in the rooms below it.

I watched on as Amber, the redhead with legs that went on forever, snagged her first John of the night, leading him off the floor toward the door to the basement. Amber was good. The guy was in for quite a night, worth every one of the hundreds of dollars he was about to fork out.

It was strange that I felt no inclination to head downstairs for the night. Memories of Amber's long legs and breathy moans just sent thoughts of Raven whirling in my head, flaming the wicked need to bury myself deep inside her body.

I shook my head, baffled. Maybe Raven was a witch. If I was a monster, why couldn't she be a witch?

"Showtime," Gabe said from where he stood beside me outside the club's office door. He nodded to the three men who had just entered the club.

Despite the wide-scale differences in Onyx's patrons, these three stood out like sore thumbs with their hair slicked back and their long trench coats. The man in the middle with salt-and-pepper hair had his coat undone, revealing a suit that cost more than most men made in a year. He was dwarfed by the dark-haired men on either side of him, each of whom looked like they were wearing inflatable rings around their biceps beneath their coats. I clicked my tongue. That much muscle might have looked intimidating to some, but so much bulk just slowed a man down and made him ineffective in a fight.

I glanced at my watch, not surprised to find Fiorenzo Avalone was right on time. I turned and stepped inside the office. I sat down behind the mahogany desk, thankful this wasn't my life. The four walls would have driven me mad.

"Tell me again why we're meeting with this prick," Gabe said as he followed me into the office. "The guy's got no territory here, no business with the Costas, and from what I hear, he's an evil son of a bitch."

"He says he's got information about who's been killing Costas and our associates," I said with a shrug that belied my own concerns about the man.

The call had been a request to meet with my father, but even if I wasn't trying to keep this information away from Lorenzo, the last time Lorenzo had a meeting was when I was still a virgin. He was more a figurehead these days, only popping up long enough to be a pain in my ass.

I wondered if that would be me in old age, bitter and hostile, holing up in the family estate like a hermit. The man's life was pointless, in my opinion. He'd pushed everyone away and had nothing but the lackeys and whores he paid to keep him company. But I was walking in his shoes, wasn't I? Looking at my father, it was a mirror reflection of exactly what was in store for me.

"And the guy is just going to hand over that information out of the kindness of his heart?" Gabe asked, eyeing me dubiously.

"No." I scoffed.

No man in this world gave away something for nothing. I did not like that I did not know what his angle was. But I didn't have a choice. I was chomping at the bit, feeling backed into a corner like this. One wrong move, and I could snap.

"So, what exactly am *I* doing here?" Gabe asked.

He wasn't used to being brought into the fold. On any other day, he'd be gathering intel, setting up meetings, and handling the small-scale operations.

"It's time you learn the ropes," I said.

He was next in line, and I firmly believed in the mantra, *"Live bloody, die bloody."* I didn't expect to live to a ripe, old age, or maybe, I just hoped I wouldn't. I didn't want Lorenzo's life.

It was strange that an image of Raven flashed through my mind at that moment. I could see her in my home, in my bed… in my life. *Ha!* I nearly scoffed aloud. Even if I wanted to saddle myself with one woman, a Luciano was not the right woman. I'd have to keep an eye on her forever, waiting for her to stab me in the back. I'd be just like Lorenzo then. Maybe that meant it *was* the right move: propose to the girl and get the ball rolling early. I could even get started on building a family of kids who hated me.

At that thought, my mind clamped down like a vise because that was *not* happening anytime soon. I was expected to produce an heir, so an heir I would produce, but not one moment before I had to. I was in no hurry to pass down whatever red liquid ran in my veins to some kid who would only grow to hate me. Maybe I'd father an heir on my deathbed.

A bouncer at the club escorted Fiorenzo and his two lackeys into the office. *Thank fuck.* I'd been itching to get out of this meeting, but any distraction was a good distraction at the moment. Thinking of kids? That was new.

"*Buena sera, Signor Avalone,*" I said, ignoring the inflatable ring goons.

"*Buena sera, Signor Costa,*" he said to me, then nodded to Gabe.

I stood up long enough to shake the man's hand, waited for him to shake Gabe's hand from where my brother stood beside me, then sat back down behind the desk.

He looked around before he sat down in the chair opposite the desk while his goons took a place on either side of him, their backs straight, hands behind their backs, and eyes alert. Avalone seemed surprised by my own lack of "reinforcements."

I laughed. "You could have a hundred goons surrounding you, Avalone. You try anything, I guarantee you don't make it out of this room alive."

He laughed good-naturedly, and his shoulders relaxed. "Yes, your reputation precedes you, *Signor Costa.*"

"Get to the point, *Signor Avalone,*" I said, leaning back in my chair in a way that belied the tension that had every muscle in my body taut and alert.

The man's face sobered. "As I said, I have information about who has been fishing from the Costa family pond," he said with a smile that told me he was pleased with his cheesy imagery.

"Why would you want to share that information with me?"

He shrugged. "Call it payment in advance."

I clicked my tongue. "Payment for what?"

"For killing the man, of course."

So, he wanted the guy dead too. Interesting. "If you know who the man is, then why not just kill him yourself?"

The smile on his face disappeared, and he sat up straighter. "I would… if I could find the son of a bitch."

The confession seemed to rankle Avalone. The grimace he wore looked like he'd swallowed something sour.

I was silent for a moment, considering the possible repercussions.

On the one hand, if the killer was someone of importance, his family's retaliation would rain down on the Costas. On the other, if the guy was the one killing Costas and framing Lucas, I didn't give a fuck. I wanted it to be well-known it was the Costas who put the guy in the ground. We were well-equipped to deal with *repercussions.*

"All right." I nodded slowly. "If you provide me with information that leads me to the man killing Costas, I will find him and kill him. That is the entirety of the deal."

Avalone nodded, seemingly satisfied, then turned to the lackey on his left. "Riccardo, give *Signor Costa* the file, *per favore.*"

Riccardo pulled a file folder from inside his jacket and placed it down on the table.

I opened the thin folder. It couldn't have had more than a few pages in it. The first of them were pictures of a dead Aunt Isabella and Abruzzo's family, all murdered, but before the fire had been set to his house. The other pages in the file folder were a paternity test, an old grainy photograph of a man in his early twenties—dark hair and average build.

The last page was a note that read, *"One family at a time. How long do you think it will take me to get to you?"*

I looked up at Avalone, waiting for an explanation.

"The man responsible for the murders is my son… apparently," he said with a sneer and the same twisted sour expression.

Yet another reason to avoid procreation for as long as possible. "Your son?"

I ran through the man's family tree in my head. He technically had a wife—a moderately attractive woman he kept locked up in his mansion who had produced a son for him five years ago. Like my own father, the man had waited until his late forties to sire an heir. Somehow though, I didn't think it was the five-year-old putting out hits. I cocked an eyebrow, waiting for him to explain further.

"Some dirty *troia* tried to cuckhold me thirty years ago." He chuckled. "The stupid cunt spread her legs more often than a whore. I thought for sure she was lying—she was lucky I didn't kill her and her unborn spawn right then and there." His face grew serious again, and anger pinkened his ears and cheeks. "It turns out, the *puttana* wasn't lying. I never figured out how she'd known the bastard was

Kiana Hettinger

mine. *Non lo so*," he said, shaking his head. "Ten years ago, the bastard showed up at the front door of my *home*." He wrinkled his nose like something smelled foul. "He wanted to play his part in my empire—collect the fruits of my labor, essentially, *si?* I had my men turn him away. The photo is from a security camera outside my home." He motioned to the grainy photo. "I lament not employing better equipment at the time," he said, clearly irritated by having to make the admission.

He had a grainy photo to go on, and that was it. But chances were, a decade ago, someone had been making a lot of inquiries into Fiorenzo Avalone—that was somewhere to start. And if all he wanted in return was the man dead, then there was little risk on my part.

"I wonder if all of this could have been avoided had you dealt with your bastard when he showed up at your door rather than ignoring him," I mused aloud.

"Yes, well, I can't argue with you there, but I assure you I'm much more careful with my whores these days," he said with a grin.

If a snake could smile, this is what it would look like.

Something about the beady glint in his eyes sent a shiver down my spine. There wasn't much that could do that. I pitied Avalone's whores, glad I'd insisted that the girls employed by the Costas were treated better. Lorenzo hadn't seen the point—they were whores, after all, he'd said—but I'd insisted on it. Though, it had been no simple task to convince Lorenzo that doing things my way meant our girls would be of better quality, they would work harder to please their clientele, and we wouldn't have to worry about a constant turnover from the girls dying.

153

Ultimately, I wouldn't have waivered no matter the consequences. I would never become the man who used women that way, no matter what I'd been accused of or what the world believed of me. It was that thread of humanity I clung to like a lifeline, using it as the defining characteristic that separated me from Lorenzo.

Maybe Lorenzo had made me a monster, but I was born of two people, not one.

I had to believe my mother's blood in my veins kept the monster from devouring me entirely.

Chapter Twenty-Two

Raven

The moment I stepped inside the dark booming interior of Onyx, I looked around, searching for Nico despite my best efforts. But he wasn't here, and while my insides crumpled a little in disappointment, it was for the best. If he was here, he'd be prowling for his next lay.

I didn't want to see that, no matter how much I tried to tell myself I was fine with it.

Two days had passed. I'd heard no more from him. Two nights of tossing and turning, waking up to the feel of his lips and teeth on my body or his cock buried deep inside me, only to find myself alone and sopping wet in the dark. I'd pressed my fingers to my engorged clit, rubbing fast as memories of him hurtled me over the brink again and again. But it wasn't the same.

All my life, I'd been satisfied with the pleasure I could give myself, but not now. It was a poor second in comparison to the cataclysmic orgasms he'd drawn from my body.

I made my way through the gyrating bodies to the bar where I'd sat next to him. The same bartender was there—Tommaso. I breathed a sigh of relief when I saw him. By the intuitiveness I'd seen in his eyes, I had a feeling that Tommaso was aware of everything that went on here.

Tommaso was the reason why I was here after all—not Nico.

Seeing Dominic alive and in the flesh for the first time the other night had thrown me for a loop, but once the shock had worn off, I couldn't help but wonder what his presence at Onyx had meant. Were he and Nico nothing more than casual acquaintances? Or was there a deeper relationship between the Lucas and Costas that I hadn't discovered in all my research?

I needed to know the answer because if the two families were already connected in some way, that meant my plan had been doomed from the beginning.

"Buona sera, signorina," Tommaso said with a wide smile when he spied me.

I watched Tommaso in fascination as he fixed me a drink. *Huh, he's left-handed.*

A moment later, he slid a sidecar in front of me. "You seemed fond of them the other night, *sì?*" he said, though there wasn't any question in his tone.

"Sì, Tommaso. *Grazie."*

Tommaso smiled again, and I couldn't help but feel a fondness for this intuitive man who looked more like he should be serving up tax advice than martinis.

I took a long sip of the orange drink. Liquid courage they called this. I took a big gulp. "Could I ask you something, Tommaso?"

"Of course," he said, putting down the empty glasses in his left hand and resting his forearms on the counter to turn toward me.

I braced myself inwardly, taking in a big inhale. "There was a man here the other night talking with Nico. His name is Dominic Luca."

"*Sì*," he said slowly.

Uncertain if I'd heard the undercurrent of reservation in his tone wrong, I pressed on. "I was just hoping you could tell me if he comes here often."

Tommaso's eyes narrowed just a little.

"He's an ex," I lied in a hurry.

God, it felt weird to call my brother my ex.

"Oh?"

"I didn't want to make a habit of running into him, that's all," I said, shrugging my shoulders and hoping it looked less rigid than it felt.

I couldn't tell whether Tommaso was buying my story or not. I wasn't that great of a liar even though I'd spent the past eleven years lying about everything from my name to where I was born.

"You can rest easy," he said, losing the creases at the corners of his eyes. "It was the first time I'd seen a *man* of the Luca family in Onyx."

I looked down at my drink, as if trying to shield myself from Tommaso's X-ray-like gaze. "I'm glad to hear it." I forced the words out of my dry throat. "*Grazie.*"

"If I may be so bold, *signorina*. The past is the past for a reason. It's meant to stay behind you, not lead you."

I nodded, but his words reverberated in my head over and over again. They drowned out the music blaring around me. They weren't all that different from what Greta had been telling me. In fact, they sounded very similar to what my own logical mind had been screaming, but I'd been wallowing in hurt and anger too much to hear it. Until now.

"Don't worry, *signorina*, you'll find your way," he said with a confident nod.

I couldn't help but notice—first, Nico and now, Tommaso. Did I have a giant *LOST* sign on my forehead?

"*Grazie,*" I said, mostly because I couldn't think of what else to say.

"*Buona sera, Signor Costa,*" Tommaso said, glancing past me.

I froze as the most delicious shiver rippled down my spine.

"*Buona sera, Tommaso,*" a man's voice greeted from behind.

The voice wasn't quite as deep as Nico's. It was gruffer.

Slowly, I spun around, mentally trying to morph whoever this man was into the man I wanted to find standing behind me. My eyes widened slightly as my mind made a connection.

A few nights ago, I would have been glad to see this man.

Dario Costa was already looking at me, glancing over my body, the twinkle in his dark eyes undeniable.

"*Buona sera, signorina,*" he said with an almost boyish smile.

Dario was handsome, not quite as tall as Nico. He was in perfect shape, and his dark eyes glittered with something lighter than the dangerous glint in Nico's eyes. It seemed all the Costas had been blessed with good looks.

But the stirring in my stomach wasn't there, the butterflies a sleeping bunch. My heart paced and beat like clockwork. I wasn't holding my breath the way I did at the mere presence of Nico.

Great, I thought with a mental roll of my eyes. Maybe he'd ruined me for all other men.

"*Buona sera,*" I replied, trying to put Nico out of my mind.

This was a Costa man I could have used for my plan. A nephew to the don, I didn't know much about him—the newspapers and tabloids could only reveal so much—but he didn't have the same lethal reputation that Nico did. So this should have been perfect.

It should have been, but it wasn't.

Tommaso's words kept playing over and over again in my head.

"The past is the past for a reason. It's meant to stay behind you, not lead you."

A few months ago, I had a pseudo-uncle I loved and a great career—a great life—ahead of me. Now, I had nothing. Nothing but a past that fueled my thirst for validation. Even if I rose to the top of the Costa empire or toppled the Lucas, it would never make my family love me, only fear me, hate me.

I'd come here tonight looking for answers but found something else instead. The glint in Tommaso's gaze refracted in my mind's eye.

It was time to embrace who I was. Who I *am*. Raven Ferrari.

Sofia was dead.

Sofia Luca died in a fire eleven years ago.

It was time to let her rest.

"I'm Dario," the man said, holding out his hand.

I know who you are, I told him in my head.

I shook his hand, trying to feel the touch ripple up my arm like it had when Nico touched me. No such luck.

"I'm Raven," I told him as I took my hand back and reached for my drink.

"What brings you here this evening, Raven?" he asked with a lopsided grin.

"A fork in the road," I told him, thinking of the *LOST* sign everyone else seemed to be seeing on my forehead.

I tried to push the past week from my mind and focus on Dario. Why not? I wasn't a virgin anymore. What harm could come from taking a page out of Greta's book and using this guy for a one good night before I went back to the life I should never have left?

No matter how I tried, though, all I could muster was a slight tingling in my veins when I thought about this man on top of me. Was it enough? Was this what Greta felt whenever she picked up a guy for a good time?

Something warm caressed my back, like the heat of the sun against bare flesh in the middle of summer. I spun around, not sure what I'd find.

He stood right behind me in a pair of black pants and a navy blue shirt with the top buttons undone. The open collar formed a V, like an arrow pointing downward to his godlike body underneath.

Nico looked just as incredible as I remembered, but the dark glint in his eyes flashed like the blinding gleam of sunlight off a blade.

So, this was what Nico looked like when he was angry.

Chapter Twenty-Three

Raven

Nico's gaze was fixed on Dario.

He stood there motionless, so close I could smell the sandalwood and leather scent of him over the mixture of sharp alcohols and perfumes.

Out of the corner of my eye, I could see the way Dario's position had changed, turning a fraction away from me, like he was relinquishing whatever claim he'd been trying to establish. Nothing about his countenance suggested he was afraid of Nico. He had an unperturbed expression on his face, but his shoulders weren't quite as relaxed as they'd been a moment ago.

I suddenly felt like the female prize in a bullfight. I wasn't a thing anyone could butt horns over. But something dark and primitive stirred the blood in my veins.

"*Buona sera*, Raven," Nico said, making my blood pump harder. He nodded to Dario, who nodded back with an easy smile.

"*Ciao*, Nico. I was just..." Dario laughed. "I was just keeping your seat warm, *cugino*." He turned his attention to me for one brief moment. "It was nice to meet you, Raven. Enjoy your evening." He slid off the barstool and walked away.

I lost him quickly. I wasn't really watching him. All of my attention was fixed on the tall, dark Adonis in front of me as he leaned down until his lips were a hair's breadth from my ear.

"Were you trying to make me jealous, Raven?" he whispered as his breath tickled my flesh.

I tried to answer him.

I tried to tell him that I had no idea he would be here and that even if he had been, I fully expected to find him with another woman. But words eluded me, so I shook my head, which made his lips graze against the shell of my ear.

"Because if you were, it worked," he said at the same time.

Shivers so strong they felt like tiny jolts rippled through me.

"I feel the urge to mark you. To make sure there's no doubt that every inch of you belongs to me," he said with his lips still next to my ear and his body so close I could feel the heat coming off him.

This was nothing like the slight tingling in my veins I'd managed to muster up with Dario. This was earthquaking panty-soaking arousal.

"And if it wasn't clear to you the other night, I leave my mark with my teeth," he finished, then leaned away, looking at me with a very different light in his eyes.

It wasn't the glint of a blade. It was like green fire.

Shouldn't a guy threatening to bite me be a clear sign to get my butt out of here? I squeezed my thighs tight against the throbbing desire his words evoked. The light graze at first, the pressure as his teeth sunk in, the sharp sting. Even now, I could feel the sensation traveling down the line and setting me on fire.

He grabbed my hand and tugged me off the barstool without another word. His grip was firm, but somehow, I knew if I resisted, he'd let go. But I didn't.

He pulled me through the heated-body crowd of club goers to a door at the back of the club. With a hard shove, he swung the door open and pulled me through, down what seemed like an oddly elegant set of wood-stained stairs for a basement. The newel post and spindles had been carved with intricate detail, forming the shapes of angels and demons, it seemed.

There was nothing ordinary about this basement.

Dark wood paneling lined the hallway walls, and rich rugs in black, red, and gold patterns covered the floors. Tall ceilings, peppered with ornate chandeliers.

He pulled me past one closed door after another, each of them carved and stained dark like something out of a Gothic mansion. Black leather benches and wing-backed chairs lined the halls.

Nico pulled me through an open doorway on the left, halfway down the hall. The moment I stepped inside, I froze.

A large four-poster bed sat in the center of a room decorated in the same black, red, and gold as the hallway. It looked like something right out of a vampire fantasy.

Is that why Nico likes to bite? I wondered for one strange moment.

I could even imagine him laying me down, mesmerizing me with the green fire in his eyes before sinking his teeth into my neck. Crazy, maybe, but at least it would explain my fascination with the dangerous man. This was what I got for binging *Twilight*.

I should have turned around and hightailed it out of that room— out of the basement and out of the club. I probably should have hailed a cab, driven straight to the airport, and caught a flight back to California. But all I could do was look around in wonder while my insides twisted up in some strange mixture of fear and arousal.

He tugged me further into the room to the foot of the bed. He grabbed hold of the hem of my dress and pulled it off over my head in one swift movement, leaving me standing in his lair in nothing but a lacy black bra and matching panties.

He left the door wide open.

I was painfully aware that someone could walk by at any moment, but I couldn't muster up the modesty to care.

"I don't know what you did to me," he said, releasing the clasp of my bra between my breasts with a flick of his fingers. "I haven't been able to get you out of my head." He grabbed hold of the side of my panties and ripped them apart, pressing the wet fabric hard against my pussy. The way Nico was looking at me, kind of like he'd never wanted something so much in his life, had my body trembling and needy—and he hadn't even touched me yet.

His eyes grazed over my body once more. Then his lips captured mine as he pulled me so close I could almost feel every plane and groove of his body through his thin shirt.

He tore his lips away and leaned back to look at me, meeting my gaze.

"If you don't want this, Raven, tell me. Tell me now," he said through gritted teeth.

"I want this," I said without a moment's hesitation.

Maybe he already had me mesmerized. Or maybe this man and this room that conjured all things sinful was everything I never realized I wanted.

He growled as he unzipped his fly, ripped open a condom, and sheathed himself. He grabbed my arms and pushed me back on the bed until my back was flat against the mattress and my legs dangled over the end. He leaned over me, one arm holding himself up while he thrust two fingers inside me.

"You're so fucking wet for me," he whispered, then withdrew.

I whimpered at the loss, but he didn't leave me bereft for long. The head of his cock pressed against me. He drove inside me in one firm thrust, groaning as he stilled, buried to the hilt, for just a moment before he began to move. He set a rhythm as every thrust stroked my inner walls, starting me on a fast climb to the cataclysmic ecstasy I knew he could give me.

He leaned away, standing up without missing a stroke, and grabbed hold of my thighs.

"Open your legs wider for me, Raven," he said.

He pressed my thighs further apart, more and more until the skin in my inner thighs were stretched taut.

I could feel the light burning in my joints, but the position seemed to grant him deeper access. All I could focus on was the way he was filling me until there wasn't a molecule of unfilled space inside me. Over and over again. The tip of his cock kissing the cap of my cervix in an unbroken tempo.

His gaze was fixed on where we were joined. It only added fuel to the fire to know the consumed look in his eyes was because of me. I wanted to see what he was seeing, so I leaned up. The movement must have clenched my inner walls down harder on him because I only got to see for a split second. He groaned a deep guttural sound and shot forward, lunging for my lips.

It was like he was starving, delving between my parted lips like my mouth held all the sustenance he needed. His tongue glided against mine, in and out, mimicking the way he was fucking me.

I thought he had forgotten about what he said upstairs, but he tore his lips from mine after a moment. His mouth paved a hot trail down my jaw to my neck. I tipped my head back, staring up at the ceiling as his teeth dug into my flesh. The graze and then the pressure. The sharp sting that shot down the line and had me arching more firmly against him.

"I don't know what it is about you, Raven," he confessed in between nips as he worked his way down and then across the upper swells of my breasts.

"I couldn't stop thinking about you," I confessed. "I dreamed about you."

Memories of the dreams slipped in, driving me higher.

"And what did you do when you woke up?" he asked with a knowing look in his eyes, just before he sunk his teeth into my nipple, making me see stars.

"I rubbed my clit until it made me come," I confessed as his pace quickened. "But it wasn't the same."

The coil had already wound up so tight I was almost there.

"Good," he said, thrusting harder. "Because it wasn't the same for me either."

The image of him with his hand around his cock, rubbing himself while images of me bombarded his mind sent a sizzling shock of heat through me. As he moved onto my other nipple, and his teeth grazed my sensitive flesh, it shot me over the brink, screaming his name and riding out the hot waves of my orgasm.

As soon as my inner walls clamped around his dick, he thrust in deep one last time. He let out a rugged groan through spurt upon spurt of his come.

Chapter Twenty-Four

Nico

Reluctantly, I withdrew myself from Raven, zipped my fly, and strode across the room to close the door.

I didn't mean to leave the door wide open, but I couldn't say it bothered me that she'd let me fuck her knowing people could walk by at any moment.

Instead of throwing Raven her dress and sending her on her way, I laid down next to her, on my side, propped on one elbow and pulled her closer.

I never much cared for cuddling after sex. In fact, I categorically avoided it. But my skin, my fingers, my body craved for hers, like all my lines and shapes were made to fit her curves and contours.

"Why were you here?" I asked.

It didn't matter what the answer was. If she came to make me jealous, she succeeded. If she came to try to coax me into another round despite my reputation, she got another point. Either way, there was only one conclusion: She had seriously fucked with my head. Maybe the Lucianos had some sort of cutting-edge drug I hadn't heard about.

"Because of you," she answered with as much of a shrug as she could manage on her back, pressed against my body. "I tried to tell

167

myself that wasn't the reason, but it was a lie. I knew that the second I saw you." There were no shadows or lies in her eyes, which made it difficult to doubt her. The light pink slashes that appeared across her cheeks told me she was a bit uncomfortable though.

"Why are you pink?" I asked.

She could spread her perfect thighs for me without flinching, but admitting she came here for me made her blush?

She was silent for a moment while she tugged on her bottom lip.

"Because it's both easy and difficult to talk to you," she said eventually.

"What do you mean?" I pressed.

I felt like a cat and she was my catnip, a dangling ball, a mouse. *A chase.*

"It's easy because the words just seem to spill out with you, but difficult because I'm not sure I want them to just spill out."

There was a moment's pause between us.

"What are you thinking?" I finally asked.

She was looking at me strangely with a half-smile toying on her lips.

More random sex facts? I wondered.

Her light blush deepened. "You remind me of a vampire."

I laughed. "I've been called a lot of things, but this is a first."

Fucking cute.

"You don't look offended," she said, tugging on her bottom lip.

"Should I be?"

She shook her head vigorously. "I love vampires," she blurted out, and her cheeks turned pinker. "I mean, I've always loved all that old-time myth and folklore stuff. I've probably watched every movie ever made about vampires. Greta and I went on a binge after finals last year. We even got our hands on this 1950s flick about a teenage vampire—"

"Blood of Dracula?"

Her jaw dropped open. "You've seen it?"

I shrugged. "I've kind of got a thing for myths and monsters too," I said, laughing to cover the way it felt like I was offering up something that was just a little too personal.

My fingers itched to touch her. I grazed along the curve of her shoulder, across her clavicle to the upper swell of her breast, where red marks in the shape of my teeth stood out against her pale skin.

I told her I wanted to mark her, and I hadn't been kidding, but less to mark my territory like an animal and more to make sure it would be a long time before she forgot. Every time she looked in a mirror, she'd see me, the proof of what I'd done to her body written on her skin.

"Can I ask you something?" she said while sparks of arousal had begun to light up in her blue eyes again.

I had a feeling the question on the tip of her tongue had nothing to do with vampire films, but I nodded anyway. "You can ask me anything, Raven, so long as you're not looking for a pretty answer," I warned her.

She seemed to consider my words for a moment and then nodded. "Why me?" Her eyes met mine, as if searching for something.

"I don't know why," I said. "There's the vampire thing," I teased, but then turned serious. "You're beautiful, and there are things I like about you that surprise me, but I couldn't get you out of my head, and that's not common for me."

It had made sense at first, I told myself, because I had to wonder exactly when she'd hand the Lucianos the information I'd given her and whether she'd be with them when they came to raid the Costas' "unguarded" warehouses. But those weren't the thoughts that occupied my mind.

Stranger still, it wasn't just the million and one ways I wanted to use her body that had plagued me day and night. It was wondering what would else make her blush and what kind of nurse she would be. What kind of quirky sex facts she was going to spout off next. And whether, when all this was over, there would be any hope of finding out all there was to know about Raven Ferrari.

The girl was a total mind fuck. The moment I saw her at the bar, sitting next to Dario—one of the few men I considered a friend as much as family—jealousy had reared its ugly head. At least, that's what I figured it was. I never experienced it before to know for sure. Jealousy was supposed to be a green monster on one's back, but this had been no pint-size monster. It had been a dragon with fire in its lungs and razor-sharp claws and teeth.

"So, um, where do we go from here?" she asked, though her gaze was busy following my fingers' path across her breasts.

"Why don't you start by telling me all there is to know about Raven Ferrari—including what got you into vampires—while I see if I can find out some of your secrets on my own," I said, turning my attention to kissing the mesmerizing red marks on her body.

She scoffed. "All right, let's see, she had an ordinary childhood, moved to California with her uncle after her mother passed away. She grew up with an awesome best friend, graduated near the top of her class, set her sights on becoming a nurse… and the rest is history. Oh, and a… friend let her watch Bram Stoker's Dracula with him

170

when she was nine years old, and she's been fascinated with vampires ever since."

It was a pretty straightforward life, read like a script she'd rehearsed a thousand times, except for the sadness that seemed to resonate in every word she spoke.

"You don't seem happy with your life thus far?"

"Are you?" she countered.

I paused. I had everything money could buy. I didn't pine for a life I couldn't have. Yet I couldn't muster up a clear resounding yes.

"I know I'm happy with my life *right now*," I hedged.

It was a shitty move, but this woman was still the enemy, even if I couldn't quite figure out her game.

She was silent again, watching my fingers move across her body. Her breathing picked up. If I laid my hand flat against her chest, I would feel her pounding heartbeat. Instead, I leaned down and suckled her nipple into my mouth, her quiet moans rippling through my veins.

Three consecutive knocks thumped at the door.

Raven's breath hitched in her throat.

Whoever was pounding at the door better have had a death wish.

"Nico, you're needed," Gabe's voice called from the other side of the door.

Fuck. Fuck. Fuck.

If it had been anyone else, I would have ignored them, making a mental note to rip off their hands and tear out their tongues later, but Gabe knew better than to bother me down here without good reason.

"What?" I called back, reluctantly slipping off the bed and away from Raven.

"There's a dead guy on fire upstairs. Someone threw him in through the window."

Raven's eyes went wide.

"Did you put out the fire?" I asked, getting dressed while Raven scrambled off the bed and yanked on her dress.

"No, I've got everyone roasting marshmallows," Gabe said, his tone so serious Raven's expression looked like she couldn't figure out whether to be horrified or to laugh.

Fully dressed, she followed me toward the door, eyeing it like the guy on fire might just come crashing through it.

"Stay here," I told her, kissing her forehead. "I'll have a man guarding the door. Lock it, and don't open it for anyone but me."

***

I strode up the stairs with Gabe at my side and my gun in hand, trying to keep my shit together. It was bad enough when someone messed with me out there, but Onyx was my territory. I cracked my knuckles. I'd been itching for the feel of my knife in the palm of my hands for a while now.

At the top of the stairs, I threw open the door, not surprised to find the place had been cleared out but for a dozen Costa men. I took a breath and then regretted it. The putrid smell of burning flesh and hair had replaced the oxygen-heavy air in the large room.

"Barbecue, anyone?" Gabe joked, looking over where Tommaso stood over a smoking mound with a fire extinguisher in his hand.

Gabe had turned a little green around the edges. The scent in the room was bad enough to make our eyes water.

The crack of a gunshot rang out.

"Down!" I hollered, crashing into Gabe and sending us both to the floor in a flash.

The bullet zipped by, grazing my arm. It hurt like a son of a bitch, but now I was pissed.

Without a second's pause, I was on my feet. All dozen of my men flew in the same direction, all of us making our way toward the rear exit door where the shot had come from. Salvatore was out first at the same time tires squealed across the parking lot.

More gunshots. Glass shattering. The crash of metal.

I stepped outside just in time to see Salvatore lower his gun.

Nice hit.

I nodded to him in acknowledgement as I strode across the pavement to the totalled black Cadillac that had tried to plow right through the '67 Mustang in the lot.

Gabe was going to be pissed.

I would have let him have a go at the driver, but when I got to the car and ripped open the door, the driver already had a bullet in the side of his head—courtesy of Salvatore. The passenger hadn't fared any better. His head was lodged in the windshield.

"Motherfucker," Gabe cursed next to me.

His eyes were wide, and the muscles of his jaw twitched spasmodically. He was staring at his car.

"I'm real sorry, boss," Salvatore said, staring at the ground in front of my feet. "I'm sorry, *Signor* Costa," he said, casting a furtive glance up at Gabe.

"It's all right, Salvatore," Gabe said, still staring at the wreck with his fingers laced behind his head. "He who holds onto his earthly possessions, and all that shit."

I couldn't help but chuckle. "You want to drag out the driver and kill him some more, *fratello?*"

Gabe looked at me like I'd lost my mind.

"No," he said, shaking his head. "But I'd sure love to find out who sent him and kill *him* a few times over."

I nodded.

But that left one glaring question: Who had sent him?

I didn't recognize the passenger—though he'd be kind of hard to recognize at the moment—but the driver, I'd definitely seen before.

"That's one of Nova's men, isn't it?" Salvatore asked, squinting his eyes and leaning closer to get a good look at the guy.

"Yeah, it is," I confirmed while trying to figure out what was going on.

Novas, Lucianos, Lucas, Avalone's kid?

It kind of looked like every family in the country had gone insane and was taking random shots at each other.

Salvatore nodded. "I'll see about getting this mess cleaned up," he said with one last apologetic glance at Gabe.

Before Gabe started quoting the Bible again, I led him back inside, leaving our men to deal with the mess. He looked around the moment we stepped inside.

"You're going to have to tell Dad," he said under his breath.

"I know." I squeezed the bridge of my nose, fighting back a migraine.

With so many Costa men as witnesses, there was no keeping this quiet. One of the Novas had just taken a shot at the next-in-line of the Costa family. And that meant the Costas were about to rain down hell on what was left of the Novas.

I couldn't help but wonder, though, if we were about to put down a foe… or if we were playing right into some unknown player's hand.

Chapter Twenty-Five

Raven

I sat next to Nico in his sleek, black car.

I had no idea where we were going. After he came back from dealing with the burning body—something I never thought I'd hear myself say—he grabbed my hand and led me up the stairs and out the front door of the club.

I expected him to send me on my way, but he drove past my hotel. I glanced at my watch. It was midnight already.

He hadn't said a word since revving the car's engine to life and pulling away from the club, and I was rather grateful for it. My mind was running a thousand miles a minute.

I'd gotten myself involved with a guy who wasn't fazed by burning corpses. A guy who had no idea who I really was or that I'd intended to use his family in some pathetic attempt to feel better about myself. A guy who I was sure had put people in a grave for far less.

He pulled into the parking lot of a pizza shop on the outskirts of town. The area didn't look safe. But then again, I was with Nico Costa. What were the chances anyone was going to be stupid enough to try to mug the guy?

"Hungry?" he asked as he shifted the car into park.

"I could eat," I said with a shrug.

I was *famished*. I could've eaten him whole if I had a bottle of ketchup in my purse.

He came around and opened my door. I realized I kind of liked that. Vito had raised me to be an independent woman who could open her own car door, but somehow, Nico didn't make me feel like any less of one for it.

Inside the pizza shop, a lone man stood behind the counter tossing a large circle of dough. He had a graying head of hair and permanent crinkles around his dark eyes, but the way he moved so agilely spoke of youth and vitality. He dropped the dough down on the counter in a perfect circle the moment we walked in.

"*Ciao*, Nico," the man said with a smile that lit his whole face, his arms outstretched wide in welcome. "It is so good to see you, *amico*." He came out from behind the counter, wiping his hands on a dishcloth as he went, and shook Nico's hand enthusiastically.

"It's good to see you too, Antonio," Nico replied with a smile in return, his eyes glimmered with something akin to warmth.

I supposed it shouldn't have surprised me to see Nico so at ease after witnessing his easy rapport with Tommaso the other evening, but it still shocked me. He was like a walking contradiction to everything the tabloids said about him. I could never ignore the ever-present shadow in his eyes that said what I heard hadn't been wrong.

"This is Raven, Antonio. Raven Ferrari," Nico introduced me. "And this, Raven, is Antonio, who I guarantee you is the best pizza maker in the country."

Antonio's smile grew wider, and he shook my hand vigorously. "It's a pleasure to meet you, *Signorina* Ferrari. Any acquaintance of Nico's is always welcome here."

Antonio's smile was infectious. "Thank you, Antonio, and please, call me Raven."

"What can I get for you two this evening?" Antonio asked while his gaze swung from Nico to me and then back again.

Nico looked at me, but I just shrugged. I was hungry enough to eat the pizza oven. Whatever he chose had to be more edible than that.

"Just a pepperoni pizza, Antonio," Nico ordered for the both of us.

When Nico reached for his wallet, Antonio shook his head.

"Your money's no good here, Nico. You know that. You see, Raven, Nico saved—"

"*Grazie*, Antonio," Nico cut in and then led me away from the counter to the empty table for two in the corner.

"What was that about? What was Antonio going to say?" I asked.

Nico pressed his lips together, looking none too pleased. "It's no big deal, Raven. Antonio's daughter wasn't well. She had a heart condition that required surgery. Antonio didn't have that kind of money, and his insurance wouldn't cover it," he said with a shrug.

"You paid for the girl's surgery," I said, filling in the obvious blank with awe.

Having spent three years studying to become a nurse, I was aware that any heart surgery an insurance company wouldn't cover generally meant the cost was well into six figures.

He nodded succinctly, clearly uncomfortable, but it took me a moment to decipher the uneasy set of his shoulders and the way his eyes weren't quite meeting mine. He was embarrassed.

"You're not what I expected," I said.

"Don't fool yourself, Raven. I'm exactly the man you expected. A bit of charity here and there doesn't change that. Ask me what I did to the insurance adjuster who rejected Antonio's claim."

I eyed him closely—he was deflecting. What else had he done for other people? But I knew the conversation was over. I wasn't going to get any more out of him.

"So, if acts of kindness are off the table, what can I ask you about?"

"You've told me about your childhood and your career aspirations. What about family? Any siblings?" he asked, altogether avoiding my question, but it provided a segue into a question of my own.

I opened my mouth to tell him I didn't have any siblings.

"I have three older brothers," I said. "But we're not close," I tried to cover quickly. "I haven't spoken to them in years."

He seemed to be mulling over this.

"What about you?" I asked, though I already knew he had three brothers. Just like me—I'd never really made that connection before. While I was the youngest, he was the eldest. "Are you close to any of them, I mean?"

He nodded slowly. "The second in line—Gabe. We're close," he said and then laughed. "Hell, for Costas, we're pretty much best friends."

"What do you mean by 'for Costas'?"

His expression turned serious, and I could tell by the calculating look in his eyes he was choosing his words carefully.

"I mean, my family isn't exactly *The Brady Bunch*. Loyalty is important—vital, in fact." A fierce light lit up his eyes. "But beyond that, close relationships have never really been my family's concern."

Antonio arrived with our pizza, served up on a tall, silver platter and steaming hot. He placed it down on the table between us, and the spicy-sweet scents wafted in the air. I tried not to be mortified when my stomach rumbled a little loudly.

"*Buon appetite,*" Antonio said. He set a knife and two plates down next to the tall tray and disappeared back behind the counter.

"*Grazie,*" Nico and I said at the same time to the man's retreating back.

Nico picked up the knife and sliced up the pizza. I watched the way his hand moved, gripping the shiny black handle and slicing through the pizza with just enough pressure to cut through each piece with one smooth stroke. Was that because he ate pizza so often, he could cut it up in his sleep? Or was it because he was so skilled with knives, he knew exactly how to wield one in any circumstance?

"Why do you do it?" The question tumbled from my lips as he transferred a slice onto each plate.

He looked up at me, cocking an eyebrow inquisitively.

"All the stuff they talk about in the news, in tabloids? You know..."

He laughed, but it was a dry laugh. There was no humor in it. "I'm the son of Lorenzo Costa. It's in my blood."

"But it's more than that, isn't it? I see the other side of you, whether you want me to see it or not. So, why choose to do *that* stuff?"

Something haunted ghosted across his expression. It made my heart ache for him.

"It's complicated," he said eventually. "And this is not a conversation I have with anyone, Raven. Just leave it alone."

The dangerous glint glittered in his eyes, but it didn't scare me the same way as it did not so long ago. It still sent a ripple of cold down my spine, but I'd seen too much of him to believe there was nothing inside him but a coldhearted killer.

"All right, then tell me what it's like?" I said, accepting another dead end.

His eyes went a little wide, like he hadn't been expecting me to ask a question like that. And I probably shouldn't have. It was morbid. But if he wouldn't tell me why he did it, then maybe what it was like was the next best thing.

Maybe a tiny part of me was genuinely curious. I could almost understand the primal thrill of holding another's life in one's hands. To feel powerful. And for me, I could understand the appeal of feeling in control, even if it was control over another's life, not my own.

But to think about it and to do it were two very different things.

He was silent for so long I figured he wasn't going to answer, but then he looked at me.

"It's messy," he said with a flicker of a smile that didn't reach his eyes.

I tried to hide my disappointment.

He sighed and scrubbed his fingers through his hair. "You really want to know?"

"Yes," I said, meeting his gaze.

"It's like a drug. You get a taste of all that power, you know what it's like to hold a man's life in your hands, and you want more of it. You feel in control in a way that no other facet of life can offer."

"How old were you when you first…" I let the words hang unspoken in the air.

181

"Fifteen," he said without hesitation.

He'd been a teenager the first time he'd killed someone. That's awful.

"I'm sorry," I said, though the words seemed too small.

"Don't be sorry, Raven. It's not something I'll ever regret."

It was the shadows that crossed his expression that caught me more than his words. There was a story there. As much as I was certain about it, I was equally sure it was not a story he had any intention of sharing with me now.

Maybe he would eventually. But I realized it wouldn't be long before he moved on to his next prey, leaving me alone with my unanswered questions.

I knew this a temporary thing, a dalliance. I knew it all before it ever started. But the thought tugged something inside me, something that could break.

Maybe Greta had been right about this too. I wouldn't be ready to get off this ride when it ended.

Chapter Twenty-Six

Raven

We had the hotel suite to ourselves. Greta had been gone the past four days, visiting cousins who'd gotten word she was in the city. Nico and I had used the time well.

"Favorite TV show as a kid?" I asked him, trying to muster the energy to lean up on my elbow. We'd christened every room in the suite—except Greta's—and then re-christened them over and over again. Our latest venture had ended us on the suite's living room floor. I was still catching my breath.

"Don't have one."

"Seriously?"

"We weren't allowed to watch television," he said with a shrug.

"Did your parents worry it would rot your brain?" I asked, half-teasing, half-curious.

He shook his head. "Not exactly. My father thought it was a waste of time. Children didn't require entertainment; they required knowledge."

I furrowed my brows. "So, you read a lot of books as a kid?"

There'd been bookshelves in Nico's house, but I hadn't paid much attention to the titles. Now, I wished I had. What did he read as an adult? Sci-fi? Mystery? "How To Be the Scariest Man in the Room 101?"

"You could say that," he said with a reluctant nod, and I wondered why.

"Seriously, how many—a ballpark figure."

He laughed but shifted at the same time, spotlighting his discomfort. "Enough that I had two undergraduate degrees and a master's by the time I was twenty-three," he said a little shortly, like he was anxious to move on.

I had to blink a couple of times. It wasn't that I thought Nico was stupid—far from it—but I hadn't really seen myself as his intellectual inferior. I was seeing it now, though.

"What about you?" he asked, and it was my turn to shift uncomfortably.

"I don't have any degrees, not yet."

He looked at me like he couldn't quite figure out why that would bother me.

"They're pieces of paper, Raven," he said like he really believed it. "And that wasn't what I was asking. I meant, what was your favorite TV show as a kid?"

"Oh, okay, but you can't laugh," I said, moving back into more comfortable territory.

He grinned. "I make no promises."

"I didn't have a favorite 'show,' but I was kind of obsessed with *Star Wars*. I watched the movies over and over again. My mother—" The rest of the words got stuck behind the lump that formed suddenly in my throat.

I looked away, trying to get a hold on my emotions, but he took my chin gently between his fingers and turned my face toward him.

Then he kissed me, brushing his lips across mine before settling against them. It wasn't like his usual kisses. Those were fiery, or demanding, or teasing. This was something else, something softer, and I melted into him as his lips seemed to suckle the sadness away. By the time he pulled back, my whole body tingled with awareness and the lump in my throat had vanished.

"So, you had a crush on Luke Skywalker?" he asked with a lopsided grin.

I laughed. "No. Han Solo, but that man's got nothing on you." I glanced over the sculpted planes of his body, noticing that his cock had already begun to thicken. God, it couldn't even have been thirty minutes since we'd finished the last round.

"Favorite place in New York?" I asked, trying to ignore the renewed pulsing heat between my thighs. Admittedly, I was a little sore.

"That's easy—right here," he said, grazing his fingers down my naked shoulder.

"That's cheating—and a little cheesy."

He gasped in mock offense, then lunged for my neck, just below my ear, and nibbled. "It's not cheating—I guarantee you there isn't anywhere I'd rather be at the moment. But in truth? My favorite place is my home."

When he went on to confess that no one but me and the caterers who cooked our meal had ever been there, it caught me off guard. He made it sound like I was special, but I'd been doing my best to keep feelings like that outside the arena of Nico and me. It was physical—that's all this was. Sure, it was great that we seemed to have a lot of common interests, but that just made the recovery times between rounds of carnal pleasure more enjoyable. That was it.

185

"Your favorite place in California?" he asked, trailing one finger down my neck from where he'd been nibbling to my clavicle.

"The Santa Cruz Mountains," I said without missing a beat while my body shivered and the heat pooling low in my abdomen grew hotter.

"Why?"

"It's so peaceful there, and some of the redwoods are three hundred feet tall. Standing amid them makes me feel so small, but in a good way—if that makes any sense."

He nodded like he understood perfectly. "The Gilboa Fossil Forest in Schoharie County has tree trunks that are three hundred and eighty million years old. I was there once, and all I could think was that they've been here through everything—dinosaurs, comets, ice ages… every war humans have ever fought—and they'll be here long after I'm gone. It's a rather humbling experience."

"And *you* are rather deep, Nico Costa. I never would have guessed it."

"Deep, huh?" He flashed me a wicked grin right before he flipped us over so that he was hovering over top of me. "I like your thinking." He grabbed a condom from the near-depleted box on the floor and sheathed his now-rock hard erection.

But I knew what he was doing—trying to distract me from my chain of thought. I'd come to recognize it in a very short amount of time.

"You know, me thinking that there's more to you than your godlike body isn't a bad thing, right?"

"I never said it was." He lined himself up.

I gasped as he pressed forward, penetrating me slowly. I was vaguely aware of the soreness, but I was so wet, he glided in smoothly. With every inch, my body stretched to accommodate him while millions of pleasure receptors fired off.

I was no longer tired.

I was awake.

Alive.

My whole body thrummed with arousal while the coil inside me started its fast wind.

"God, I never thought…" I caught myself before the rest of the words spilled out.

"You never thought what?" he asked, stilling inside me. He stayed there, eyes meeting mine expectantly.

"It's nothing," I said, writhing my hips, trying to make him move, to create the friction my body craved. *God, I need him to move.*

He flashed another wicked grin and withdrew until just the head of his cock remained inside me.

"You never thought what?" he asked again, not moving, waiting, driving me crazy.

"I never thought sex would be like this," I blurted out.

His body jolted, plunging in to the hilt. "Christ, Raven, don't say things like that."

"Why not?" I asked, breathy and reeling in sensation.

"Because I might be a hypocrite for it, but I love that no other man has been inside you, and when you remind me, it very much makes the less-than-civilized side of me want to come out."

"Oh? And what would the less-than-civilized side of you do?" I asked, grazing my fingers down his biceps, silently begging him to let that side out.

He groaned and shook his head. "You've got to be sore, and I'm doing my damnedest to play nice."

"I don't want you to play nice, Nico."

The noise that rumbled from his throat sounded like a growl.

A shiver of trepidation raced down my spine, but I was too high on pleasure to care.

He leaned his weight onto one arm and grabbed my wrists, pinning them above my head.

"Fuck, Raven, you're perfect." He thrust in harder. And harder. Again and again. "So fucking perfect." He lunged for my neck and sunk his teeth into the column of my throat.

Sensation came from everywhere. His teeth, his tight grip on my wrists, his slick chest rubbing against my breasts, the friction as he slammed inside me over and over again.

It came out of nowhere. One second, the coil was winding inside me; in the next, I was screaming as an orgasm took me hard and fast, jolting all the way out to my fingertips.

"Raven," Nico groaned, and I waited for him to follow me into orgasmic bliss, but he withdrew instead, so fast, I didn't know what was happening until he'd flipped me over and drew me back onto my hands and knees.

He grabbed hold of my hips and thrust inside me none too gently, driving in deep. It should have hurt. God knew, I was going to feel it afterward, but at the moment, the ebbing ripples of my orgasm had switched direction, like the sudden turning of the tide. I was climbing again, so fast I felt almost dizzy with the constant flood of ecstasy.

He leaned over me, fisting the hair at the nape of my neck and turning my face to his. He kissed me, fierce and demanding, while his free hand sought out my breasts, palming one and then the other, catching my nipples between his fingers. My god, I was going to die of sensory overload.

"I can't get enough of you, Raven. You're like a drug," he ground out between gritted teeth. He released my hair, moving his hand to my clit. He rubbed me the same way he was fucking me—hard and fast.

I dug my fingers into the carpet. I could see the precipice this time, so close, my whole body shook. I wanted to tell him he'd made me insatiable, that I was addicted too, but my tongue wouldn't form the words. All I could do was scream as he sent me soaring over the edge and joined me on the free fall that left me weightless and euphoric.

It could have been seconds or eons later when he withdrew from me and we collapsed back onto the carpet. He threw an arm over me and drew me close against him. I felt boneless, and exhausted, and absolutely right where I was supposed to be.

That probably should have been the first warning that my feelings weren't as free from the arena of Nico and me as I'd thought.

Chapter Twenty-Seven

Raven

I still hadn't gotten off the ride.

Nico and I spent the better part of the past ten days together before he had to drop me off at my hotel to "tie up loose ends."

He didn't come out and say it, but I saw the headlines over the past two weeks.

Paulo Nova shot dead in New York condo

Retired accountant Giuseppe Nova stabbed to death at Long Island hotel

The Nova family—the men responsible for murdering my mother. If I'd really managed to put my family to rest, I would have been indifferent.

The twisted sense of satisfaction inside me every time I saw one of the headlines concerned me. But it meant one less Nova. One less of the monsters who killed a woman in her own home. *My* home. At least, it used to be my home. My home was in California now with my *Zietto* Vito.

I stood in the elevator of my hotel with my cell phone in my hand.

"The past is the past for a reason. It's meant to stay behind you, not lead you." Tommaso's words played over in my head like a broken record.

If Sofia was dead, then it was time to breathe life back to Raven.

190

I did not know how to do that without Vito.

The elevator door opened, and I stepped out, crossing the hall to my room with my finger hovering over the call button. I unlocked the door with my key card, but the moment I pushed it open, a hand latched onto my arm from inside and yanked me into the room.

The door slammed shut as my assailant shoved me face-first against it, my arm twisted behind my back, pressing my cheek hard against the cold wood.

It happened so fast, I hadn't seen his face, but the faces I'd seen in the newspaper flashed through my mind, making hot fury mingle with the fear that coursed through my veins. The man who had snuck into my hotel room, who'd attacked me, might have been some random psycho, but he could just as easily have been one of the men who'd murdered my mother.

"Don't move," my attacker hissed.

The blood in my veins was too hot to obey. I slammed my foot down on my attacker's foot with every ounce of rage I felt.

"*Merde!*" my attacker cursed. He still held my arm, but his grip had loosened, and I yanked myself out of his grasp and spun around.

"What the..." The rest of the words got stuck in my throat.

I squeezed my eyes shut, half-expecting to see someone else when I opened them.

Nope. He was still there, standing right in front of me, staring at me like he was looking at a ghost.

"What are you doing here?"

The words felt like sandpaper in my throat.

I stared up at the face I knew so well, a face I hadn't seen in a decade. A face I thought had been burned to ashes.

"Sofia?" Dominic said. It came out even more strangled than my words had. "Is it really you?"

He took a tentative step forward as his eyes grazed over my face, taking in every slope and wrinkle.

My tongue felt glued in place. Even after all the hurt and anger, Dominic was my brother. I imagined seeing him again so many times in the past eleven years.

Now words eluded me.

When his gaze had passed by me, *right through me*, that night at Onyx, I told myself that was it. Whatever tether left hanging between me and my family, *Dom,* that I thought I could still cling to was gone. Cut off.

Dominic stood in front of me, alive and breathing and real. But my feet felt like they were drilled to the carpet, my jaw hammered shut, my lungs pressed flat against my rib cage.

He took another step forward, closing half the space I'd put between us. It was like a line drawn in the sand. The moment he crossed it, he was no longer the brother I lost, or the brother who didn't want me, or the brother who had forgotten me.

"Dominic," I whispered right before he wrapped his arms around me and drew me into a hug I thought I'd never feel again.

Sobs clambered up my throat and escaped, one on top of the other as I shook against his familiar tall frame.

"You're bigger," I choked out between sobs, even though he was always bigger than me.

"So are you," he said, pulling away enough to look at me. Tears rimmed his eyes, and when he blinked, one fat drop spilled over and trickled down his cheek. "You're all grown up." He pulled me back into his embrace. "I've spent months looking for you. I didn't know. I didn't know that you were alive until *Mammina* passed away."

They lied to them too. Maria and Vincent Luca had lied to the rest of the world. They locked me in a cold, steel room and threw the key away. I wanted to be angry, I could feel the stirrings of it in the pit of my stomach, but it fizzled unto itself.

I could feel Dominic's chest pounding against my cheek. He was *alive*.

"I missed you so much," I said, my voice cracking. "I thought you were dead. Vito told me you were all dead."

I couldn't say how long we stood there. A tiny part of me was afraid that if I let go, he would vanish.

I held on tight, trying to figure out how I felt. Dominic was from my past, but I couldn't place him in my present. He felt like a familiar stranger.

I closed my eyes. Memories flooded back in, memories I tried to bury down. Dominic taking me for a drive the day he got his license. Dominic letting me watch Bram Stoker's Dracula with him even when our parents said no. Dominic bringing me home birthday cake when I was too sick to go to Aunt Ginevra's seventieth birthday party—he kept it hidden from the other two until I was well enough to eat it. Dominic picking me up after school in the second grade when Matteo Bianchi kept yanking on my braids. That boy never bothered me again after that, though he did ask me to go steady with him in the fourth grade.

My brother was always there. As the oldest of us, he should have wanted nothing to do with his clingy little sister, but he never stopped me from following him around like a lost puppy. More than that, he never once made me feel bad about it.

I had just as difficult a time making friends in elementary school as I did in college, so it made all the difference in the world to have been able to hang out with my big brother.

Dom pulled away just a little, just enough to look at me again like he needed to confirm I was still here.

"How did you find me?" I asked, my voice thick.

He scoffed. "The next time you go looking for information, pick someone other than Harry Belemonte. No secret is safe with that man."

"But I didn't tell him who I was. How did you know?"

"I didn't. Belemonte said a dark-haired woman was making inquiries about the Luca family, and he pointed me here. I assumed..." He swallowed hard and looked at my arm where his grip had left red marks on my skin. His brow furrowed.

"It doesn't matter, Dom. I'm fine. Besides, I think I got you back pretty good." I glanced down at his foot.

He smiled ruefully but then his expression turned serious. "*Dio*, Sofia, I've been looking everywhere. Dad, and Dante, and Leo are going to be so happy to see—"

"No," I said, stepping out of his embrace. "I'm not ready, Dom."

I took another small step back. It was happening too fast. Sofia's heart had barely started beating again.

"What do you mean you're not ready?"

"I mean, I spent half of my life thinking my whole family was dead. When I found out it was a lie, I was so heartbroken, and confused, and angry. I thought you all wanted to get rid of me, and I still don't understand why our parents did it."

But maybe Dominic knew why. Maybe he could tell me why they sent me away, letting me believe they were dead.

194

"Why did they get rid of me, Dom?" I asked.

I held my breath, waiting for an answer I wasn't certain I was prepared to hear.

His shoulders sagged, and his expression looked torn. He was angry too, though he was trying to keep it buried beneath the surface. Like me.

"I don't know, Sofia. I don't know what *Mammina* was thinking. We had your funeral. We…" He swallowed hard. "I don't know why she did it, but I know she must have had a good reason. She loved you. We all loved you."

By the way he was talking, it sounded like *Mammina* was the only one who knew. It was only my mother who plotted to send me away with Vito, never to see me again? It should have provided even a modicum of relief to know at least one of my parents had wanted me, but somehow, it was worse.

I could picture my mother, her kind smile, her warm eyes. I could still feel her arms around me and the brush of her lips whenever she kissed my cheek. But this woman, whom I loved so much that I could remember every detail about her, didn't want me.

"Not even our father knew?" I pressed.

As a child, I grew up admiring the way my father always kissed my mother in the morning before he left. I couldn't imagine there being any secrets between them, never mind the death—or not death—of their daughter.

Dom shook his head, then held out his hand like he explained away everything and wanted me to go with him. Right now.

Panic flooded my chest. "I can't. Not yet. Please, Dom, just give me a little time."

"Give you a little time? Sofia, the minute I tell them I found you—"

"Then please don't."

Seeing Dom was like a gift that jump-started a piece of me I'd been ready to let die, but I wasn't ready to walk right into their home and act like nothing had ever happened.

While I'd already given up on my reckless plans, it seemed that despite Tommaso's good advice, I hadn't made peace with my past yet.

I wasn't ready to move on.

Chapter Twenty-Eight

Nico

Gabe and I had been sitting side by side for the past few hours, sifting through haystacks for a conniving needle—Avalone's illegitimate son. Phone calls, research, countless hours of scanning surveillance footage.

Thus far, no needles. Nothing resembling it either.

I itched to go out, make deals, chase a bastard, carve him up, get some answers. Not sit behind a desk and work until my skin's all pruned up.

Our men were out there taking down Novas like dominoes, yet I found it hard to believe that a retired accountant would have anything to do with this.

Gabe was scanning through Avalone's decade-old phone records, looking for any number out of the ordinary. Avalone had probably already chased this lead, but we were too close now to leave any stone unturned.

Our men had gone through everything with a fine-tooth comb, but they were missing something.

They had to be.

On the screen in front of me, I scanned through hour after hour of surveillance footage I found from anywhere near Avalone's estate.

Street cameras. Security footage. Anything that could give me a better picture or a relevant license plate. This guy was out there somewhere, making plans for his next hit.

For some reason, ever since Abruzzo, it felt like there was a bull's-eye on the back of my head. I could feel the red dot like a hot laser beam.

"I've got nothing," Gabe said, sighing and scrubbing his fingers through his hair. "No weird calls to the guy's house or his cellphone. Maybe Avalone is bullshitting us."

"No," I said with more certainty than the situation seemed to warrant.

For the first time, something about this whole thing seemed clear to me, the haze lifted. Whatever else Avalone was, he wasn't a liar.

At least not about this.

"Is your Spidey-Sense going off?" Gabe asked with a grin.

I smirked. "Something like that. I just know we're on the right path."

"All right." Gabe yawned and stretched his arms. "I guess we just keep following the yellow brick road, Dorothy."

I barked out a laugh.

I was just about to make another coffee run—*and if I happened to stop by Raven's hotel room along the way, who could blame me?*—when my phone rang.

I cringed, pulling my phone out of my pocket. There hadn't exactly been a whole lot of good news lately. I glanced down.

Lorenzo appeared across the screen.

I could have passed the phone to Gabe—what else were younger brothers for?—but I answered the phone and put it to my ear.

"*Ciao*," I said in a short clipped tone then waited to hear my father's voice like waiting for nails to scrape across a chalkboard.

"You've been keeping secrets from me," he said, seething.

All I had to do was find the goddamn needle.

"What are you talking about?" I asked, playing dumb.

"I'm old, Nico, not blind. And certainly not deaf. I've been hearing plenty of whispers."

I never thought that when the day came I had it out with Lorenzo, it would be over saving Dominic freaking Luca's life. But if he put out a hit on the Lucas, what was I going to do? The only options were to stand by or put the man down. Kill my father to save the Lucas? Lorenzo was a *Costa*. It scraped across my sense of loyalty like a grater to even *think* of it.

"I don't know what you're talking about," I said, trying to delay the inevitable like these few seconds could somehow make any difference.

"The girl, Nico. I hear the girl you've been fucking looks an awful lot like a Luciano."

Part of me sighed with relief while another part of me surged with rage. If he dared to threaten *one* hair on her head, I'd rip him apart.

So, where's your loyalty now? a voice taunted from inside my head.

"How would you know that?" I asked, keeping every drop of emotion out of my tone. Lorenzo knew how to weaponize every sign, wink of weakness.

"There is nothing coincidental about it if a girl with Luciano blood has showed up at the same time we've been plotting against the Lucas," he said, ignoring my question. "That girl is *using* you."

199

It would never cross Lorenzo's mind that any girl could be possibly interested in me, not the Costa empire. I wanted to be angry with him for it, tell him he was wrong.

But even I didn't believe it. It would never cross *my* mind that Raven would be interested in *me*, not the Costa empire. Still, questions and doubts niggled at the back of my head.

Raven had ample opportunity to deliver information to the Lucianos. But I haven't heard a single peep from Enzo or his men.

Why did she stick around? If she wanted a good time in bed, I was the man for the job. But if that was all she was interested in, it should have fizzled out by now.

She should have been long gone. Because no one could convince me she hadn't bolted for my charming personality.

Nobody wanted to get deep and personal with a monster.

"Not that it's any of your business, but the girl's got nothing to do with anything," I said.

"I want you to bring her home for dinner. If she is a Luciano, I'll make the bitch squirm."

Ignoring the insult—for now—I tried to imagine just how that encounter would go. Raven and the Costas sitting down to eat spaghetti, Lorenzo's glare trained on the girl like a hawk while my mother and brothers mustered up pathetic attempts at dinner conversation. If she was innocent, she would just chalk it up to a lousy night out.

If she was guilty, she'd be quaking in her pretty strappy sandals.

One way or another, I'd have my answer.

"Fine," I barked. "But if you call her that again, I'll cut out your tongue."

200

The line went silent, but he hadn't hung up. I could just imagine Lorenzo's stunned face. Nobody talked to him that way. Nobody threatened him, not until I waved a gun at his face years ago.

But the apple didn't fall far from the tree. If he sent his men after me, it would almost have been worth it just to picture the slack-jawed look on his face.

"You watch what you say to me, boy," he said when he recovered from the shock enough to speak.

"I'm just being the man you raised me to be," I said, then turned off the phone.

I clicked my tongue. I couldn't stand it when my own head was a mess. *Raven, Avalone, Lorenzo.*

"What the hell was that about?" Gabe's eyes widened, brows knitted together.

"Nothing a few bullets or knives wouldn't fix," I muttered, trying to shake off the grimy feeling that dealing with Lorenzo had left on my skin. It was like a thick coat of dirty, black oil.

"He found out about the girl?" Gabe asked.

I narrowed my eyes. *Had Gabe gone running to Lorenzo, looking to get into his good graces?*

I looked at him, perhaps for the first time in my life as the man he was, not as my younger brother. He was a man, full-grown, with a place of his own and a regular stream of women moving in and out of his life. He was skilled in combat and experienced with weapons. He knew the ins and outs of the family business. He'd even undertaken business ventures of his own on the side, which attested to his interest in climbing the ladder. In truth, I didn't even have a clue what those ventures were.

It was entirely possible he'd used what he knew about me to try to further himself. But the same loyalty that ran through my veins ran in his. I could see it in the hard-set of his eyes, in the look that said that for all the gold in the world, he couldn't be bought.

"He wants Raven over for dinner," I told him, accepting that I could trust him.

Gabe scoffed. "And she'd be the main course, no doubt. Why the hell did you agree?"

"Because it wasn't the worst idea."

"Seriously?" he asked, looking at me like I've lost my mind. "She's put up with your shit, isn't that enough? Why the hell would you do that to the poor girl? You do remember what a good old-fashioned Costa family dinner looks like, right?"

"What difference does it make to you?" I turned to him.

"Some girl has actually managed to grab your attention for longer than it takes for you to fuck her? I guarantee you that's one hell of a girl. She deserves better than whatever our father has got planned, *si?*"

"He just wants to see if it rattles her." I shrugged.

"*Ohhh.* I see," Gabe said with a knowing look that also said he was none too pleased with what he saw. "This isn't about Dad. This is about *you. You* want to see if it rattles her."

"So what if I do?" I growled.

"Hey, she's yours, not mine," he said, holding his hands up. "But you know as well as I do that she's no evil spy. If you want to fuck up the first good thing you've had, then be my guest. I've seen her. I wouldn't mind taking her out for a whirl." He waggled his brows.

"Over my dead fucking body," I said, seething as I bunched my fists so tight my knuckles cracked.

"Exactly, *fratello*." He chuckled. "Admit it, you're afraid because you're getting close to her, and you're just trying to hang on to your *out*."

I cocked an eyebrow, not bothering to hide the muscles spasming in my clenched jaw.

"My *out*?" I ground out.

"If you keep her at arm's length because she's the enemy, you can't get hurt, right? But you might want to start considering the possibility she means more to you than an easy lay before she gets smart and dumps your ass."

The muscles in my jaw were still ticking.

"So then what's your advice, genius?"

I had to admit: I was out of my element. Dates, teddy bears, flowers—all that relationship stuff was not my expertise.

Not that I *wanted* a relationship.

He shrugged. "Just accept she sees something in you, and stop looking for her angle."

Everyone had an angle. There was no such thing as free lunch. Everyone wanted something for something. No one gave away anything for nothing. There was a reason for everything, from why a man had only one sugar in his coffee to what kept him awake late at night.

How do you call someone "dumbass" nicely?

"*Grazie, fratello*," I said, clapping him on the back.

If he wanted to believe he could moonlight as Oprah, who was I to burst his bubble?

"You're bringing the girl to dinner, aren't you?" he asked with his eyes narrowed.

"Yes, I am, Gabe, but never think it's because you're shitty at giving advice."

"*Vaffanculo, fratello,*" Gabe cursed, though he wore a giant goofy smile.

"*Sì,* I think I will *'fuck off.'* You see? *That* was good advice," I said, standing up and stretching my legs for the first time in too many hours.

It meant absolutely nothing that I couldn't wait to get out of here so I could see her.

Chapter Twenty-Nine

Raven

Dom was alive.

And he loved me.

He'd never forgotten me.

It should have been a dream come true. My father, my brothers, they all missed me. Dom said they would be thrilled to see me, and I believed him because he was my brother.

But a festering wound in my heart refused to close up, heal nicely. Like how I thought it easily would.

My mother was the one who didn't want me. And she was the one person I couldn't see. I couldn't do a thing to prove she'd been wrong about me because she was gone. I thought about going to the Luca estate, *my* home, hugging Leo, Dante, feeling my father's arms tight around me. I thought of Bullet and how his claws would skitter against the floor when he came running the second he heard my voice.

But a gaping hole remained in my chest.

There would always be something missing because my mother was *gone*. Even if she wasn't, she wouldn't have wanted to see me.

"Penny for your thoughts?" Nico asked from where he sat next to me in the grass.

He had picked me up a half hour ago. On a whim, it seemed, he drove us across town to a pretty park complete with a pond and half a million ducks. We sat down against the back of an old oak tree, about twenty yards from the water, scattering the ducks and making them quack incessantly.

But neither of us had spoken since.

It was strange how much I wanted to answer him truthfully. Or maybe it wasn't so strange. I'd ignored the warning signs. I'd pretended what was going on between Nico and me was casual. But it wasn't, not for me. I wanted to tell him all the thoughts whirring in my mind, but I couldn't do that because he didn't know who I really was or why I came here. I couldn't tell him about seeing Dominic or how I couldn't sort out how I felt about seeing the rest of my family.

I'd well and truly sunk myself in a pile of lies so deep there was no hope of getting out even if I tried to climb out.

"The people you… *hurt*…"—I couldn't think of another word— "…what if they were sorry for what they did?"

"What do you mean?" he asked, plucking at the long blades of grass.

"I mean, if you somehow knew the person was truly sorry, would it change your mind about what you felt you had to do?"

I waited with bated breath, suddenly desperate for the answer like a starving woman desperate for sustenance. But the silence stretched for so long I began to grow a little light-headed.

He shook his head. "I think if someone was sorry for what they did, they wouldn't have done it in the first place. No one can truly ever be forced into doing something, can they? There's always the option of choosing another path, even if it isn't a palatable one."

It felt like a heavy weight had slammed into my chest. There was no way Nico would forgive me if I confessed now, and I couldn't even fault him for it. He was right; I could have done things differently. I could have asked Vito about my family the night I saw the news about my mother. I could have chosen to confront them like an adult. I could have told Nico the truth from the beginning, or told him nothing at all.

I turned to him. "What made you choose your path?"

He was silent again, but it had to be more that he was deciding whether to tell me, not that he wasn't sure of the answer. He was too cocksure of a man to not know the reason behind the decisions he made.

"Cowardice," he answered.

The word seemed to be gibberish coming from his lips. It took me a moment to be sure I heard him correctly.

"I don't understand. I can't even imagine you as a—"

"Coward?" He scoffed and drew his knees up closer to his chest while fiddling with a long blade of grass between his fingers. "Someone was threatening my family, hurting them. I had every ability in the world to stop them, but when it came time to following through, I balked. I couldn't do it. So, when they offered to remove the threat, and all they wanted in return was my soul, I jumped to it gladly," he said with a shrug.

"Your soul?"

That sounded like no small price.

"What I do, it changes a man. It eats away at his soul a little at a time until what's left inside isn't quite human anymore."

"You don't think you're human?"

Nico was capable of great violence.

But as the days came and went, his shadow slowly faded, until only a dangerous glint in his eyes remained. It was a warning, a predator warding off a prey.

It was gone when he spoke with Antonio the other night, or when he answered Gabe's calls.

And when he looked at me, his eyes glittered like the moon on a dark night.

Nico was capable of great violence, but I thought this was only possible because he was capable of great love.

I remembered reading about vampires and how they *did* have hearts. They just didn't need to pump oxygen through their bloodstreams. Essentially, there was just no *need* for their hearts to beat.

"I am what I am," he said thinly, *ice-thin.*

"I don't think you're a monster," I said, hoping it broke the sheet of ice that caged his heart.

He was silent for a moment.

I was just beginning to wonder if there was a draft out here when the slightest upturn lifted the corner of his lips. "Just a vampire?"

I laughed softly. "I do believe I have an Edward Cullen poster stashed somewhere in my room…"

He flashed me a toothy grin. "I'd like you to come with me to dinner with my family this evening, Raven."

My heart raced. I could feel my pulse in my temples. Not so long ago, it was precisely what I wanted. But even if I hadn't laid my ridiculous plan to rest, I couldn't do it, not now. I couldn't— *wouldn't*—use Nico that way.

"I'd love to," I said.

He smiled wryly. "I'd hold the comments until after you've spent an evening with the Costas. We're more like the Sopranos than the Brady Bunch."

I took his hand, keeping my gaze fixed on the twirling blade of grass between his fingers, suddenly shy. "Well then, take me to meet Tony."

His grip tightened around my fingers, but when I chanced a glance up, the look in his eyes said his mind was faraway.

***

I sat on the edge of my bed while Greta ran a brush through my freshly washed hair with slow, even strokes. The tangles were long gone, but she kept going, making my scalp tingle.

I couldn't imagine what I would have done without her.

"Thank you, Greta." The words just bubbled up and spilled out.

"You know I love you, babe." She kissed the top of my head then went back to brushing my hair. "But you didn't answer my question."

I told her about Dom.

"I'm feeling… I don't *know* how I'm feeling. He didn't know the truth. None of them knew, except for my mother." I shrugged, trying to brush off the hurt that ran bone-deep. "Dominic never forgot about me," I said, letting that truth assuage some of it.

"But you didn't see the rest of them?" she asked as she started to twist and pin my hair into some elaborate updo at the crown of my head.

I shook my head. "Not yet."

When I was at the park earlier with Nico, I decided that I wanted to see my family. I'd put it off long enough.

"I'm going to tell Nico the truth tonight," I told Greta with a confident nod that belied the way my stomach churned at the thought.

"Are you sure that's a good idea?" she asked.

I could see the worried furrow between her brows in the reflection in the mirror.

"I promise you won't find me at the bottom of the Long Island Sound tomorrow." Nico wouldn't want to see me again after I told him the truth, but he wouldn't hurt me.

She pressed her lips together, but nodded. "All right, but you know if he takes it badly, it could all end. Are you sure you're ready for that?"

"No," I said without hesitation.

I was terrified that this painful, uncomfortable feeling in my chest at the thought of losing him was just a tiny taste of what it would feel like soon.

"But I'm going to do it anyway," I added.

Greta secured the last pin in my hair, and I reached for my suitcase. I only had enough money left for two or three more days here, so I'd started packing. Even my bank account was telling me my time here was up.

I rummaged through my bag for an outfit for the evening. Dinner with Nico's family wasn't really how I would have chosen to end the thing between us, but Nico deserved the truth.

"I guess the next best-friend thing I'm supposed to do is have lots of ice cream ready?" Greta said, pulling out the underthings that matched the peach-colored halter-style sundress I pulled out of the suitcase. "Though, I'm also good with having a rebound guy ready. More my style, you know?"

I did know that. "Ice cream will be fine."

She frowned exaggeratedly but then laughed. "Then I guess all that's left to do is get you dressed? What time is lover boy going to be here?"

I checked my watch. *Crap.* "Twenty minutes." Then added, "Could you request a new card key for me? Mine stopped working."

Greta nodded. "I'll call the front desk later."

Nico had only dropped me off long enough to run some sort of errand, then he said he would be back for me.

I stripped off my clothes, heedless of Greta's presence in the room.

Ever since Nico, I felt differently about my body. It wasn't that I was ashamed of it before, it was just different now. The way his eyes grew heated when he looked at me, the way he worshipped every inch of my body with his hands and his lips; I felt a kind of confidence I wasn't sure I would ever have known without him.

It took me precisely three minutes to get dressed and then I tried to sit still long enough for Greta to coat my nails and toenails in a peach shade lacquer that matched my dress.

I wanted to make a good impression, I supposed, but really, I knew Nico liked the nail polish. Well, he liked to watch the color on my fingertips disappear when he had me put my fingers inside myself.

I shook my head, as if the physical act of it helped any.

It's over, I reminded myself over and over again.

A knock sounded on the hotel room door. I shook my fingers and blew on the tips one last time. I hugged Greta in the living room, but she followed me to the door.

When I opened it, my breath hitched. His emerald eyes flashed with both fire and steel as they held mine. His full lips were quirked in a smirk. My ears tingled at the memory of his deep growl vibrating through me.

I glanced down, my cheeks flushed.

After tonight, I might never see him again. *That freaking sucks.*

His eyes flickered to Greta and dismissed her before his heated gaze settled on me.

"Ready?" he said, holding out his hand.

He looked a little disgruntled, like perhaps he intended to slip in a little sex before heading to dinner.

It was probably for the best that we couldn't since I couldn't imagine sitting at his parents' dinner table just moments after sitting on their son's cock.

Chapter Thirty

Raven

The drive to the Costa estate outside city limits was longer than I expected. Or maybe it just felt longer because Nico's grip on the steering wheel was so tight that his knuckles looked like white stars.

I realized I'd only ever heard him speak to his brother, Gabe, on the phone. I knew he had two other brothers, younger. Both of his parents were still alive. But he never spoke with them, at least not in the time I spent with him.

As we pulled up the long winding drive of the Costa estate to the tall Greek Revival-style mansion with its impressive columns reminiscent of the Parthenon, a knot of fear began to churn in my stomach. Not only was this my last evening with Nico, but I was spending it in the home of Lorenzo Costa. *Was I freaking crazy?* But when Nico's forest-green eyes met the tumultuous waters in mine, the storm calmed. I was safe.

I laughed in my head. It was a strange feeling to feel safer than I've ever been with Nico Costa—of all people. The tabloids would beg to differ.

"It's not too late to back out," he said, shifting the car into park at the top of the drive. His voice was light, but there was a seriousness in his gaze.

If I told him I wanted to leave, what would he do? Would he take me somewhere he and I could be alone for the night? My core tingled at the memory of his flesh against mine; the hole inside me seemed to open even wider, as if waiting to be filled. The craving was intense, consuming. *Carnal.*

I glanced at Nico, tilting my head to the left. I was also curious about the pieces that made up the puzzle next to me.

"I'm good." I nodded at him.

He held my gaze for a moment longer. Behind his eyes were a murky haze that I couldn't make out. Seldom did he let anyone see right through him, always keeping his thoughts close to the vest.

I felt like I had a face made of glass in comparison to him. It was a wonder he didn't see right through every lie I'd ever told. *Guess he was too distracted,* I thought with a smirk.

"All right, let's do this," he said, getting out of the car and coming around to open my door just as the front door of the mansion opened.

I recognized the man who stood in the doorway right away. Even if I hadn't seen pictures of him in newspapers, I would have known who he was. Gabriel. He looked like Nico, but a bit younger and a little less lethal. Something about his easy posture, maybe. But while it could have been any one of his brothers—they all bore a great deal of similarity—it was the friendly smile he wore for Nico that gave him away. I felt an instant pull to him.

"Nico." He came down the steps to meet us in front of the car. He clapped Nico on the back while some sort of silent communication passed between them. Then he turned to me. "You must be Raven," he said with a warm smile.

214

It was the kind of smile Nico reserved for people like Antonio and me, but Gabe seemed to flash it indiscriminately.

"And you must be Gabe," I said, smiling easily while he took my hand and grasped it between both of his.

"So, my brother has been talking about me, has he? Don't believe a word he's said. I guarantee you every one of them is a lie," Gabe quipped.

I laughed. "Nico hasn't said a bad word about you."

In truth, Nico had said very few words about Gabe or any other member of his family except to say they weren't the ordinary dysfunctional family. Funny that I knew so much about him and so little at the same time.

"If you two are done talking about me like I'm not here," Nico said, motioning toward the stairs.

He didn't look the least bit disgruntled, but the energy that came from him had changed. Or maybe intensified. He was definitely uncomfortable.

"Well then, step right up and come on in, ladies and gentlemen. The show is about to begin," Gabe said, gesturing grandly.

I didn't miss the irritated glare Nico shot him right before he took my hand and started up the steps.

Just before we reached the top, more bodies appeared in the doorway.

Two younger versions of Nico eyed us curiously. They stood side by side, wearing their inherited features well, the same green eyes Nico and Gabe had dilated.

Standing rigidly by the side was a much older version of the Costa boys. He wore neither the young ones' wide gaze nor Gabe's easy smile. His mouth was the mix of purple and black, coiled into a permanent grimace. Uneven stubble docked below it along with a scar across his neck and jaw.

Life had turned Lorenzo Costa ugly to the core.

The three Costas stepped back, and Nico led me inside into a grand foyer with lustrous Italian marble floors and an ornate crystal chandelier in front of an imperial staircase. What struck me more than the rich architecture were the flowers.

They were everywhere. Mostly roses, in crystal vases of all different sizes. The floral perfume wafted lightly in the air, a surprisingly delicate scent despite the plethora of blooms.

"Lorenzo," Nico said as Gabe closed the door behind them. "This is Raven Ferrari."

Nico clenched his jaw, the hard-set of it visible beneath his skin.

I took the hand Lorenzo offered and shook it. His hand was warm, but it was a degree colder than I expected.

"It's a pleasure to meet you," I ventured.

"And you, *Signorina Ferrari,*" he said, not a single genuine note in his voice. He let go of my hand, as quickly as he had taken it, at the same time his eyes landed on mine, looking away a second earlier than I had.

"These are my brothers, Caio and Sandro. And you've already met Gabe," Nico said, gesturing to each of the young men, two of whom were rather difficult to tell apart aside from the way they styled their hair.

Caio's was cut close to his well-shaped head, whereas Sandro's was perhaps shoulder-length, drawn back in an elastic at his nape.

The three men smiled warmly at me, though only Gabe seemed relaxed. Caio and Sandro were definitely the youngest in the family. While their backs were ramrod straight, their countenances were slightly turned to each other and they were muttering something to themselves, like they were memorizing something.

A woman walked into the foyer from the parlor beyond it. Slim and beautiful, with silvering dark hair knotted at the nape of her neck and emerald eyes I would have recognized anywhere. Instead of the steely glint that glittered in Nico's eyes, there was a strength in hers I almost missed for the cloud of sadness in front of her irises.

The moment her gaze settled on me, my breath caught in my throat.

She looked at me, not with polite curiosity but with a spark of recognition that sent my heart racing. Had she seen me since I arrived in New York? Or did her recognition stem back further? The way she tilted her head just a little and she squinted like she was trying to bring me into focus made me fear she was reaching back further in her mind than the past few weeks.

My heart pounded ten times louder than the quiet footsteps of her approach.

Please don't recognize me, I prayed. Not now. Not yet.

I was going to tell Nico everything after dinner. But if she made the connection now, in front of the entire Costa family, I had no way to predict what could happen.

I held several lungfuls of air in my chest.

She stared at me for a moment then glanced down to where Nico's hand held mine.

"*Mamma*, this is Raven Ferrari," Nico said when his mother had come to a stop.

There was something overly gentle in his voice. It was sweet, but it reminded me of the way a parent would speak to a fragile child.

Could he not see the strength in her eyes?

217

"Raven, this is my mother, *Signora* Victoria Costa."

She held out her hand, and I took it. Her skin was soft and warm, nothing like her husband's. She gripped my hand tightly, like she was holding onto it rather than shaking it while she continued to stare at me. Could she feel my pounding pulse in my wrist?

"It's nice to meet you, Raven."

Not Sofia. I let out the breath I *definitely* knew I was holding.

"It's my pleasure, *Signora Costa*," I said in the steadiest voice I could find.

"*La cena è pronta,*" an elderly man in a black uniform said, appearing from a door on the right and motioning for us to follow him into the dining room.

Thank God. I tried to hide the whooshing breath of relief. Maybe with the distraction of dinner and conversation, Victoria would abandon her attempt at placing me.

The large wood-paneled dining room smelled of basil and oregano, but the scents just turned my stomach.

A healthy distance was kept between the wing-backed chairs set around the table. Victoria and Lorenzo took their seats at the opposite ends of the table. The deep fissure of cold that tethered the two seemed to expand the length of the dark walnut table. The division was so tight, so potent that it sent a chill through the room.

Nico pulled out a chair for me, then sat down next to me. Gabe took the seat on my other side. Flanked by the Costa brothers, it should have put me at ease despite Lorenzo's dark gaze, but the way Victoria continued to look at me kept me unnerved. My muscles were so taut it was a wonder I didn't spring from my seat at every sound.

Fortunately, the scraping of serving spoons, the clatter of forks, and the quiet *glug, glug* noise as Gabe filled his wineglass to the brim were the only sounds that accompanied our food. Nico filled my glass and then his. As tempting as it was, it might have drawn unwanted attention if I downed the glass in one gulp.

It was too warm in here. Though my hands felt cold and clammy, the back of my neck was damp with perspiration. Lorenzo's gaze on me was like two hot lasers on my face, but I didn't dare look up. If Victoria recognized me, then certainly, her husband wouldn't be far behind.

"Nico tells us you're visiting New York, *signorina*. Where are you from originally?" he asked, but it felt like every word pierced right through me, digging deep like the lasers, searching below the surface for the truth.

Oh god, I'm going to have to look up. It felt like my head weighed a hundred pounds as I forced it up and met the man's cold, dead-eyed stare. "Um, California—Los Angeles," I squeaked and then silently cursed my monumental lack of backbone.

"Hmmm, and do you visit often?" he persisted in a tone that said he wasn't buying a word I was selling.

"No, this is my first time," I lied.

"Is that so?" It seemed like a rhetorical question, but he looked at me expectantly.

I nodded. My throat was too dry to force another word out.

This was a *bad* idea. This was the absolute motherload of bad ideas of all time. This would go down as one of the worst ideas in the Hall of Fame of bad ideas. *I'll wait for my plaque in the mail.*

The man didn't believe a word I was saying, and somehow, I had a feeling in the pit of my stomach that Victoria *recognized* me. It was beyond me, though, how she remembered what Sofia Luca looked like. Were she and my mother friends? How was she able to recognize me despite the decade that had passed, despite the toll puberty and a life without Italian marbles had taken on me?

She knew who I was. She knew the truth.

Every time her gaze landed on me, the heat around the room seemed to gather around me, the way I imagined the single bulb in interrogation rooms felt like on the skin. The fact that I was eating dinner with the Costa family was just now sinking into me.

I was in a den of lions.

A naive kitten in a den of sharp-fanged lions.

Nico's gaze kept swinging back and forth between me and Victoria. It didn't take long for the dawn of recognition on his face to fully break.

I was definitely getting eaten alive—and I didn't think Nico was going to use his tongue this time.

I stood up without thinking. *Stupid!*

"Can you please tell me where I could find the bathroom?" I asked Nico in a quiet enough voice I hoped the trembling in it was less noticeable.

"Third door on the left," he said, pointing toward a hallway off the left side of the dining room.

I nodded my thanks, pushed back my chair, and tried to walk out of the dining room with anything but the composure of a girl whose death was faked a decade ago and was supposedly buried six feet beneath the ground.

If Nico didn't kill me, I had no doubt Lorenzo Costa would have no qualms about doing it. Despite his age, he looked like a man who'd have no trouble ripping a person's heart right out of their chest with his bare hands.

I walked right in here. *The Costa estate.* This was basically suicide. I might as well have pinned a name tag to my chest next to a big, round bull's-eye.

Down the hall, the closed doors prickled my curiosity despite my fragile situation. They always did that. When I first walked into my hotel room, I checked all the rooms and the closed doors, drawers, and cupboards, just like I'd done the first day in my dorm.

Vito had taught me the importance of knowing one's surroundings. *"You know what curiosity did to the cat, passerotta?"* Vito would ask whenever he caught me snooping in the kitchen cupboards, the linen closet, or the side tables next to the sofa.

I did know what curiosity did to the cat.

I walked right past the closed doors and headed to the bathroom near the end of the hall. Inside, I stumbled to the marble sink and splashed water on my face.

A naive kitten in a den of sharp-fanged lions.

No one ever said anything about what curiosity did to the *kitten.*

I stared at the girl in the mirror, my blue eyes brewing a storm beneath. I looked around the bathroom. There was a window on the left. I walked over and checked it closely; it wasn't the kind that slid open on tracks. I would have to smash the window to get out.

I wasn't dumb enough to set off a security alarm. I'd be caught before I even climbed through.

I plopped my butt on the toilet lid and pinched my nose, the peach hue on my fingers a blur in my peripheral vision.

I could ask to speak with Nico for a moment, just the two of us. I'd get him alone and tell him the truth. I could only hope that he asked me to leave quietly instead of throwing me to the lions.

But I didn't want to do that. I didn't want to tell him the truth. I didn't want him to ask me to leave.

It felt as if someone was taking a bone out of my rib cage out and using it to pierce my lungs.

Greta was the type to rip off the Band-Aid all at once.

"Easy peasy, see?" she'd say. *"Just get it over with!"*

I did it the opposite way—peeling it off one painful inch at a time. Preserving the pain, suspending the blood that would spill out, delaying the inevitable.

I glanced at my watch. I was running out of time.

Maybe I was just being paranoid. Maybe Victoria *didn't* recognize me.

Or maybe she did, and I was wasting what precious little time my life had left before I was served up on a silver platter.

I stood up and glanced at my reflection in the mirror, surprised to see tears glistening on my cheeks. They often surprised me. It was like I got so caught up with what was going on inside, I forgot to notice what was happening outside.

When Greta warned me about my plan, I waved her off, certain I wasn't going to be distracted. *I'm focused,* I insisted then. But she was right. I enjoyed the ride too much. And now I didn't want to get off the roller coaster.

I became careless and did the stupidest and most dangerous thing: *I've fallen for Nico Costa.*

I breathed in deep, trying to stem the flow of tears.

Then as if a staccato beat was drumming to the pulsing of my heart, leather shoes clicked and clacked against the marble floor, the sound awfully near.

The door swung open behind me.

Chapter Thirty-One

Nico

I could feel every eye boring a hole at the back of my head as I turned left into the hallway. *Lorenzo, angry. Mom, concerned. Gabe, smug son of a bitch. The two, giving Alicia Silverstone a run for her money.* It played like a reel in my head, like the opening sequence of a sitcom.

How had I missed this?

I watched Mom stare at Raven like she was looking at a ghost the moment we arrived. But seeing Raven act like she was fucking Emily Rose purged the haze for me.

Or maybe it had always been clear as day and I was just looking the other way.

The reason I was never able to find information about Raven's past was because she did not have one. Raven Ferrari did not.

Raven Ferrari didn't exist until the night Sofia Luca died.

A Luca right under my nose, on my bed, in my mind, on my lips. She played me for a fool. A deceptive vixen acting like a kitten, wearing naïveté as a costume so well it looked like her own skin.

I threw open the bathroom door so hard it slammed against the wall.

Raven was hunched over the sink, tears flooding her eyes.

The muscle in my jaw spasmed.

She spun around, eyes widened in shock.

The rage flowed inside me like electricity. It zapped inside me, flaring through my veins like wire. Yet the moment I met her eyes, the blue sea in them put out the fire blazing through me.

I couldn't do it. I could never hurt her.

And I resented that. Despised it.

She had stripped me of the one thing by which I defined myself. Who I was down to the core.

Doing what needed to be done was like breathing oxygen to me. It was who I am.

I did what I had to do to protect my mother and brothers. I did what I had to do to prove myself to Lorenzo. I tortured, murdered, all in the name of loyalty. A twisted sense of it.

A Luca knocked on my door, and I willingly let her walk right in and shit on my bed.

The sense of betrayal, whether intentional or not, made me sick to the stomach.

It was the Lucas behind everything after all.

I was wrong about Aunt Isabella and Abruzzo. Their blood was on my hands because I listened to my dick and not Gabe.

Costa blood was on my hands.

"So what exactly was your plan?" I sneered, walking toward her in three long strides.

She stared up at me with tear-filled eyes, stretched to the brim.

"Sneak your way in like a rat, and try to tear this family apart from the inside out?"

I planted a hand on either side of her, pinning her against the sink. She was so close that her light jasmine scent filled my nostrils, traveling all the way to my head and down to my middle.

I grit my teeth and thrust it out of my mind.

"I-I don't... I m-mean, I d-didn't..." She stuttered.

"What's the matter, Raven? Or should I call you Sofia?"

Her eyes stared back at me, a million things running through it.

I didn't miss the way they did not fly wide in surprise at the mention of Sofia.

She knew.

She knew she was busted the minute Mom saw her.

My gaze fixed on her, I watched her closely, trying to search for answers. But all I could find were tears, pink-stained cheeks, cupid-bow lips I'd kissed hundreds of times and wanted just as much as the first time.

"Please, let me explain—"

I swooped in and crushed her lips beneath mine, unable to resist the way they seemed to call to me. Her lips grew pliant beneath me, but it made me draw back even angrier.

"Come on, Sofia, you can do better than that."

Her lips were still parted, and I took them again. Despite the way she was trembling, I could feel her body sparking up. But she made no move to reciprocate. She didn't lace her fingers through the hair at the back of my neck. She didn't grab onto my shoulders like they were her lifeline.

"What's the matter?" I said, wrenching my lips away. "You fucked me to play your game, didn't you? That was quite the price to pay, wasn't it?"

"I didn't... I-I mean... that wasn't..."—she shut her eyes closed, as if what she was about to say next pained her to say it—"a game."

Rage coursed through my veins so hot I expected to see it burn right through my skin.

"I mean, that wasn't supposed to happen…" she added lamely.

"Are you trying to tell me I made you… that I forced you to fuck me?" I seethed, fisting my hands so tight, my knuckles popped. "I've ripped men apart, Raven. I've carved them up piece by piece. I've done plenty of things you couldn't even imagine. But I have never raped a woman. Never, do you understand me? So if—"

"No!" she cried as her face seemed to fracture into a thousand pieces. "I didn't say that, Nico. I would never."

In all the pieces that made up her beautiful face, there wasn't a spot of doubt. For some fucked up reason, it mattered to me. It mattered that she didn't see me that way.

"She got rid of me," she cried.

It was the most anguished sound I've ever heard. It pierced my eardrums and shot through my body, laying waste to everything inside of me.

"What do you mean 'she' got rid of you? Who got rid you?"

I couldn't stop the question from slipping out. As angry as I was, the thought of anyone treating Raven like garbage topped it tenfold.

"My…" Sobs shook her chest as tears ran in steady streams from her blue eyes. "My mother."

I eyed her closely. The pain in her voice was so raw, but it was difficult to tell if it was real. Everything had been a lie with her so far.

"She wanted people to believe I was dead. She sent me away, and Vito told me they died, all of them. I had to become someone else or the people who killed them would kill me too. But then I saw her on the news," she said, and then the whole story spilled out about the fire, about her Aunt Francesca's house, and the morning after when she was picked up. Somehow, as she narrated everything, she went from being pinned against the sink to walking back and forth across the room, arms gesticulating wildly.

I listened as she told me about her new identity, her life in California, and what she did after finding out her family was alive.

"I was just so angry." She spun back around to face me. "I wanted to prove to them I wasn't useless. I couldn't be useless if I was able to do what they never could."

With my back against the sink, I stared at the wide blue sky of her eyes and realized with crystal clear certainty that I believed her.

I ate up her whole act, every single crumb of it. Even though the truth was staring at me right in the face. I even understood why she came for me. Even still, how do you call yourself a dumbass nicely?

"That's where I came in, right? My family?" I cracked my neck to the side.

She nodded. "But it wasn't supposed to be you... I'd read about you and..." She pressed her lips together.

The smallest smirk tilted my mouth upward, gone as quickly as it had come.

"So, when I met you that night, it wasn't me you were after?" I asked quietly.

She suddenly looked guilty as she bit her lower lip, pursing it to the side.

If I hadn't been her original target, then it wasn't all lies.

I thought of the way her nimble fingers filled the spaces between my hands so perfectly. I thought of the way her ebony hair lay flat on her back when I fucked her from behind. In my head, I listed all the sex facts I knew now like a roll call.

Raven was real, at least some part of her was. It certainly explained why nothing happened with those warehouses I set up as traps.

"I had no idea what you were talking about when you told me about those shipments," she confessed with a small laugh that was more like the Raven I'd come to know.

The air around us no longer snapped with anger. Instead it was sparking up like the electricity in a storm before a lightning strike.

I needed to kiss her, taste her, *inhale* her.

For the first time, there were no secrets between us. Nothing but the thin fabric of our clothes. There had never been so little between me and another person. I felt exposed, like a wound still raw.

I slammed my lips against hers, soft and sinful. My teeth nibbled into her lower lip, tasting a single rivulet of blood as I drew away.

"Take off your clothes," I said, needing it more than ever before in my life.

"Here?" She eyed the bathroom door.

"Now."

I was harder than I'd ever been, throbbing so painfully, desire twisted like pain in my gut.

Her fingers trembled as she unknotted the tie at the back of her neck, but the heat in her eyes flared so bright it turned them into molten blue pools. When her dress fell to the floor and she slipped off her lacy bra and panties, I took the only three seconds my pulsing cock could stand to look at her and take in every real, untainted, honest inch of her.

One, thin strands of her dark hair veiled her pink nipples.

Two, a single drop of wetness dripped from inside her right thigh, resting delicately in the small curve beside her pussy.

I licked my lips at the sight of it.

Three, smooth planes of her stomach that felt like silk underneath my hands when I held her in place as she rode me.

Almost instantly, she reached for the buttons on my shirt, working them open with none of the hesitation that was there before.

Her breathing was coming faster and heavier, the lower swells of her breasts starting to dampen.

She tugged my shirt off when the buttons were undone and moved right on to the button and fly of my pants. The second she finished, I kicked off my shoes, whipped off my pants, and lifted her up onto the counter.

Without having to be told, she spread her thighs for me, leaning back while a knowing light flashed in her eyes.

I let my eyes take one greedy look of her perfect body and then I lined myself up and drove into her hot, tight pussy. I fucked her hard and fast, incapable of gentle and slow, incapable of being without her slick walls clenching my dick for a second longer.

Her eyes seemed to glue mine to them, sewing an unbreakable tether. My hands explored her body as if I'd never touched her before. Getting to know every line, shape, contour all over again.

My name fell from her lips over and over again, first as breathy sighs, then as broken screams.

I could tell when she became aware that she was getting a bit too loud by the way she bit down hard on her lip, trying to stifle her moans. Her nails scraped down my back harder as she imploded within, her thighs tightening their grip around me.

Kiana Hettinger

Not for the first time, I felt connected to her in a way I never experienced before. I was heady. *Obsessed.* It was like a drug, and I knew I'd never be able to get enough. Not ever.

I was hooked.

I speared my fingers into the sweat-dampened hair at the nape of her neck and forced her head up.

I needed to see her unguarded. Open.

The tingling at the base of my spine intensified as she stared back at me. She didn't say a word, too engrossed in trying to swallow back all the sounds that begged to escape.

But I swore I could *see* her. I couldn't put a name to it, but something was shining bright in her eyes. Something that brought me to the peak, until I erupted, my white seed gushing inside her. The very tip of my cock continued to convulse, kissing the wet, warm muscle of her cervix.

It only took the light in her eyes to wrench the most exquisite, earth-shattering orgasm from my body.

Her pussy clenched rhythmically around me as her nails drew blood and one tidal wave after another crashed through me in the ultimate release.

Panting heavily, I let go of her hair, and she dropped her head against my chest. In a move that was the most foreign and most natural thing I'd ever done, I wrapped my arms tight around her and held her there. I never wanted to let go.

Several moments passed before our rugged breathing finally began to slow to something that resembled normal, but still I held her. She seemed so small in my arms, and I couldn't help but relish in her.

No matter how it had turned out, she came here determined to infiltrate one badass mafia family—that required a special kind of gut I bet only she would have.

I dropped hard back to reality. She was still a Luca in the Costa estate. A Luca who had paraded herself as a complete stranger. It was bad enough that Lorenzo was under the impression she was a Luciano, but his recent interest in the Lucas made this terrible situation even worse, if that was possible.

I didn't even want to think about Raven being a pawn in Lorenzo's game.

Over my dead body, my mind seethed. There wasn't anything I wouldn't do to keep her safe. I'd put that gun to my father's head all over again, but pull the trigger this time if it meant she got to draw one more breath.

Lorenzo *would* understand that there was a line here he was not allowed to cross.

But while I'd do anything for the dark-haired Juliet to the twisted version of *Romeo and Juliet* that was my life now, I wasn't exactly thrilled about the idea of patricide. So I needed to get her the hell out of here.

If I was able to figure out who she was, Lorenzo wouldn't be far behind.

Reluctantly, I withdrew from her warm heat that felt way too familiar already. I froze when I saw my come dripping down her thighs.

My heart raced.

Oddly enough, I wasn't filled with dread the way I knew I would have if this had happened with anyone else.

I thought of a mini Raven running around the house, peals of laughter filling the house.

Huh. Raven was strong. Maybe she could keep whatever evil ran through my veins at bay.

I helped Raven down from the counter, tucked the wayward lock of hair behind her ear, and retrieved our clothes.

Once we were dressed and she leaned down to fiddle with the straps of her sandals, I paused.

Raven was beautiful, kind, and strong. She was thrust into a new life, a new identity, and she came out fearless. She was everything a man could want. Everything *anyone* could want.

I counted down the days in my head until she realized I was not what she wanted, what she deserved. I couldn't sleep in a house surrounded by a white picket fence. Monsters slept in cages.

Wherever her imagination had taken her about me would soon come crashing down.

"I don't think you're a monster."

Wrong. You just don't know what I plan to do to my father if he laid a finger on you.

You would be repulsed.

You would be scared.

You would stop rattling the cage that has served as my home.

She stood up and took my hand as if on schedule. I wanted to close my hands in a fist so she couldn't warm my calloused palms with her soft skin. I wanted to let go. Instead, I said nothing.

I led her back down the hallway, through the dining room, straight out the front door, in my car.

Only then did I let go of her hand, just in time.

Chapter Thirty-Two

Raven

I'd been transported to another dimension, an alternate version of the same reality. The "multiverse" they called it, yes? That's why we can have more than one Spider-Man?

How else could I explain what happened tonight? It wasn't like I didn't know Nico had another side to him, a side that was nothing like the stone-cold killer he showed the rest of the world. But even knowing the kind, warm, and fiercely loyal man he tried to keep buried beneath the surface, it was supposed to end tonight. But it hadn't. And I had no script, no playbook to tell me what to do next. I didn't even know where we were going.

He had both of his hands on the steering wheel, and though he was watching the highway in front of us, it looked like his mind was someplace else.

"You're staring," he said with a quirk of a smile that didn't reach his eyes.

"I am." I couldn't stop looking at him. "I don't understand why you didn't kick my butt to the curb."

The words spilled out unbidden.

"Have you seen that butt? No man lets go of something so fine." He smiled again, but it didn't quite reach his eyes.

There was something he wasn't saying, or didn't want to. He was hiding something. I could practically see the shroud of smoke surrounding him.

Do you regret it?

For once, the question on the tip of my tongue did not slip out. It stayed there, settled itself, refused to budge.

"Where are we going?" I asked instead.

"We're—"

Nico's phone rang. He stopped talking and pulled it out of his jacket.

"What is it, Gabe?" he asked as he turned off the highway.

I couldn't hear what Gabe was saying, but with every passing second, Nico's countenance changed. He seemed distracted a moment ago, but now he was alert. His spine was straight and his shoulders back.

There was an energy radiating from him.

"Finally," he said. It came out like a sigh.

There was no relief in his expression, though. It was hard as steel, and the dangerous glint flashed in his eyes.

"We move on him tonight. Put out the word: it's all hands on deck. I'll be back at the house in an hour."

He hung up the phone and slipped it back into his jacket.

My heart was beating harder, and my hands felt sweaty. I wanted to pry, but I kept my mouth shut. Not because I was afraid to ask, but because I was afraid of what he would say.

Nico lived in a dangerous world—I knew that even way before I met him. Everyone in this life did. Dom did, Leo, Dad, Dante, Victoria, Vito. *Me*, and even Greta somehow.

But until this moment, Nico had been this invincible force to me. Not flesh and blood, but impenetrable steel.

"We move on him tonight…"

Suddenly, I was struck with the cold reality that it didn't matter that Nico seemed invincible to me because to the rest of the world, he was mortal. He could be injured, killed, shot in the chest, kicked in the gut.

He could be gone in the blink of an eye. My mind went into SOS mode as a thousand possibilities flashed through my mind like a slideshow, each one scarier than the one before.

"I have to take you back to your hotel," he said as my stomach twisted into knots.

And you *might not come back.*

I opened my mouth, but no words came out. It felt dry, like there was a drought. All the water was inside me, drowning me out, flooding my insides, spilling into every nook and cranny.

"Raven?" he repeated, glancing at me.

"Um, sorry, what did you say?"

"Are you all right?" he asked, putting his hand over mine.

"No."

The confession slipped out.

"What's wrong?" he asked. He seemed genuinely perplexed.

"I don't want you to go."

His brow furrowed, and he squeezed my hand. "You don't even know where I'm going."

"Maybe not, but I know it's somewhere dangerous."

He smiled. It lit his eyes this time. "*I'm the world's most dangerous predator, Bella,*" he quoted.

I rolled my eyes, but couldn't keep from laughing. "And everything about you invites me in?"

"Damn right." He leaned over and kissed me as he turned into the hotel parking lot, but his attempt at distracting me wasn't working.

"I—"

"Don't, Raven." He shook his head. "Someone's been trying to mess with the families for the past several months. We found him. We'll be in and out before the guy even knows what's happening."

"Then let me help."

The words were out before I even realized I was saying them.

Nico's eyebrows reached for his hairline.

"*I* could help," I said for a second time, meaning the words this time.

Vito trained me at hand-to-hand combat for years, and I was quite the proficient marksman. On days we both didn't feel like working up a sweat, *Zio* Vito made sure I knew how to use a gun.

Nico stole a glance at me, looking me at like I had fangs in my mouth. "You'd do that... you'd fight with Costas?"

I didn't really think about it that way. All I knew was that it was going to be dangerous wherever he was going. If I could help keep him safe then I'd fight with Costas. Yes. Sofia Luca would fight with Costas.

I'd fight alongside a pride of dancing lions if it meant keeping Nico's heart beating.

"Yes."

He squeezed my hand once more then released it. "I can't let you do that."

Pop.

I had a vagina. No one would ever let me be useful or do what I could do because I had a freaking vagina—which, mind you, could take quite a beating. *Certainly more than ding-dongs can, I'm sure.*

"What are you thinking, Raven?"

"I'm thinking that I spent eleven years learning how to fight, how to use weapons, and I don't know why Vito even taught me all that stuff if women are expected to shut up and sit pretty."

Nico scoffed. "Not wanting you there has nothing to do with what body parts you have—though, I am very fond of yours. I don't want you there because I'd spend every second watching you, worrying about you, because…" He clamped his lips shut. "Because…" He looked away, glancing out the window. "Because you'll always be a Luca."

He might as well have just stabbed me in the heart with his finest knife.

I thought of the way his eyes blazed earlier as he filled me, in and out until I was stripped bare. No lies, no barriers between us. No one else had ever come so close.

But I held on to a single thread of hope I knew was more brittle than my strength could make up for.

There was always something that would come between us.

I chuckled. The only person who had come so close needed to be as far away as he could be.

I stepped out of the car and closed the door behind me as gently as I could.

I headed to the concierge, my movements feeling slow and heavy.

"Miss Raven Ferrari?" the receptionist with a cleft chin said as she handed me my replacement card key.

238

I nodded once.

I didn't let a single tear escape until I was behind the closed door of my hotel room.

It's Sofia Luca, I guess.

Chapter Thirty-Three

Nico

"Nico, can I speak with you, *per favore?*" *Mamma* asked the minute I arrived home. She caught me as soon as I walked back inside the house like she was waiting for me.

My mind was elsewhere.

My own words rang in my head, the vibrato of my own voice bounced around the walls.

"Because you'll always be a Luca."

The truth was, after this web of lust, loyalty, and suspicion that bound me to Raven was untangled, what was left was *chickenshit*.

I was too much of a chicken to tell her the truth. I was shit-faced scared. Shit-faced scared of my heart continuing to twitch and spasm, as if being revived.

She scared me.

So instead of protecting her, I shattered her, broke her.

Chickenshit.

"*Si, Mamma,*" I said, clenching and unclenching my fists. My knuckles were sore from punching the steering wheel on the drive home.

I followed her through the foyer, past the parlor to the sun-filled solarium where she spent most of her days. I watched as she walked, one foot in front of the other, prancing along the invisible straight line she never veered away from, much like trains ran on tracks, unfailingly, that led them to their destinations.

"Sit down, Nico," my mother said, motioning to the sofa that sat facing the wall of windows.

I stood in place. A million things ran through my head.

Raven. Sofia. "Because you're a Luca." Maria Luca. Lorenzo. Avalone's son. Fiorenzo. Diego Berlusconi—a nobody who managed to lure soldiers from families all over the country. And his most abundant source: what remained of the Novas.

Eventually, I sat down on the sofa. It overlooked the rose gardens behind the house. My mother's rose gardens. When she wasn't in the solarium, she sat on the bench in her garden, surrounded by hundreds of roses.

I waited while she retrieved something from the chest she kept locked in the corner. She sat down beside me with a file folder in one hand, her other free hand gently placed upon mine.

I glanced down. I ached at the memory of my mother's hands damaged, her wrists broken.

"I know what happened that day, Nico," she said with a knowing look I found myself not liking one bit.

I was brought right back to three days after my sixteenth birthday. The first day my mother had ever looked at me the way she looked at Lorenzo.

"I don't know what you're talking about," I replied, keeping a straight face.

She laughed, a sad sound. "Of course, you do. You might be able to fool the world with that face, but I know you, Nico."

"*Mamma*, I—"

"Hush," she said, pressing her hand down more firmly on mine. "I know you didn't do it, Nico."

Rosalie Santo had been a maid in my family's home for two years when she snuck into my bedroom. She was young and hot. I was just young.

One night, Rosalie snuck into my bedroom, and I woke up with her mouth around my cock. She thought she could blackmail my family into keeping her silence with the bruises she wore a few hours later. They must have bought her story because the problem went away fast.

"I thought you believed I did it," I said, my voice thick and raw at the memory of *that* day.

"I wish I could tell you I didn't even consider it, but your father had gotten hold of you by then. I can't deny I wondered, but then I saw the truth in your eyes," my mother said.

Even all these years later, it was like another boulder off my shoulders.

"I know you didn't do it, but I also know that what that woman did to you changed you, maybe as much as what your father did to you. I feared you would forever be angry and bitter, and under Lorenzo's tutelage, it would be far too easy for you to lose sight of who you really are."

"Why are you telling me this?"

She sighed, but her jaw hardened with determination I couldn't remember ever seeing in her. "In all my years as the wife of Lorenzo Costa, I seldom used the power the position granted me. Only twice."

That sounded ominous, but I couldn't imagine my mother hurting a fly.

"What did you do, *Mamma*?"

She sighed again, placed the folder down on my lap, and released my hand. I opened it up.

Dark eyes that paralleled dark hair looked back at me. I used to think that the glint in her eyes was just innocent mischief. I'd grown enough now to know that it was malice after all.

I squinted my eyes at the mug shot on my lap. I'd distorted Rosalie's face in my head so much that it was a shock to see how pretty she'd been.

"I could have had her killed for what she tried to do to my family, to my son," my mother said in a voice so hard I barely recognized it. "I could have forced her to work in the whorehouses until it killed her. But none of that seemed right. I didn't want her dead. I wanted her to live a long life, remembering every day the consequences of what she did to you."

I flipped over the old photo and looked at the next page and then the next. "What is all this?"

"It's the case I had fabricated against *Signorina* Santo. The case that has kept her in prison, and will continue to keep her there for the rest of her natural life." My mother didn't flinch, her green eyes unwavering, not an ounce of remorse.

I stared at the pages, not quite able to process what she was saying. My mother, the fragile, abused wife of Lorenzo Costa, had wreaked vengeance on her enemy.

"You said 'twice.'"

"*Sì*, I did."

I waited for her to continue, but the silence stretched and grew louder until it was ringing in my ears.

"*Mamma?*" I said when I couldn't take it any longer.

"Sofia was a good girl, Nico. She was bright and beautiful. She had everything she could have needed to make a glorious future for herself."

Prickles of apprehension ghosted down my spine. I had no idea where she was going with this, but I had a feeling I wasn't going to like it.

"And then your father made an agreement with Vincent Luca," she said.

I almost chuckled at me and Raven falling in line, even unknowingly, with what Vincent and Lorenzo originally wanted. Well, at least until I ruined, shattered, destroyed, and burned my relationship with Raven to the ground until they were just mere ashes, speckles of dust. What did this have to do with…

My stomach bottomed out.

"You and Maria Luca."

I could almost see the two brunette heads pooled together at the nook in the solarium. Half empty glasses of what I thought was orange juice back then, ash trays, and cigarette sticks with pink lipstick on them. I could easily see the two of them scheming to make sure the marriage never happened. *She* was the one who needed to be safe from *me*. And no place was safer than six feet beneath the ground.

Raven had thought her own family didn't want her, had no use for her, had gotten rid of her. Because of me.

The knife at the back of my mind felt like it was being twisted in place, by my own mother. My own blood and flesh. She had gone to great lengths to keep Sofia Luca away from me. To keep her safe from me. To keep her away from the monster.

The click of a key turning rang in my head, the locks clanking against the steel bars of the cage. *My* cage.

"I thought I was doing it for you, and for her. We arranged to send Sofia off with one of the Lucianos' men. I had to believe that one day, you'd come to see that what your anger and your father were turning you into… It wasn't… It was *wrong*. That's not who you want to be. That's not who you are. I know *you*. I didn't…" She paused and turned slightly away as if she was weighing her words in her head very carefully, like there was a balance scale inside her head. "You couldn't be the man your father wanted you to be and have people close to you, love you, care for you. They… *she*… wouldn't have survived it."

The haunted look in my mother's emerald orbs reminded me of how close her words were to her reality. She knew what it was like to have to care for a monster. She had to learn how to survive. She almost didn't.

If I hadn't done what I'd done, what would have happened to *Mamma?*

If *Mamma* and Maria hadn't done what they did, what would have happened to Sofia?

Every part of me rejected the possibility, but for every part of me that did, a tiny twinge of doubt knocked at me, continuously, incessantly until it was difficult to ignore, until I was forced to look up.

I saw *Mamma's* bruises on Raven's flushed cheeks, her broken bones protruding through Raven's skin. I saw the fresh wound bleeding copiously into Raven's eye from the thin scar above my mother's eyebrow.

"Do you think…" I had to swallow down the lump in my throat. "Do you think I would have been like him?"

"No, Nico, I don't. That is what I'm trying to tell you. I was wrong. When I saw you this evening, the way you looked at her, the way you held her hand. Even when you figured it out, it wasn't rage in your eyes. You felt betrayed. There can only be betrayal when there's trust. I don't believe your father is capable of love, but you are not like him, and I was wrong."

I was the reason why Raven was torn from her family, kept in the dark for more than a decade. I was the reason why Raven had to be Raven, why Sofia had to start a new life. Maria Luca didn't abandon her daughter. She did what she could to protect her. From me. The monster.

My mother thought she was wrong to have gone on with the plan, but I didn't necessarily think so. It made me sick to the stomach just imagining hurting Raven tonight. But who's to say that wouldn't change a few years from now?

All monsters were the same. Lorenzo bred me well.

I ignored my heart rattling in its cage.

"You should have done a better job keeping her away."

I couldn't remember ever being angry with *Mamma* before.

But the anger was chaotic, consuming me like wildfire. I was angry with her for keeping Raven away. And for not doing a better job keeping her away. And for hurting Raven with her lies. And for not lying better.

If it had been me, I would have sent ten-year-old Raven and her "Uncle" Vito across the Atlantic, maybe to Italy, to live off the grid and spend their lives making wine on a vineyard or growing potatoes in a farm in Peru.

But then I thought about the way she lit up when she talked about Greta, or when she told me the story about that nice nurse from when she was young. Or the way her whole body seemed to buzz when she talked about her dreams. I couldn't imagine being the one to keep all that brilliance away from the world, to be the to one dim her shine, until she was nothing but a flicker of her once prosperous luminosity, void and exhausted from trying to survive.

I glanced at my mother.

"Why were our fathers so hellbent on the union between our families?"

It hadn't escaped my notice that without it, Raven would have been free to live the life she should have had, surrounded by a family who loved her.

My mother shook her head. "It was your grandfather's and Sofia's grandfather's most fervent wish. They were friends, Nico. Good friends from the time they were children in Italy. But since both men only sired sons, it wasn't until Sofia was born that the possibility of a union between the families was possible. Vincent Luca swore to his father on his deathbed that he would see that wish fulfilled. I think perhaps, he regretted it later," she mused aloud. "But Vincent Luca is not a man to go back on his word. That's why Maria was worried.

Vincent Luca ruled with an iron fist, but he was a fair man, and even more than that, he was an honorable man.

"Vincent couldn't possibly have known what your father had been like at home or what he was grooming you to become. It's never the men who know those private things. It's the women, Nico. The women who, in our families, have no voices. As much as Vincent loved Maria, she couldn't risk her only daughter on the chance that she would be heard and he would go back on his word. She only wished to protect Sofia."

"What is your most fervent wish, *Mamma*?" I'd spent more time with my mother than any other woman. I tried to protect her. I did my best to show her the respect she deserved. But looking at her now, I found it difficult to see beyond the dense forest in her eyes.

She smiled. "That's simple. My most fervent wish is for your happiness. I know what you did for me, what you have continued to do for me and your brothers. If I could go back..." Her thoughts seemed to turn inward and her eyes looked far away.

"If I could go back, I wouldn't change—"

My mother put her finger over my lips. "You're a good boy, Nico, but there's no sense in worrying over the past. Any of it. I told you the truth because both you and Sofia deserve it. Sofia deserves to know that her mother loved her enough to do what she had to do to keep her safe. But now it's time for you to go to her."

She stood up and held out a hand to me, healthy and supple as I liked to wish it always would be.

I stood up, and like every time before, I went to swallow down the fears and doubts that ate at me, but I stopped myself. Here, with my mother, was perhaps the only place in the world I could voice them. And though the words scraped up my throat like razor blades, I forced them out.

"What do I do when she realizes she's too good for me?"

I looked away.

She sighed and shook her head, then placed her hands on either side of my face. "I know what you think of yourself, but you're wrong. You're no monster, but if there's no one around to remind you of the man you really are, you will become what you fear most.

You two really were made for each other. The way she was looking at you tonight, that was not the look of a woman in lust. It was the look of a woman in love, Nico. Don't throw that away."

I nodded, hoping I hadn't done exactly that. If nothing else, my mother had shown me I wasn't ready to let it go just yet, whatever it was.

The rattling of steel bars in my chest continued to hiss and clank like a train announcing its arrival.

With a grin, I thought, *It's about damn time.*

Chapter Thirty-Four

Raven

"I don't think ice cream's going to do it, hon," Greta said, hugging me tight. "You sit tight, and I'll be back in fifteen minutes with an entire liquor store, I promise."

She swiped her purse off the coffee table and darted out the door.

Greta was probably right. I had little experience with getting drunk, but it didn't sound like a terrible idea at the moment.

My eyes were red and swollen from crying for the past half hour. My chest hurt from all the heaving and sobbing. I didn't even know why I was crying. The tears just spilled out of my chest, real chest-wracking sobs. I knew there was a good chance I wasn't going to see him again after tonight. But if I was being completely one hundred percent I-swear-on-Sofia-Luca's-fake-grave honest, I nurtured a small bubble of hope for us. To see it burst and by Nico himself with his shiny knife, and his words that tasted like rust on my tongue.

"Because you'll always be a Luca."

He could never trust me. He could never sleep soundly at night knowing he was sleeping with his enemy on his bed. It was some twisted irony that the name that had been stripped from me held so much sway over my life.

I stood in the middle of the room, fidgeting with my phone in my hand. I lifted it and began to scroll through my contacts.

I brought my phone to my ear, waiting as the other line rang, all the while scrambling for what I was actually going to say.

I just wanted to hear his voice, maybe apologize.

"What's wrong, Raven?" he barked the moment he answered.

I could almost feel his panic coming through the phone in waves.

"Nothing's wrong," I said, feeling the tidal wave of guilt crash down on me for what I put him through. I struggled to find the right words, but ultimately, I only needed two. *"I'm sorry."*

He was silent for a brief moment. I could hear the way his breathing changed from short and shallow to slow and deep.

"No, I'm sorry, *passerotta*. It was never my intention to hurt you. I wish I could have told you about your family."

My insides sagged with relief. Deep down, I knew he didn't want to hurt me, which made the way I reacted all the more abhorrent.

A knock sounded at the door.

He came back?

My stupid heart started doing cartwheels.

"I'll have to call you back," I said, moving to hang up the phone but then putting it back to my ear at the last moment. "I love you, *zietto."*

Uncle Vito and I could figure out everything else later.

"I love you too, *passerotta*," Vito answered.

Smiling, I hung up the phone, tossed it on the sofa, and crossed the room to answer the door. I turned the handle, anticipating the sight of *him* on the other side.

Then it flew wide open with so much force, it slammed against the wall.

Four men stood in the open doorway. Four men I'd never seen before. All of them taller than me, broader than me, more muscular than me.

I stumbled back as cold terror shot down my spine and surged through my extremities.

There was a tall, gangly man unconscious on the floor in the hallway with a bloody bump on the side of his head, right over the top of his temple. I'd seen him at Onyx, but I knew next to nothing about him.

Like they were one being, the four men stepped forward, crossing the threshold into my room, my space.

I stumbled back another three steps with my heart pounding a staccato beat like the victim in some slasher horror movie before it hit me.

Running is pointless.

Everyone dies in *Final Destination*. Jamie Lee Curtis practically gets killed off in ninety percent of her movies. Victims who try to make a run for it either get caught, killed, or something else worse.

I hadn't been away from the gym for more than twenty-four hours since that time I turned green from eating those questionable fish tacos at the taco truck by the gym. But even when I was out cold with food poisoning then, Vito still managed to drag me to the gym as soon as I could manage to hold my head up and do some simulations by himself along with a lecture. The man was determined to train me. I wouldn't be surprised if I found out that Vito had made some kind of deal with some dead Italian mobster to raise me as if he was preparing me to star in the next *Kill Bill* movie.

He trained me, taught me to read and anticipate his next move, taught me to respond with my body and react. He taught me how to defend myself.

He taught me how to survive.

I tried to slow my pounding heart and focused on reading my enemy. Looking at the four men, it was clear which of them was in charge. Tall, dark hair, handsome aside from his crooked nose, he stood just apart from the others with his chin tipped a smidge higher, his hand hanging loosely at his side.

He wasn't going to attack. He would let his burly lackeys do his dirty work, at least so long as his lackeys held the upper hand.

I turned to the other three. They all leered at me like I was a hapless deer, and they were starving hunters. And like a hunter with a deer caught in his sights, they were confident they had me. In their arrogant eyes, I was as good as dead, or whatever it was they intended to do to me.

I could use that, at least for now. I kept my features arranged in a terrified mask, mimicking my inner Jamie Lee Curtis and maybe summoning a little Bella Swan too—not difficult to do given the way fear was coursing through my body, making my lungs work overtime and my palms turn sweaty. I deliberately skittered back a little further as the three strode closer while the fourth, the ringleader, hovered back.

A little closer. I wanted to attack. I wanted to run. The urge to do something useful made my legs tremble.

You'll lose your focus, I chastised myself.

They continued to corral me, corner me, as my steps led us back toward the corner of the room. Their beady eyes gleamed with something that made my stomach twist. I continued to pace backward, precisely leading us to the corner of the room where none of them would be able to get behind me. The solid wall could be useful as part of my offensive.

Just as my shoulders made contact with the cool, unyielding wall behind me, two sets of hands reached for me. They were reaching low like they were going to grab me by the forearms, so I shot my arms out higher and grabbed the nearest one by his shoulders. Startled, he barely resisted as I yanked him toward me with all my might, just askew so that his forehead slammed into the wall next to my head.

I barely heard the telltale thud when one meaty hand wrapped around my forearm.

I yanked my arm downward and shot my knee into his groin at the same time. His grip around my arm loosened as he stumbled back, groaning, trying to hold himself upward.

Yes! Two down, two to go.

There was no way I would be able to incapacitate all four of them. All I could hope for was to inflict enough injuries in quick succession to buy myself a few seconds. Just enough time for a clear shot at the door so I could hightail my butt through it before they could follow.

The third guy was faster than the other two.

I barely had my foot back down on the ground when his hand shot out.

I ducked to avoid the blow, but I misjudged his intention. He grabbed hold of a fistful of my hair and yanked my head back.

His free hand went for my throat.

I picked up my foot and slammed it down, heel first, into his foot. His hands loosened its grip on my hair and my throat as he roared and fell.

I slipped sideways, not willing to relinquish the wall that served as my offensive. But he had recovered quickly, standing upright again.

I cocked back and struck him with an uppercut to the jaw.

Pain shot up my hand, all the way to my shoulder, as he stumbled back for a second time.

If I could hold out for just a little longer…

I caught sight of the ringleader. He stood in place, a small grin tugging his mouth upward, like he was amused.

I paused.

For a second.

A fraction of a breath.

My breath hitched as I felt a meaty hand wrap around my throat, the man's rough skin scraping against the jut of the bone. He tugged me forward as another man snagged my arms from behind my back.

I lost.

I lashed out without rhyme or rhythm, kicking at the man who had his hands around my throat while I tried to writhe out of the other man's grip.

But all my fists and feet connected to were air. Every moment tugged painfully at my shoulder joints as the hands around my throat began to constrict my airway.

They had me and they knew it. The air around me had changed.

I didn't need to see their faces to see their smug looks.

"Release her, Sergio," the ringleader said to the man who was trying to strangle me to death.

The guy instantly let go and stepped back. While I could breathe a little easier, it came with no relief. The ringleader stepped forward while his lackeys dug their fingers into my arms, making sure they had a nice, snug grip.

"You really are a magnificent creature, aren't you?" he mused.

I sunk my teeth into my lip, biting back every filthy word I could imagine. Vito had taught me to be smart. Provoking a bear was not a smart move no matter how bad things looked for me at the moment.

"Where are my manners?" He laughed. "Allow me to introduce myself. My name is Diego, and I'm afraid you're going to have to come with me."

"Over my dead body."

I yanked against the hands holding me, ignoring the burning in my shoulder joints.

He shook his head. "I don't think so, *Signorina* Luca."

Nobody but Greta, Vito, and Nico's immediate family knew who I was.

"It's too bad we're in such a hurry." He sighed, glancing over me in a way that made me want to vomit. "Now, we could do this the old-fashioned way, but it would be such a shame to mess up that pretty face, don't you think?"

He produced a syringe from the inside pocket of his jacket.

An overwhelming wave crashed down on me, leaving me grasping for breath. My whole body shook uncontrollably.

It was unlike anything else I'd experienced before.

I'd never been knocked unconscious before.

I'd never been rendered dead to the world, unable to react, powerless and helpless.

I wouldn't be able to fight them. I wouldn't even know what they were doing to me because I'd be unconscious.

I struggled harder. I kicked out in every direction I could. I whipped my head around and tried to sink my teeth into anything I could reach. All futile efforts. I might as well have been a child throwing a tantrum.

He jabbed the needle into my neck, and I could feel the liquid cold spread out. My heart was pumping so fast, I had seconds left at best.

I glanced around frantically, looking for anything that could help me.

My gaze settled on my phone I tossed on the sofa earlier.

Something dropped inside me.

"It doesn't matter what's happening," Vito said, "you hit that button, and I'll find you, passerotta. I'll tear apart every man in my path to get to you, but I will get to you. Always."

Vito had programmed a panic button on my phone. Over the years, he drilled into my head to call him if I ever got into trouble.

It hadn't even crossed my mind and I had just spoken to him.

My eyelids fluttered to a close. It was starting to feel heavy. Which made it even more strange, because my body felt weightless. I felt like nothing at all. My legs seemed to have vanished into thin air from under me. All feeling in any part of me was slowly whistling away. Maybe because I wasn't the one holding myself up any longer.

I felt like I was watching a black-and-white film as meaty hands replaced gravity. Or maybe they let me go.

And I was just floating up to the ceiling.

Up, and up, and up…

Chapter Thirty-Five

Nico

"You know who she is, don't you?" I stood in front of Lorenzo's gleaming mahogany desk, staring down at the man who'd sired me.

He smiled, though like always, it didn't reach his dead eyes. "Sofia Luca, you mean? Of course, I recognized her. I am rather disappointed in you, though. To be deceived by the complicitous offspring of Vincent Luca... I thought you were smarter than that." Every word out of his mouth dripped with arrogance and disdain.

"I'm smart enough to make you my first stop, Lorenzo. If you—"

He held up one wrinkled hand. "The girl is of no use to you. She's a lying snake, and that is not the kind of woman you'll have for a wife."

I scoffed. If he thought he was going to tell me who I could or could not have for a wife, then my father had clearly lost all of his mental faculties. "If you wanted an obedient, little puppet for a son, you shouldn't have raised a monster. I'll do what I damn well please, and you know it. If you want to kill me for it, I'm right here," I said, holding my arms out wide. "Take your best shot."

I stood still, waiting, part of me begging for him to try, to finally have an excuse to end this.

But he shook his head and sat back in his chair, laying his hands across his stomach. "I'm not going to kill you, Nico. It wouldn't do me any good. I've seen the way your brothers look at you. You've sunk your claws into every one of them. If I do away with all of my disobedient, disrespectful offspring, I'll have no heirs left, will I?" He sneered.

That was all that kept him from putting a bullet between my eyes. Not love, not anything that resembled affection for his son. Only his empire. His legacy.

The image I'd had of my father cracked and shattered into a thousand pieces. I'd always thought of Lorenzo as a brave monster, but the man wasn't brave, he wasn't fearless. He just had nothing to lose. For all the people in Lorenzo's life, there wasn't a person he truly cared about. He had nothing to fear because there was no one that could be taken from him that would cause him a moment's grief. He had nothing.

He wasn't brave; he was pathetic, but with almost nothing to lose, it made him a difficult man to scare. So, for Raven, I played the only card I could.

"If you so much as have one hair on her head harmed, Lorenzo, I will burn your empire to the ground."

He scoffed, not believing me for a second. "It is your empire as well, my son."

"I don't care." I met the man's lifeless stare, letting him look his fill, letting him see that I wasn't bluffing one fucking bit.

He stared for a long time. Maybe he was hoping to see some flicker of doubt in my eyes. Maybe he was just stalling for our men to get here and put a bullet in my brain. I didn't think so, though. Over the past several months, there'd been a shift, a subtle change in the way our men looked at the two of us. Men like Cesare and Salvatore, they'd take a bullet for me. They'd follow my orders to the ends of the earth. But for Lorenzo? I wasn't so sure anymore.

His hands clenched together across his stomach, knuckles turning white. It seemed he'd noticed the shift as well. "More deals then, is it?" he asked, his tone flippant but with an undercurrent of tension that gave him away. "You never seemed happy with the last deal you made me."

"I'll be happy when you're dead and buried, Lorenzo. Until then, you'll give me your word."

He was quiet for a moment like he was mulling it over, but there was nothing to consider. He'd do it. He'd make the deal because his empire was his only friend. The only thing in the world he was afraid to lose.

He nodded once, but that wasn't good enough. I cocked an eyebrow, waiting. I wanted to hear him say it.

"You have a deal. So long as my empire stays strong, your snake remains safe."

"Her name is Raven. Do not disrespect her again."

I strode out of the room before he could respond, closing the door behind me.

It was done. Raven was safe. The knots in my stomach loosened, and I took the first real deep breath since I'd walked into that office.

Now all I had to do was stop the scumbag Berlusconi from chipping away at the goddamned Costa empire.

***

"A Luca, huh?" Gabe asked from the passenger seat of the Porsche, grinning like a seven-year-old at Disneyland.

I scoffed.

Gabe needed to get his head in the game. Even though I spent the past few hours reciting apology speeches in my head, I was never going to admit that to Gabe. That kind of ammunition just wasn't something a smart man handed over.

"Don't you think you have more important things than my personal life to worry about?"

He looked around exaggeratedly as if he was looking for something then shook his head. "Nope. Your personal life is pretty much at the top of my list at the moment."

Stronzo. "You need to get a life, *fratello.*"

"I don't think so. I get all the excitement I need living vicariously through yours."

Gabe was smiling, but there was something guarded about him—like he was keeping secrets, but now wasn't the time to pester him about them.

"So, when are you going to pop the question?" he asked as I slid off the highway and merged into city traffic.

I had a feeling Gabe was watching way too many *Sex in the City* reruns.

"You're going to have to close your mouth eventually, you know?" he said. "And that was our turn, wasn't it?" He was still grinning while he pointed as I drove right past the intersection.

I clicked my tongue. I watched in my rearview mirror as our men made the turn I missed.

I had to wait to make a U-turn because there was too much traffic. I glanced at my rearview again then did a double take. The same black car I saw a few miles back was still tailing us, keeping two cars' distance between us as it had earlier.

There was about a negative zero chance of it being a coincidence.

I should have noticed sooner. I tightened my grip on the steering wheel.

I'm getting sloppy.

I pushed all other thoughts out of my mind and led the car off the main road. I slammed my foot on the gas to get ahead of them just long enough to bring the Porsche screeching to a stop and get out before the car turned onto the side street behind.

Gabe and I faded into the shadows cast by the tall red-brick buildings that flanked the narrow street. Thanks to the tinted windows on the Porsche, whoever had been following us would have to get their asses real close before they realized no one was in the car.

Their car sat idling for a full minute before all four doors opened and four men stepped out, all of them with inflatable ring arms and bulging neck muscles. It was a wonder they fit inside the black midsize sedan.

They all had their guns drawn as they approached my car. Their eyes seemed to be fixed on the driver's side door, so much they didn't even bother looking around. It would have been so easy to take them out. Four quick shots, and they'd be the suckling pigs at the next Costa meeting.

But I needed them alive to know what the hell was going on.

No one in their right mind would be stupid enough to try to get the jump on me. Everyone knew that.

I had a lot of questions that I needed answers to. Fortunately, I didn't need all of four of them for that. One would suffice.

I signaled to Gabe, and we fired bullets into two of the thugs' heads. They dropped to the ground as the gunshots reverberated off the building walls of the narrow street. The remaining two spun around at the same time Gabe and I lunged.

I knocked the gun out of the hand of the man nearest me while Gabe cracked the other guy over the back of the head with his gun.

"I want him alive," I said to Gabe as I grabbed my guy's arm and twisted it behind his back.

Gabe's guy swayed as he spun to face his attacker.

"You got it, boss," Gabe said as he cocked back and connected with an upper cut that sent the guy's head snapping back. His body followed, and he slammed into the Porsche before dropping to the ground like a two-hundred-and-twenty-pound sack of potatoes. Two blows to the head, and the guy was down for the count.

"Nice work, *fratello*," I said as I twisted my guy's arm back further until his shoulder popped out of its socket.

I probably would have toyed with the guy before—Nico Costa had a reputation to uphold—but I was done. I just wanted it over with, so I pulled the trigger. The guy's body jolted against my hold while the crack of the gunshot reverberated off the walls, and then he joined his comrade, facedown on the cracked pavement.

I nodded to the Porsche. Gabe popped the trunk before he returned to help lift our one piece of unconscious luggage inside.

It took a bit of bending and shoving, but eventually, the luggage fit.

Chapter Thirty-Six

Nico

"Gabe and I will be there shortly," I told Salvatore over the phone as I revved the engine and headed toward Onyx.

A trip down to that stone-walled room hadn't been on the agenda tonight, but I needed to be sure.

"Make sure our men are in position. We move on Berlusconi at ten PM."

I looked at my watch.

9:14 PM, it read.

"You got it, boss. Ten PM on the dot."

I hung up the phone and cursed while I navigated the short drive toward Onyx. Gabe was smart enough to keep his mouth shut the entire ride. I caught him casting furtive glances at me, though, like he couldn't quite figure out my state of mind.

"I'm just pissed," I told him as we pulled into the parking lot. "I'm sick of…" I slammed my lips closed on the words that had nearly slipped out.

I'm sick of this life, I nearly told him, and that was no thing for a big brother to say. I needed to be strong, committed, leading the rest of my brothers without a shadow of doubt.

"I get it," he said as I slipped the car into park. "I said some things I shouldn't have."

I turned to him and tilted my head to the right.

"I called you a monster before, but I didn't mean it. I just wanted… I wanted you to *fight* me," he said as anger flared in his eyes.

"You want to fight me?" I repeated, not bothering to hide my confusion.

"Not a fist fight, you moron. I wanted you to tell me I was wrong. I wanted you to tell me to go to hell. I wanted you to give me some sign you don't actually see yourself that way," he said, nodding toward Onyx's rear entrance.

I shrugged then moved to open the car door. "I am what I am."

"Would you stop drinking the goddamned Kool-Aid?" he hollered, slamming his fists down on the console.

"The Kool-Aid?" I said, cocking a brow while I clenched my jaw, my hand still hovering on the door handle.

"No matter what you think, you're not like Lorenzo. You've always done what you had to do. He did the shit he did because he enjoyed it."

"And you think I don't?"

Gabe paused. "I think you like it because it's the only way you could make yourself do it. It was the only way to survive it."

"Thanks for the advice. Let's go," I said, popping the trunk and getting out of the car.

I slammed the door shut behind me, effectively putting an end to the conversation.

It was no simple task to get the thug out of the car, but I managed to get him over my shoulders, hefted him downstairs, and dropped him on the wooden chair in the middle of the stone-walled room.

I grabbed a bottle of water. I found one next to my row of knives, all neatly organized. I twisted the cap off, turned the bottle upside down, and dumped it over our special guest's head.

He came awake slowly despite the cold shower.

It was showtime. *This is who I am. This is who I always will be.*

The monster came awake, sending blood pumping through my veins. The monster cracked his knuckles, the sound of bone popping echoed in the thick air.

Then the smallest wrinkle furrowed my brow. Something was wrong.

I could feel the blood in my veins, pumping almost languidly, enough to feed my muscles. But not my brain.

Where's the high? The instant buzz?

The guy looked up at me with cold, bleary eyes.

I felt it pump a little faster, a little harder. I grabbed something from the table and tossed it at him.

"You want me dead? Here's your chance."

The Bowie knife landed neatly on his lap.

He reached for the knife but grabbed the wrong end. He cursed before readjusting his grip.

It was only now that he'd fully roused. Wide awake, his dark-eyed gaze took in the room, his head swinging back and forth between me and Gabe.

"I wouldn't worry about him." I nodded at Gabe without taking my eyes off the thug in the chair. "My brother knows I don't like it when other people play with my food," I said with a grin.

His eyes widened.

"Fuck you," he said with more bravado than brawn. And then he spat, catching the bottom of my pant leg and my shoe.

I cringed inside but kept my features smooth.

I could accept a man hitting me, stabbing me, shooting me. But a man spitting at me told me all I needed to know about where his dignity was.

On the bottom of my pant leg and my shoe.

I wouldn't be surprised if he started throwing feces at me like a donkey.

"I'm good, thanks. Too bad I can't say the same for you," I said, not wanting to waste any more time than I already had. "I'm only going to ask nicely once. Who sent you?"

He pressed his lips shut and stared me down.

I struck out with one quick swipe of my knife, severing the tendons in the wrist of his free hand.

He screamed and surged to his feet, stumbling back, making the chair scrape loudly across the stone floor.

"Who sent you?" I asked again.

It was a simple question that only required a first name and a last name for an answer. I only wanted two words from him and he would be free to go.

But they were all the same. They never gave in quickly.

They needed the gashes, and the pain, and the blood to see the truth.

And the truth was, I always got what I wanted.

"Nobody had to send me," he spat, pressing his bleeding wrist against his torso while he gripped the knife in his good hand and prepared to attack.

He surged forward, but I stepped aside, sinking my knife into his side, not deep, just enough to let him feel it.

He let out another roar and stumbled back, looking up at Gabe almost pleadingly.

I stepped back, waiting for him to recover. "Answers, *amico*. You give me what I need, and this is done."

I was even tempted to let him walk away if he gave me what I wanted. I just wanted the guy to talk so I could get out of here. The walls of the room seemed to be closing in on me. The ceiling hung lower. This place where I'd felt most alive before was threatening to crush me.

He lunged, and the dance continued like a never-ending salsa.

More blood, more screams. I even gave him a chance to get in a decent slice, leaving my torso unprotected in hopes the pain would rile me up.

He barely managed to break the skin.

I feinted and jabbed like I was on autopilot until it seemed he wore more blood than flesh. He toppled back, slamming his hand against the wall behind him. He dropped the Bowie knife just two seconds before his knees gave out and he followed it to the floor.

I stood in front of him, and it was my turn to stare pleadingly into his eyes.

"Who the fuck sent you?" I repeated for what felt like the hundredth time.

And then he smiled.

He looked at me with the same defiance that had flared in his eyes when he came to earlier after his cold shower.

"You're too... *late*," he choked out between gasping breaths.

"Too late for what?"

I usually didn't fall for the stupid lines that were generally just lame attempts to delay the inevitable, but something about the pleasure in his tone caught me.

"We've got her now—your fucking Luca bitch," he said, wheezing, "and after he gets what he wants from her hot, little body, he's going to kill her. Hack her up into—"

All I could see was red as I drove the knife straight into his heart.

Raven's blood, thick, it coated everything in my dark world. I could see it all over my hands. It was on my hands because I let this happen. Because the bull's-eye I felt like a hot beam on the back of my head hadn't been aimed at me. Not directly, at least.

It was pointed right at her.

And I didn't see it.

"Fuck!" I screamed, yanking out the knife and chucking it across the room.

"Nico, you don't know. The guy could have been full of shit," Gabe said, trying to calm me down, but he couldn't hide the look of horror in his eyes.

But maybe they haven't gotten to her yet.

I surged to my feet, not sure when I'd sunk to my knees.

I was out of Onyx without a word and in my car so fast, I couldn't remember climbing the stairs. I was still covered in the thug's blood.

I threw the car into reverse and squealed out of the parking lot, weaving around every car that got in my way while my heart pounded like a hammer inside my chest.

Less than a minute away, I got stuck behind traffic at a red light, and it took every ounce of restraint I had not to slam right into the bumper in front of me.

My limbs shook and my chest felt tight as image after image of all the vile things that could have happened to her ran through my head. Seconds ticked by. Too many seconds.

I pulled out my phone and scrolled through my contacts for her number. I pressed *Call*.

If only I could just hear her voice...

The phone just kept ringing until it went to voicemail.

I pushed down on the pedal, swerving around cars. Maybe she didn't hear her phone. She could have been in the shower.

Fear coursed through my veins. I'd never felt it before, not like this.

I dialed Cesare's number. He was supposed to be keeping an eye on her hotel, just until we settled the Berlusconi mess.

"Your call has been forwarded to an automated voice message system."

Stronzo! I tossed my phone aside as I pulled up right in front of the hotel, squealing to a stop, then got out and made my way through the hoard of people coming in and out of the hotel, making them jump to get out of my way.

Inside, I took the stairs three at a time. There was no way I could have stood there waiting for the elevator. My heart was pumping so hard, I couldn't hear the thud of my own footsteps over the blood pounding past my ears.

On her floor, I slammed open the stairwell door and started down the hallway.

She was going to be here.

She was going to be fine.

And then I caught sight of the open doorway to her room.

Chapter Thirty-Seven

Raven

It was dark, and the ground vibrated beneath me. All I could remember was floating, higher and higher.

Why was I floating? I couldn't remember. My brain felt like it was wrapped in a thick shroud, and I was an outsider trying to look in.

I squeezed my eyes shut and tried to force my way through. The answers were right there, and a small voice inside me told me I needed to reach them. I needed to know why I could feel rough floor beneath my cheek. It smelled like cigarette smoke and dirt. I held my breath and turned my head to search for something less repugnant. Then the fabric over my eyes rubbed against the bridge of my nose.

A blindfold.

It opened the floodgates.

The hotel room, the corner wall, the four men who had me outmatched from the get-go. The syringe. The phone.

My breath came faster, drawing in more and more of the potent cigarette-dirt smell.

The ground beneath me bounced, jostling my body and making my face thump against the floor. Wincing, I tried to reach up to remove the blindfold, but I couldn't move my hands. They were stuck behind my back, bound together.

They tied me up.

Tears welled in my eyes, but they couldn't fall. They just spilled over and soaked the fabric over my eyes, making it stick to my eyelids.

I wanted to scream, but even as the sound rose up my throat, I fought it. Whatever drug they gave me had left my brain muddled, but it was beginning to clear, enough that I knew the worst possible thing I could do was let them know I was awake.

I swallowed it back and forced my breathing to slow to something that resembled normal. And then I listened.

That's what Vito would have done. He would listen. He would pay attention to every detail. The hum of the car engine. The crunch of gravel beneath the tires.

I was in a car. In a van, more likely, and it was moving. The gravel meant they weren't driving on a main road, and that meant they were taking me somewhere secluded.

Fear climbed up my throat as my mind tried to shy away from the truth, the reality of my situation. I squeezed my eyes shut despite the blindfold, like I could hide from it.

Vito wouldn't have hidden from it. He would have faced it head-on, looking for every opportunity to turn the tables in his favor.

The van slowed. I could hear every piece of gravel crunch beneath the slowing tires. Slower and slower until it jolted to a stop, scraping my cheek against the abrasive carpet.

Two doors squeaked open. The driver and passenger side doors, I assumed.

I could only hear two sets of footsteps crunching through the gravel, around to the back of the van. Only two sets. *Two men.*

If I had my hands free, I could have taken them on. They didn't know I was awake. I'd have the element of surprise. But my hands *were* tied. My ankles? I shifted my legs, trying to ascertain whether or not they'd been bound, but they moved unimpeded.

I was blindfolded. My wrists were bound. But they left my legs unfettered. Without sight, trying to run the moment they opened the door would be pointless, but a few well-placed kicks could take down an opponent.

The creak of a rusty door sounded near my feet and a cool breeze raced across my bare calves. I tried to envision the two men, imagining where they were standing and how I might be able to incapacitate them.

I would only have one shot—and it could very well be my last.

"I'll take him. You bring the girl," a gruff, heavily accented voice spoke from outside the van.

He was close, but not directly at my feet. The sound had come from just left of me.

"My pleasure, *amico.*"

This voice was raspy, equally accented, and right in front of me.

Two assailants, but if luck would help me out just a little, one of them would have his hands full with whatever "him" they'd been talking about—probably the tall, gangly man from the hotel hallway floor.

Warm hands latched onto my ankles. I forced my body to remain lax while he tugged me toward him, painfully aware of the way the movement hiked up my dress.

It didn't matter. Nothing mattered but landing a kick that would do the most damage. The solar plexus or the head. I needed to hit one of them.

He released my ankles and my legs dropped, dangling out of the van. I couldn't see him, but I could envision him there, leaning forward to grab hold of me and heave me up.

The moment his fingers made contact with my ribs, I attacked, drawing up my leg and kneeing him just beneath his rib cage, dead center in his chest.

He stumbled back, gasping over and over again, trying to draw a breath.

Yes!

I surged to my feet, still blind, but with one less assailant for at least a few more seconds. I started to run, but the click of a gun being cocked somewhere in front of me made me freeze.

I'd heard that sound hundreds of times, maybe thousands, but it had never rippled down my spine like ice water before. Despite the blackness over my eyes, I could see the barrel of the gun, aimed right at me.

Stupidly, I tried to reach out with my mind to feel it, like I'd developed some sort of sixth sense. Was it aimed at my head? My heart?

"I admire your spunk, *Signorina* Luca, but don't make me drug you again, *per favore.*"

I nodded because the last thing I wanted was to be rendered unconscious again. At least awake, I could watch for every opportunity to escape.

"That's my girl."

He spoke right in front of me. I could kick him. Headbutt him. *Where was the gun?* If he still had it pointed at me, either move would be a mistake.

Fingers slid up my temple. I flinched at the contact, but then forced myself to remain still as he removed the blindfold.

It was dark out, but not as dark as I'd been anticipating. I'd been imagining a dilapidated cabin in the middle of nowhere, but he'd taken me to some beat-up industrial site. The few streetlamps overhead that hadn't burned out flickered their light on the dismal scene around us.

At least if I escaped—*when* I escaped—it wouldn't be a long trek back to civilization.

"Now, Sergio is going to take you inside," Diego, the handsome man with the crooked nose said, motioning to the peeling paint-covered warehouse behind him. "But don't worry. I'll be back to collect you shortly. I trust you'll behave until then?" He cocked an eyebrow while he pulled out a syringe from his jacket pocket and held it up in front of me.

Though my mouth was dry, I swallowed hard, staring at the needle in his hand, the silver tip gleaming under the streetlight.

I nodded. I had to do whatever it took to stay awake, to stay alert... to *stay alive*.

"Words, *signorina*. Answer me with words."

"Yes." I forced the word out no matter how repugnant it tasted on my tongue.

"Yes, what?" His lips quirked up in a smile that reminded me of those plastic vampire fangs kids wear for Halloween.

I glared at him, hating him with every fiber of my being.

"Yes, I'll behave," I spat out.

He slipped the syringe back into his pocket then reached out and grazed his fingers along my cheek.

My body from shuddered at the contact. It was like slugs sliding down my skin.

He dropped his hand and nodded to the man who was still slightly hunched over, his breathing labored.

The man—Sergio—glared at me as he grabbed my wrists roughly and shoved me forward. I wanted to fight him. I wanted to do something—anything—as he pushed me into the dark, cavernous interior of the warehouse.

But I didn't fight him.

I went willingly. Pathetically.

Like a lamb to the slaughter.

Chapter Thirty-Eight

Nico

Noise came from inside Raven's hotel room.

Someone was inside.

I wasn't too late.

I drew my gun and crossed the hallway in four long strides, squaring my shoulders. I was ready to do whatever it took to keep her safe, to defend her, to protect her.

Not because I enjoyed it, or because I relished the buzz of a kill snaking through my veins.

I thought of the way her lips slightly parted when she was asleep, and the way her chest felt pressed against mine, and the way her breath hitched whenever she looked at me.

I wanted Raven alive and safe.

It was all that mattered.

Outside the doorway, I saw a spatter of blood on the carpet. My stomach turned in a way it never had before. A lump formed at the back of my throat as a single thought pushed itself at the forefront of my mind.

Is it hers?

I rounded the doorway, peering into the empty hotel living room. Empty but for the specks of blood that stood out in sharp contrast against the pale carpet near the back wall.

The lump at the back of my throat grew as I stepped inside. I could feel it—the strange sensation that something terrible had happened here.

If they hurt her, if they…

The room grew hazy as something hot and violent pounded through my veins.

Footsteps sounded in one of the rooms down the hall. I snapped my head to the right.

Raven?

I shut my eyes as I said a silent prayer.

A blonde stepped out, her face stained with tears. The minute our eyes locked, her face contorted.

"You," Greta hissed, storming straight at me.

If there had been any doubt in my mind about what happened to Raven, it vanished as Greta stared me down, her hazel eyes snapping with sorrow and anger.

The open door.

The blood.

Something inside me cried in a voice I didn't recognize. It was raw and filled with so much anguish that the sound inside my head threatened to drown me.

"This is your fault, you son of a bitch," she shouted, stopping right in front of me and pounding on my chest, over and over again. "If you'd left her alone… if you'd just been your usual goddamned selfish self…" Tears streamed down her cheeks as she continued to hit me.

Kiana Hettinger

I remained in place as she continued to punch me with her fists, like she was a violent little energizer bunny. I'd certainly never been in this position before, but Greta had every right to her anger. So I stood there, letting her pound away until her batteries ran out.

This was my fault. I let them get to Raven. I let them take her. I let them hurt her.

"Greta, calm down," said a tall, bald man as he walked in through the open doorway.

He glared at me with eyes so cold, it felt like an Arctic blast. If looks could kill, I wouldn't just be dead, I'd be a thousand bloody shards of ice on the hotel room floor.

I'd have to remember to quake in my boots later.

He was a man I vaguely recognized as it took me a moment to place him. Vito Agossi—a Luciano man who'd fallen off the radar. Word was he'd died more than a decade ago.

He didn't look dead to me.

He had no weapon in his hand, but I could see the bulky outline of the guns beneath his jacket.

"Don't tell me… to calm down, *zietto*," she told the man, but she stumbled back.

Vito Agossi was Greta's uncle? Raven's "uncle" was named Vito. Dominic was looking for a man named Vito. *Mamma* mentioned a Luciano man when she was plotting with Maria.

The pieces of the puzzle fell into place perfectly.

Something fell from Greta's hands as she leaned over, putting her hands on her knees while she gasped, catching her breath. It was a crumpled-up piece of paper.

I picked it up and smoothed it out. The words on the paper stared back at me.

I've got her now—B

My heart flared up, clattering the steel bars it had been locked behind for years. It wanted free just so it could be ripped out of my chest.

I glanced at my watch. "Fuck!"

I yanked my phone out of my jacket and punched in Salvatore's number. The phone rang. Then it rang again. The sound oddly resembled the ticking of a time bomb in my head.

Answer the fucking phone.

Halfway through the third ring, he picked up.

"What's up, boss?" he whispered.

"Fall back. Right now."

"What's that, boss?"

"Raven and Cesare are in there. Fall the fuck back. Now."

"*Dio santo!* It's too—"

Raspy static. Screams. Shouts.

"Fuck." I resisted the urge to chuck the phone at the wall and shoved it back in my jacket.

Berlusconi had her. She was there, right in the middle of a firefight. Of the slaughter we had planned.

"Leave no man standing and burn the place to the ground," my own words echoed in my head.

I stormed toward the door, but Vito stepped in my way.

"Where the hell do you think you're going?" he spat.

It would have been so easy to shoot him or break his big, meaty neck. But I had a feeling this man meant something to Raven.

"I'm going to get your niece—or whatever she is to you," I said, eyeing Vito, then Greta. "Berlusconi's got her, and soon, there's going to be nothing left of Berlusconi—or anything else within a hundred yards of him. *Capisce?*"

Vito eyed me for one long moment. At least, it felt that way. My pounding heart had only thudded twice when he nodded and stepped aside.

I was out the doorway and down the hallway in four beats. Another ten beats down the stairs, and I flew out the hotel's front door. I was vaguely aware of two sets of footsteps following me, but I didn't stop until I reached the Porsche, still parked askew in front of the hotel.

When Vito threw open the passenger side door and got in, I paused for one beat. Greta followed, getting into the back seat. I tilted my head to the side.

I'm not James fucking Corden, this isn't a car pool.

"Let's go, Costa. Drive," Vito Agossi barked.

"Don't fucking tell me what to do," I snapped back and then did exactly as he said.

There wasn't time to argue with Vito, but I had no intention of letting the little energizer bunny wander into a war zone.

"She stays in the car," I said, pointing a thumb at the back seat while I revved the engine and sped away from the hotel.

The temperature in the car plummeted. Greta and Vito scoffed at the same time.

"I don't think so," Greta said. "I've been watching over Raven for years, Nico. A few weeks riding on your roller coaster, and she's…"

Her voice cracked, and my dumbass heart cracked right along with it.

Whatever happened to Raven, it was on me.

Images flashed through my mind, making my heart beat faster and cold sweat trickle down the back of my neck. It felt like I was going to come right out of my skin.

Focus, damn it.

The road in front of me. The route to Berlusconi's place. The wonderful, horrible, inhuman things I was going to do to him when I got my hands on him.

I squealed around the corner and stepped on the gas. But my heart was beating just as hard. My breath was coming faster. I reached for something—anything—to get me through the next several minutes without coming apart.

"What do you mean you've been watching over her?" I asked Greta because it seemed like a rather strange way to describe a friendship.

"I mean I've done everything I could to keep her safe," she shot back, then turned to Vito. "I don't understand why you didn't stop her from coming here, *zietto*."

"You're a plant," I concluded.

"I'm her friend. Her *best friend*," she said. I didn't miss the thick layer of defensiveness that coated her words. "But I also happen to watch over her."

She seemed to shrink into herself as she spoke. Raven most certainly was not aware of the full scope of Greta's role in her life.

Chapter Thirty-Nine

Raven

It was dark inside the warehouse. Almost black, aside from the sliver of moonlight and lamplight that flickered in through a broken window somewhere above me. The temperature inside had been cool at first, but with every passing minute, the coolness had seeped inside me until my skin was covered in gooseflesh and I couldn't stop my teeth from chattering.

I sat down on the cold, hard floor. Sergio had untied my hands only to cuff my wrist to a chain attached to a post in the middle of the dark building. He'd cuffed the unconscious guy to the same post and then he'd left. An engine had revved outside a moment later, and there'd been no sound aside from the blood still pumping heavily past my ears ever since.

I felt across the floor until my fingers met with semi-warm flesh—the unconscious guy's arm. I moved my fingers downward to check his pulse, then upward, searching briefly for injuries as I went until I reached his neck. I prodded upward gently, but it didn't take long to find the swollen lump at the back of his head, just above the nape of his neck and about the same size as the goose egg-size bump I'd seen on his temple. His pulse was strong and steady, and he was still breathing, but if his brain continued to swell, there was nothing I could do about that here.

I closed my eyes, trying to divert all my body's resources to listening, hoping for the faintest indication that there was someone—anyone—nearby.

There was no sound, not even the distant hum of traffic.

I opened my mouth and screamed as loud as I could.

"Help!" I cried, over and over again. I had no idea when Crooked-Nose—Diego—and his thugs would return, but I sure as heck didn't want to be here when they came back.

I screamed more. Louder.

Over and over again until my throat was raw and every scream felt like broken glass shredding its way up.

There had to be someone, somewhere.

But no one came.

No voices. No crunching gravel footsteps. Nothing.

I slumped against the pole. It had been a useless endeavor. If there'd been any hope of finding help nearby, Diego would have had me gagged to keep me quiet. It felt like worms writhing beneath my skin to sit here and wait to die, but I couldn't think of anything I could do.

I squeezed my eyes shut, and an image of Nico flashed behind my eyelids. Strong, powerful, lethal. He'd know what to do. He'd know how to escape, and even better, he'd know how to make Diego and his lackeys pay for what they'd tried to do.

Sobs clambered up my chest as warm tears trickled down my cheeks. I was never going to see him again. There was no bubble of hope this time. I'd tried to escape twice, and I'd failed.

I felt around for the unconscious guy's wrist and checked his pulse again. There wasn't much point. Diego was probably going to kill him too, but still, the almost-nurse inside me wouldn't just sit idly by. And in truth, it felt less lonely to know there was another beating heart nearby.

This time, though, as I counted out the beats, his arm twitched. Then it twitched again, like a weak effort to pull his arm out of my grasp.

I held on, waiting with bated breath.

"Hello? Can you hear me?" I asked when he made no more movement. *Please, wake up.* I didn't really think there was anything more that could be done with the two of us awake, but I shook him anyway. "Hello?"

He pulled his arm free this time and stirred. Then he groaned and seemed to be trying to get his arm beneath him.

"Wait," I said, then felt around to get a supporting hand beneath his back. I was little help with one hand fettered, but it was something.

He yanked on his hand, seemed to realize it was shackled, and shifted his position to sit up, gripping his head between his free hand and the pole.

"Where?" he rasped after a moment.

"I'm sorry, I don't know. It's some old industrial building, but I couldn't tell you where." It was all the bearings I could help him get.

I thought he moved his head incrementally in a nod, but it could have been the play of shadows.

"Who are you?" I asked after a moment, hoping my guess that he was friend rather than foe was correct.

"I'm—" He gasped. "*Merde!*" he cursed, looking this way and that, though I imagined he couldn't see any better than me. He stopped and his shoulders sagged. "I'm sorry, *signorina*. I don't know what happened." He put his free hand on my arm, but removed it quickly. "*Signor* Costa wanted to make sure you were protected—it was just a precaution." He scoffed. "Or, I suppose it wasn't. I failed you, *signorina*. I failed *Signor* Costa."

He sounded so crestfallen that I felt the urge to say something, anything.

"It wasn't your fault. You couldn't have known."

"I should have—"

"Don't," I said, putting my free hand on what I hoped was his knee. "There's no sense in regrets at this point. We're still alive. I say we figure out a way to keep it that way."

I didn't really think there was a way out of this, but since he'd woken up, it felt like there was maybe a tiny shred of hope. If this man had been watching over me on Nico's orders, then it was possible Nico knew I'd been taken.

It didn't escape my notice that it also meant this man was here—injured and trapped—because of me.

"*Sì*, you're right," he said, tugging on his shackled wrist. "I don't suppose you have a paper clip… or a bobby pin?"

My breath caught in my throat. I reached up and felt my hair for the pins Greta had put in it. "*Thank you, Greta*," I whispered, pulling one out. "I do. Here." I reached out for his hand and waited to be sure he had a grip on the pin.

Then his hand was like a dark shadow in front of the pole, but I could feel his movements against my wrist and hear the quiet scrape of metal against metal as he fiddled with the lock—my lock.

How many people would work to free someone else before they freed themselves?

"What's your name?" I asked, trying to occupy my mind with idle conversation while the knot in my stomach twisted up tighter and tighter. Now that there was maybe something that could be done, I could feel the passage of every second again. Waiting, listening for the sound of a car engine approaching.

"Cesare, *signorina.*"

"Have you worked for Nico, I mean *Signor* Costa long?"

"Just a few years, but I owe my life to *Signor* Costa. I will be with him for my whole life—if he'll have me." He spoke with so much conviction, I didn't doubt his commitment for a minute. I did wonder, though, if Cesare was yet another one of Nico's "good deeds" that he didn't like to talk about.

Cesare kept fiddling, but the sound of a distant car engine broke through the near-silence.

It was coming closer.

And closer.

My heart started to pound again, and my breathing came so fast, I got light-headed. I wanted to beg Cesare to go faster, but it wouldn't help. He was moving as fast as he could. I imagined it was no simple task to break out of handcuffs with a bobby pin in the dark.

And then I heard it—the quiet click of the mechanism turning. The metal fell away from my wrist, clattering against the pole.

"You did it," I whispered as car tires rolled over gravel right outside. The engine turned off.

Oh no.

"Hurry," I said despite my assertion there was no sense in rushing him, but instead of hurrying, he stopped.

"Hide," he said.

Just one word, but it echoed over and over again inside my head.

"No, please, just—" I groped for his hand and yanked it toward his own shackle.

"Go. Hide now. Tell *Signor* Costa I am sorry."

I couldn't move. I couldn't just leave him.

"Please, *signorina*. You cannot let me be the reason... I could never live with myself."

"Nico wouldn't punish you, Cesare. Please. This isn't your fault."

"Not punishment. Honor. Please, let me do this one honorable thing. I beg you."

Footsteps crunched over gravel outside. I was out of time. *Stay here, get recaptured, and be of no use to Cesare? Or hide, and hope the opportunity to help him presented itself?*

I could feel his pleading expression even if I couldn't see it. I could only hope that was the reason I kissed the top of his head and darted off, sneaking quietly as far back as I could go and feeling around for somewhere to hide and anything I could use as a weapon.

The door squeaked open.

I froze, listening.

The beam of a flashlight spread out across the floor, shining in the direction of Cesare. I held my breath, trying not to move despite the way my whole body trembled.

The beam and the footsteps stopped, right in front of Cesare, but it was silent.

No one spoke.

Maybe Cesare was pretending to be unconscious. Maybe they'd just leave him there and go search for me.

The heavy clang of metal echoed throughout the building all of a sudden.

"Where is she?" Diego's voice roared, followed by the thud of flesh hitting flesh.

Cesare grunted.

More fleshy thuds.

"I said, where is she?"

"She's… long gone," Cesare panted.

"Is that so?" Diego said in a voice that was suddenly too calm.

Silence.

No clang of metal. No fleshy thuds. Nothing until the ominous click. The sound of a gun being cocked.

My heart lodged in my throat.

"*Signorina* Luca? You have until I reach ten to show yourself or I will decorate the floor with this young man's gray matter. One. Two."

My heart was racing. I could barely hear him counting over the whooshing of blood past my ears.

"Five. Six."

"No, *signorina*, don't do it," Cesare cried, but I couldn't.

I couldn't hide like a coward while Cesare died because of *me*.

I stood up, willing my legs to hold me up. I put one foot in front of the other while my knees tried to give out with every step.

"Eight. Nine—"

"Stop!" I screamed, running the last few steps. I stuttered to a stop directly in front of him, right in the beam of light cast by the flashlight in his hand.

He didn't even look at me.

He kept his gaze on Cesare, and his gun was still aimed directly at him.

I'd done what he asked, and he was still going to kill him.

I stepped in front of Cesare. It was the only thing I could think to do—there was no way I could out-strength him, not with a cocked gun in his hand. But before I could open my mouth, before I could demand he put down the gun—though what leverage I thought I had, I wasn't sure—I felt Cesare's hand on my back. He shoved me forward. He shoved me so hard, I stumbled and fell, slamming my knees against the hard concrete floor.

"No!" I screamed, trying to regain my footing, but I was too late.

The crack of a gunshot pierced my eardrums and reverberated off the walls all around me. I swung around just in time to see Cesare's body fall to the ground like a rag doll.

He looked back at me with sightless eyes, a bullet hole dead center between them.

And then I felt the sharp jab of a syringe tip in my neck.

Chapter Forty

Nico

The staccato beat of gunfire filled my ears as I stepped into a war zone.

Men running, bullets zipping past. The air was rich with the metallic zing of the gunfight.

I drew it into my lungs over and over again as I glanced across the yard toward Berlusconi's metal-and-glass monstrosity.

If he had her here, if she was in there, no men or bullets were keeping me out.

But I couldn't move.

For the first time in my life, I was frozen. Not in fear, exactly. I didn't fear being shot at or wounded. It might hurt like a son of a bitch, but I wasn't afraid of it.

She was all I could see. Her chest riddled with bullets and covered in blood. Her blue eyes, lifeless. The lump at the back of my throat got bigger, so big it felt like I could barely breathe past it.

"Let's go, Costa," Greta said.

I'd underestimated the violent energizer bunny. Though her eyes were wide with fear, her shoulders were squared and her spine was straight. She had a gun in her hand and looked more than ready to shoot her way straight through a battlefield for her friend.

Vito and I flanked her as I forced myself to move, walking right over the human-shaped mounds on the ground. Dead men, but not one of them were Costa men. What was left of Berlusconi's men had been corralled in the house. It was only a matter of time before every last one of his men was dead. The thought should have sent a ripple of satisfaction through me, but it only added to the heavy weight of dread in my stomach.

Where is she?

The big window at the front of the house exploded as a body flew through it. Whether it had been thrown or it jumped, I didn't know. *I don't fucking care.* I put a bullet in the guy's forehead then strode through the open front door.

The gunfire was louder inside, echoing off the walls, but the staccato beat had slowed dramatically. The fight was winding down. Only the occasional pocket of resistance remained, and my men would have them snuffed out soon.

I looked around.

We'd cut the power, but moonlight spilled in through the plethora of open windows, shining on the shattered china across the dining room floor, the overturned furniture in the living room, and the bullet holes that pockmarked every wall.

Where would he have taken her? I glanced up the winding staircase. Upstairs? In one of the bedrooms? My blood boiled thinking about what he could be doing to her there. But all the doors I could see were hanging wide open, most of them riddled with bullet holes like the walls.

Salvatore strode through the living room with a gun in each hand and a bloody rag wrapped around his arm.

"She's not here, boss, and neither is Cesare. I checked myself," Salvatore said, his eyes not quite reaching mine.

I kept my face blank and nodded. "Berlusconi?"

Salvatore shook his head. "I checked every face, I swear. He's not here either, boss."

I didn't know whether to be angry or relieved. He wasn't one of the dead bodies here—which meant Raven wasn't either—but where the hell had he taken her? What was he doing to her? Questions swirled around in my head. What if I didn't find her in time? What if I was already too late?

I had no answers. I didn't even know where to fucking start.

I was coming undone. I could feel it no matter the blank expression I tried to keep pasted on my face.

Whatever Raven had done to me, I sure as hell didn't like it. I felt weak, helpless, useless—things I hadn't felt in a very long time.

I nodded to Salvatore and turned away, doing my damnedest to stay in command of my legs as I strode back toward the door.

I needed to get out of the fucking house.

Outside, I sat down hard on the smooth concrete front steps. The impact jolted through me. It tried to wrack loose something in my chest, clambering up my throat until I swallowed it back.

"You really care about her, don't you?" Greta said, sitting down next to me.

She draped her arms over her knees, but despite the casual repose, her whole body was strung taut.

"I…" I swallowed hard. *Care* felt like too small of a word. "Does she know about you?" I asked instead.

Greta shook her head, staring at her dangling fingers. "When we were kids, I wasn't allowed to tell her that Vito was my uncle, but

293

other than that, we were just friends." She shrugged her shoulders. "When I got old enough to understand more, to understand what was going on, it just felt normal—to watch out for her, you know?" She glanced at me, but went on without pausing. "I didn't like lying to her, but Vito said the truth was dangerous. I didn't know her family was alive. If I'd known the truth…" She trailed off.

"The lies they told her were because of me."

The words slipped out unbidden, an error to which I was not accustomed.

Greta looked at me, her brow crinkled.

"Our mothers—hers and mine—plotted to hide Raven to ensure the marriage our fathers planned never took place." And if they'd lied better, she never would have been here. Berlusconi never would have gotten his hands on her. He never would have been able to hide her… where? Where the hell was she? There was no other property under his name.

Merde!

We were looking at the wrong name.

"Salvatore!" I shouted and heard his heavy steps shuffle toward the door. "I need every property under the name Diego Avalone. Now." Few people knew that Berlusconi had wanted Avalone to acknowledge him ten years ago. It would be the alias he'd use.

"Right, boss. Right away."

I was back on my feet, every muscle in my body thrumming with renewed purpose.

Berlusconi had to have property under that name.

I paced back and forth across the front steps. There was only wide, open space all around me, but I felt like a caged animal, trapped until Salvatore could point me in the right direction.

Greta stood up as Vito stepped outside.

"All of this because of some stupid marriage arrangement?" Greta looked confused, still focused on the information I'd dropped inadvertently.

I nodded. "Would you want your friend married to a man like me?"

"No," she confessed. "Not to a man *like* you. But to *you*…" She shrugged. "I hate to admit it, but I've never seen Raven as happy as she's been with you. And that says a lot given the bomb that was dropped on her a few months ago. If anything's happened to her though…" Greta's tough façade fractured. Her pain was written across her face.

"Got one hit, boss," Salvatore said from the open doorway. "An old, run-down warehouse. Hasn't been operational for years."

"Where?"

"I sent the directions to your phone, boss. We're ready to head out." He nodded to the Costa men who'd assembled behind him. The rest were busy gathering dead bodies from around the house. There would be one hell of a bonfire going pretty soon, but I wasn't going to be here to see it.

I nodded and practically jumped down the stairs, Greta and Vito still close on my heels.

Then a sharp prickling sensation raised the hairs at the back of my neck.

"Where's Gabe?" I asked Salvatore as he followed behind us.

"He's not here, boss. Never showed up."

Chapter Forty-One

Raven

I forced my eyelids open despite the heavy weights that were trying to keep them closed.

The disorientation was fleeting this time. It felt like a jarring drop from the top of a cliff.

I slammed back into consciousness, could even feel the jolt through my body. I whipped my head around in search of Cesare. My loose hair flung in my face. Diego had removed the pins. Little did he know it wasn't me who knew how to pick a lock with a bobby pin, it was—

Cesare's prone figure laid close by, one arm twisted up awkwardly, shackled to the post. I could still hear the gunshot reverberating inside my head. I could see his lifeless eyes, bright in the beam of the flashlight. The flashlight was gone, but the image had been burned indelibly into my brain. He'd pushed me out of the way. He'd died… *because of me.*

Fresh sobs clambered up my chest, but before they could slip out, the sound of a voice forced them back in my throat.

"*Buona sera,* Raven," the voice spoke from my other side.

I whipped my head around, recognizing the voice.

"Gabe?"

"Fancy meeting you here, *signorina*." His words came out sluggish like he was just coming awake too.

He was sitting on the floor next to me, his knees drawn up and his back against the post, caught in the thin sliver of light from the lampposts outside. It took a moment to recognize his awkward position.

He was shackled to the post like me.

From our brief meeting, Gabe had struck me as a man with perhaps a more easygoing countenance than Nico, but he still gave off the same lethal energy as his brother. He would have been no easy man to capture, and his presence here blew up the tentative theory I'd been formulating that Lorenzo Costa was somehow behind my abduction.

"What are you doing here?"

He shrugged. "I had some time on my hands."

I scoffed. "And this was your idea of a good way to spend an evening?"

"I hear it's good to mix things up every once in a while. The spice of life and all that, right?"

"How can you be so calm?" I glanced at Cesare.

And yet, he laughed. "If you grew up in my home, you'd find that not much fazed you. Besides, Nico might not be aware of *my* current predicament, but he knows you've been taken."

My heart clenched painfully in my chest, but at the same time, bubbles of hope surged through my veins before I could tamp it down. I squeezed my eyes shut and thrust it away, letting his parting words play over in my head.

"Because you'll always be a Luca."

"I'm sorry, Gabe, but I wouldn't count on him calling in the cavalry." The bubbles popped, and I had to fight to keep my voice from cracking.

He reached out and put his free hand on my arm. "My brother will move heaven and earth to find you, *signorina*. And I don't envy what he's going to do to the people who took you."

I shook my head, not trusting my voice. I would never be more than a passing entertainment to Nico because in the end, he'd never trust me. And no one moved heaven and earth for a passing entertainment.

He sighed and squeezed my arm. "My brother can be confusing at times, but once you learn to read between the lines, he's much easier to understand. Whatever he said to you, Sofia, he said because he's afraid. You bring out a side of him he tries to keep hidden. A side that can be hurt... rejected."

Hurt? Rejected? They just didn't seem like words in Nico's dictionary. He was strong, confident, nearly invincible. The other words just made him sound so... *human.*

But it didn't matter. Well, it did, in my heart, but I didn't share Gabe's confidence that anyone was going to find us. How could they? I didn't even know where we were.

I never thought I'd face it so calmly—the end. Death. It wasn't that I wasn't terrified—my whole body was shaking and, if I was being honest, it wasn't entirely due to the cold. But I would have expected more tears, more silent bargaining with whatever deities might have been listening.

My mind tried to shy away from it, but I couldn't help but wonder if this was how my mother had felt, afraid of the void, the blackness that was coming, but almost resigned to the inevitability of it.

If it weren't for the people I was leaving behind, perhaps I could have resigned myself entirely, but I couldn't stop the images of Nico from flashing through my mind. And Dominic, Greta, Vito. I'd never see them again.

Tears trickled down my cheeks, and I swiped at them angrily. All I had left was my composure. I couldn't let Diego take that too.

"How... how did you end up here?" I asked, grasping for something, anything.

He laughed. "I can't quite say. One minute I was heaving a dead body up off the floor and the next..." he said, motioning around us.

My eyes widened at his suddenly free hand.

"Shhh," he said before I could open my mouth. The sound was little more than a breath. "We've got company," he whispered just as quietly.

I resisted the urge to glance around and struggled back to the conversation at hand. "What were you doing with a dead body?"

"I told you I don't envy what Nico's going to do, and I certainly didn't envy what he did to that one."

"He killed a man... because of me?"

Gabe nodded. "'Killed' is the pretty way of putting it. Heavy, right?"

All this time, I'd thought Nico was off doing whatever dangerous thing he had planned, but he'd been trying to find me and killing people in the process?

"Gabe, do you think..." I had to swallow. "Do you think he'll get here in time?" It came out like a strangled whisper.

Gabe nodded without missing a beat. "He'll get here." He stopped talking, but I could feel the weight of the words hovering on his tongue. "I just hope he's levelheaded enough to recognize the trap he's walking into."

"Trap?"

My stomach contracted, threatening to heave up the meager food left in it. Suddenly, I didn't want him to come. I wanted to scream at the top of my lungs for him to stay away, to stay safe, to stay alive.

"I'm afraid it's no coincidence you and I are sitting here together. Though, if I have to be sitting here with anyone, I will say that I can't imagine better company."

"Then, why?" I asked.

"The Lucas and the Costas, *bella*. If you've got one of each, then you've got two families who will go to great lengths to get them back. Two families who maybe won't mind shooting at each other if it looks like one is standing in the other's way."

The sound of clapping resonated through the warehouse, not close by at first, but the slow, steady *clap, clap, clap* continued and grew louder until a dark figure loomed just outside of the lamppost light.

The clapping stopped, and the figure stepped out of the shadows.

My breath caught in my throat.

It wasn't Diego, the crooked-nose stranger.

It wasn't a stranger at all.

Chapter Forty-Two

Nico

I slammed on the brakes on the rough gravel road.

I could just make out the roof of the old, dilapidated warehouse about a half mile in front of me. As much as I wanted to drive up to its rusted front door and plow right through it, I wasn't that stupid.

Berlusconi had to know I was coming. He'd planned well, getting hold of the two most important people in the world to me.

Cars pulled up behind me, stopping a few feet away and killing the engines. A few cars kept coming. Cars I didn't recognize at first until a Maclaren slowed to a stop right beside me.

"What the hell is he doing here?" I barked.

I glanced over at Vito, but he shook his head. "Wasn't me."

I got out of the car at the same time Dominic Luca stepped out of the Maclaren, both of us with our shoulders back, stretched to our full height. We might as well have been on fucking Animal Planet.

I didn't mind that I bested him by a good two inches.

Car doors clicked open then slammed shut as the rest of the vehicles behind us emptied. Every man had a gun in his hand and a finger on the trigger.

There were too many Costas and Lucas in one place. I could feel the tension in the air like gunpowder. One spark, and it would ignite.

Vito and Greta moved to stand beside me as the doors of a black Rolls-Royce Ghost opened up and Raven's two other brothers stepped out.

I suffered a moment's uncertainty; just a moment when I had to consider the possibility that I'd been wrong about the Lucas, that they'd been part of this from the beginning. But one look in Dominic's eyes and the moment was gone. Pain, uncertainty, fear; things I'd never expected to see in a Luca's eyes.

He was here for Raven.

I hadn't considered it before, but there was no way Berlusconi could have guessed what lengths I'd go to for a woman I'd only known a couple of weeks. And that's why Dominic was here. Berlusconi had taken Gabe, thinking he could draw me out. He'd taken Raven to draw out Dominic to the same place at the same time.

This was the same goddamned game he'd been playing all along.

I looked around at my men and the Lucas' men, all itching for a reason to pull the trigger, all unknowingly letting Berlusconi pull their strings like puppets. I was wound up too tight to play arbiter, but I wasn't letting Berlusconi play me.

"Why are you here, Costa?" Dominic asked. His voice was level and his gray eyes assessing. Maybe I hadn't given him enough credit.

"He's got my brother in there," I said, nodding toward the warehouse.

Letting him know I'd been fucking his baby sister probably wasn't conducive to the arbiter role.

Dominic nodded. "I don't know who Berlusconi is," he admitted, though it seemed to pain him. It was a testament to how important Raven was to him that he'd make such an admission in front of more than a dozen Costas.

"He's Fiorenzo Avalone's son. He's been scooping up men from wherever he can and has been trying to pit one family against another for quite some time now."

"Then what the hell are we waiting for?" Dante piped up then turned to his brother, "I say we gun them down and take back what doesn't belong to them, Dom. Right now."

"It won't work," I said, wishing like hell I was wrong.

Berlusconi was smart. He was prepared for a gunfight. He'd let the Costas walk right in and gun down his men just to see what he was up against. Going in with the same old tricks now wasn't going to work.

Dante glared at me, but it was Dominic who spoke up, his expression a mask of indifference.

"How can you know that?" he asked.

My respect for the man grew. He could keep his wits about him no matter the situation, and that was no simple task.

"Salvatore," I called and held out my hand.

Salvatore handed me a pair of infrared binoculars, and I held them up to my face all the while hoping I was wrong.

"That's how," I said, then handed the binoculars to Dominic who handed them to his overzealous brother.

Dante took a look at the same scene I'd been looking at.

"Fuck me," he breathed and lowered the binoculars.

Despite the two dozen men between us, we were outnumbered at least five to one, all of them strategically situated around and inside the building.

One of the Lucas' men sidled up next to Dominic.

"You want me to call for reinforcements, boss?" he asked him.

Dominic didn't answer right away, but it looked like he was considering it.

"No," I said.

"No?" Dominic asked, an eyebrow cocked. "What do you mean, no?"

"I mean, my brother and the woman I love is in there, and…" I clamped my jaw shut. My stomach bottomed out. "Look, I don't give a fuck about families or turf wars or pissing contests. We do this my way and we do it now because if there's one thing I know how to do, it's how to take down a fucking monster."

Once again, Dominic's intelligent eyes were busy assessing. "How can you be so sure?"

"Because I am a monster."

For the first time, I was grateful to Lorenzo. He'd made me this way. He'd made me the monster who was going to save Raven and my brother, and bring Berlusconi to his knees, and anyone stupid enough to try to stand in my way.

Dominic nodded. "What's your plan?"

"We go in dark, and we go in silent. We take down everything that breathes along the way. Everything. No man left standing to give Berlusconi the heads-up. If anyone has any qualms about that, now's the time to walk away."

Dominic and the youngest one—Leo, I thought—nodded, but Dante's eyes were troubled. "Killing isn't exactly quiet. They'll know we're here in three seconds flat."

I smiled. "No, *amico*, they won't."

I popped my trunk and my eyes grazed over the racks that held not just guns, but knives. Lots and lots of knives.

Very quiet knives.

Chapter Forty-Three

Raven

My heart was pounding.

I could feel my pulse all the way to my fingertips.

But it was the bitter taste of betrayal that stood out above everything else.

"I tried to warn you, *signorina*." He stood right in front of me, but I still couldn't believe my eyes. "I told you, didn't I, that your past was best left alone?"

"The past is the past for a reason. It's meant to stay behind you, not lead you," he'd said.

Those words were the reason I'd abandoned my stupid plan to use Nico and his family. I'd never imagined they were words of warning.

"Tommaso? I don't understand?" The words came out strangled, little more than a whisper. He still looked just like the intuitive man behind the bar at Onyx. His hair slicked back. His outdated suit.

"Don't you?" He reached down and ran his fingers along my cheek.

I batted his fingers away, then wished I'd left them where they were and bitten them off instead.

He *tsk*-ed me and stood back. "I tried to help you, Sofia. Your brother was so distracted looking for you, I told Diego we didn't need you."

"Indeed, you did," Diego's voice came from far too close.

He was right behind me. His hands reached under my arms and dragged me up onto my feet.

"Let me go," I demanded, trying to shake him off.

"Leave her the hell alone," Gabe hissed. He'd shot to his feet, but as he took a swing at Diego, Tommaso yanked him back.

"Calm down, Gabriel." Diego chuckled as he moved around me until he stood right in front of me. "*Signorina* Luca and I are merely having a chat, aren't we?"

I pressed my lips together and glared at him.

"Tommaso thought we didn't need you, but I wasn't so sure." He leaned in close until his lips were just a hair's breadth from my ear. "To be honest, I didn't care. You're much too enticing of a prize to pass up," he whispered, making my whole body shudder in revulsion.

He was too close.

I could feel the warmth of his body radiating in the small space between us, but it only made me colder.

I started to pull my arm away, at least as far as the chain attached to my wrist would allow, but then I stopped.

If I was handcuffed to the post, then reasonably, there had to be a key to the handcuffs.

I forced my eyes wide in fear and tried to make myself appear smaller, like I was trying to disappear inside myself.

Nothing but a frightened little kitten.

He grabbed my wrist and drew me back toward him. The urge to shake off his hand was overwhelming, but I kept it in check.

Where would the key be? In his jacket pocket? His pants pocket? He was pulling me with his right hand, so likely his dominant hand. That meant it was reasonable to narrow down my search to the pockets on his right side, but jacket or pants? Jacket or pants?

He'd pulled me as far as the chain would reach.

"Please don't hurt me," I pleaded in a voice that quivered with fear. *No need to try to fake it.*

"Now, why would I do that, *signorina?*" he asked as he slipped his arm around me.

Because you get off on it, you twisted freak. I could see it in his eyes. The more frightened I looked, the brighter the lascivious light shone in his eyes. But I kept my thoughts to myself and didn't resist when he pulled me closer, molding my body against his larger frame.

Giving my body leave to tremble and shudder all it wanted, I moved my hand slowly, envisioning where his jacket pocket would be and slipping my fingers inside gently. Slowly. Ever so carefully.

He was busy sliding his hand down my back lower, pressing me disgustingly closer. I could feel every ridge and plane and jutting part of his body.

I'd reached the bottom of his jacket pocket, but it was empty.

"Disappointed?" He cocked an eyebrow, letting me know he'd been aware of what I'd been doing. Then he forced me backward in two long strides, pressing my back against the post until every pit and bump in the concrete must have been etched into my skin.

Each time, he'd bested me. I wanted to scream in frustration just as much as fear.

"His balls, Sofia," Gabe barked, and my body responded from years of practice without conscious thought.

I drew up my knee and slammed it into Diego's groin.

He hollered as he doubled over, and I slammed the same knee right into his nose. I hoped this was what Gabe had in mind because I was out of moves as Diego stumbled back, still hunched over while one hand attempted to stem the flow of blood from his nose.

"Well done, *bella*," Gabe said.

I chanced a glance at him while Diego stumbled back further. He had an arm wrapped around Tommaso's neck. Tommaso was flailing, but his face was red and his lips had begun to take on a bluish hue.

"His pocket, Raven," Gabe said, ducking his head to avoid a random strike from Tommaso's thrashing arm.

I delved into his right pocket but came up empty. *Crap.* Tommaso was left-handed. I shoved my hand into his other pocket, careful to avoid his limbs, and my fingers closed over the cool, smooth metal I sought.

I pulled it out, smiling victoriously when a click I'd heard far too often today sounded close behind me.

"Drop it, *signorina*," Diego said, his voice far more nasally than it had been before I'd smashed my knee into his nose.

My gaze shot up to Gabe's, but while he still held onto Tommaso, his jaw was clenched in frustration. He nodded once.

I couldn't do it. I couldn't force my fingers to release their vise grip on my freedom.

Despite the irate light in his watering eyes and the handkerchief he held against his nose, Diego chuckled and lowered his gun.

"All right, *signorina*. Go ahead. Unfasten the cuff."

308

I paused.

"Don't do it, Raven," Gabe whispered.

How could I not? Whether it was a trick or not, I'd be able to defend myself a whole lot better unshackled. So, keeping one eye on my bleeding captor, I shoved the key in the lock and unfastened the cuff. It clattered against the post, resonating the metallic sound throughout the warehouse.

I kept the key in my hand, gripping it tight, though I wasn't sure why. I noticed Gabe no longer had Tommaso in a choke hold.

Tommaso was on the ground, his eyes closed, his lips purplish, maybe, but not blue. Unconscious then, not dead.

Diego hadn't even spared his accomplice a glance.

"Your feistiness is refreshing, *signorina*," Diego said with a smile that was pure evil. "I'll tell you what. If you can make it to that door..." he said, pointing to the door through which I'd been brought in, "...you and *Signor* Costa will be free to go. Do we have a deal?"

I glanced over at the door, then back at him, then the door.

It couldn't have been more than thirty feet to the door.

I returned my gaze back at Diego.

Only thirty feet, but with the gun in his hand, I wouldn't make it three.

He chuckled, following my gaze to his hand.

"Fair enough."

He bent to place his gun on the concrete floor then kicked it away.

"Don't," Gabe warned.

He was right. Of course, he was right.

There was no way I was making it to the door in one piece, and even if by some miracle I managed it, I didn't believe for a second he'd let Gabe go.

So I ran three steps in the opposite direction amid the deafening crack of gunshots that seemed to come from all around me.

And I dove for Diego's gun.

Chapter Forty-Four

Nico

It was like fireworks. I couldn't see them, but I could hear them, cracking through the silent night from the warehouse.

Gunshots.

My heart beat double time as I fought the urge to plow straight ahead, but I couldn't fight the images that came.

The blood and the screams, Raven and Gabe dead or dying on a cold, concrete floor.

But it was too many gunshots for an execution. An internal squabble? I could do nothing but hope neither Raven nor Gabe had been caught in the crossfire.

Weak, helpless, useless.

The words echoed around in my head, trying to chip away at the steel bars. The bars that separated the monster from the man.

"We move now," I barked at the men still assembled around me. "O vinciamo o moriamo."

Either we win, or we die. The Costa battle cry.

"O vinciamo o moriamo," Salvatore repeated back with a nod, then he veered off to the left with Dante while Vito, Greta, and a man named Marco veered right.

Costas and Lucas working together. Who would ever have thought it? But then again, according to my mother, our grandfathers had. The Lucianos were an unexpected addition, but desperate times called for desperate measures.

To save Gabe's life, I didn't think my grandfather would have disapproved.

The rest of our men were already back in their vehicles, driving around to approach the warehouse from the opposite direction.

I was flanked on either side by Dominic Luca and his brother Leo, making this the weirdest job I'd ever done.

But it was a job.

It had to be just a job.

Feelings and emotions and the potent need to charge right through the warehouse wall led to mistakes.

And there was no room for mistakes.

Adrenaline vibrated through my veins as the three of us slinked silently up the middle, heading straight for the warehouse. Fifty yards in, I spotted the first pair of Berlusconi men. Thanks to the burned-out lampposts, they were little more than shadows in the trunk bed of a rusted old Chevy.

We ducked behind another beat-up car.

"Keep an eye on them," I told Leo, handing him the binoculars. "Signal if any more start coming."

He glanced at Dominic, who gave him a quick nod, before nodding to me.

I bit my tongue. If the roles were reversed, I'd expect Gabe to run every order by me, too.

Dominic and I took off. He moved like a shadow beside me. I'd never worked with him before. There was every possibility he'd mess this up, but he moved with a confident step, and the way he held the knife, his wrist bent at just the right angle to slice a man's throat wide open, told me he was no stranger to using one.

They never saw us coming.

Like we'd been working side by side for years, we struck simultaneously, grabbing the two men from behind. We dragged the blades across their throats in quick, smooth motions, deep enough to cut right through vocal cords to keep them from crying out.

Thick, warm blood spurted down my arm as the dying man's limbs flailed futilely.

It was only a matter of seconds now.

Five... four... three... two... one...

The man went limp, and I lowered him to the ground just as silently as I'd killed him, and Dominic's man joined him there a moment later.

Two down. Too many still to go.

Chapter Forty-Five

Raven

Pain tore through my left arm as I wrapped my right hand around the gun on the floor. It was too late for me to stop now. Bullets zipped by from every direction. I could hear Gabe's voice, but I couldn't make out the words.

Amid the chaos, all I could think was that this was how I would die, bleeding from gunshots all over my body. I was going to die, but I was taking at least one of them with me. *At least one,* I pleaded. I couldn't die for nothing.

I rolled onto my back just as a dark shape dove on top of me, smothering me beneath the hard wall of a chest and knocking the gun out of my hand.

No!

I groped blindly but couldn't find it. I tried to buck him off, assuming it was somehow Gabe who was trying to shelter me from the downpour of bullets, but he wouldn't budge.

"Diego, stop!" the figure on top of me barked.

To my surprise, the room went silent.

It wasn't Gabe's voice.

Crooked-Nose—Diego—scoffed. "I should have known you were too much of a pussy for this, big brother."

Brother?

Tommaso sat back on his heels. "*This,*" he said, looking down at me, "was never part of the plan."

"Plans change." Diego shrugged. He'd managed to stem the blood flowing from his nose, but even in the dark light, it seemed more crooked than it had been. Clearly broken. At least I'd managed to do that much. "Besides, it makes no difference if I have a little fun with our guest. Tell me you haven't thought of all the fun you could have with Costa's pretty little whore?"

My jaw clenched. I tried to wriggle out from under Tommaso, but he put a restraining hand on my hip and shot me a warning look.

"This was never about 'fun,' Diego," Tommaso said, turning his attention back to his brother.

Diego laughed, though it sounded more like a bark. "You don't think I know what this is about? You don't think I've fantasized about this day every minute since this whore's family killed our mother?"

"What?" The word slipped out before I could stop it. No member of my family would ever have murdered a young mother. They were criminals, yes, but heartless killers, no. I couldn't believe it.

Tommaso was glaring daggers at me, but Diego was laughing. "Don't act so surprised, *signorina*. You didn't think your father was a saint, did you? It was *his* job to watch over the whores who made him his fortune—the women, like my mother, who spread their legs to help keep Vincent Luca a rich man. But he couldn't always be watching, could he? He let my mother slip through the cracks, didn't even know that some nameless john had beaten her to death until it

315

was too late. I was nine years old, and all I had was *him,"* he said, pointing an accusatory finger at Tommaso, "to watch over me."

"I did my best, Diego. I was a kid too," Tommaso said, his shoulders slumping.

"Your best?" Diego cocked a doubting eyebrow. "Your best landed you a dead-end job in a Costa skin club. If it weren't for me, you would have been stuck there the rest of your miserable life."

"This was never about me, Diego. The moment I agreed to help dig you out of the hole you've gotten yourself into, my life ended. I die tonight, and you know it."

"I don't know what you're talking about," Diego said, but even I could hear the insincerity in his tone.

"Don't lie to me, Diego. You never were very good at it." Tommaso sighed.

Tommaso sounded tired. His hair had been mussed in his scuffle with Gabe, and now, with it framing his face, I could see the vague resemblance between Tommaso and his brother. Similar jaw structure and high foreheads, the same sharp eyes, but there were dark bags beneath Tommaso's eyes now and a hollowness within them.

Diego chuckled. "I suppose not. Now, stand the girl up, would you? I don't imagine we have much time left, and I'd like to enjoy these few moments."

Tommaso clenched his jaw, but he grabbed me beneath my arms and hauled me to my feet. Instead of gift-wrapping me for his brother, he shoved me behind him and walked us backward.

"No more, Diego," he said as another arm wrapped around me and drew me back into the solid wall of a chest.

From behind, Gabe felt so much like Nico, it made my heart ache like an open wound.

"You still don't get it, do you, brother?" Diego said, still unperturbed. He had a gun in his hand again, and he held it up menacingly. "You don't call the shots anymore."

Then he fired his gun.

Chapter Forty-Six

Nico

One gunshot.

It shot through my eardrums, louder than any sound I'd ever heard.

Raven or Gabe?

The question beat along with my heart, faster and faster.

Blood dripped from the blade of the knife in my hand. I'd lost count of the number of throats we'd slit. Two dozen? Probably more. Most of them were clean kills—quick slices from behind.

At first, every step next to a Luca had felt like it went against the grain, but now, despite my pounding heart, we moved like a well-oiled machine.

Dominic was intuitive and skilled, anticipating every move I made. It wasn't much different than working with Gabe by my side.

It surprised me that Leo worked as efficiently as Dominic. Usually, the youngest family members tended to be coddled longer, less prepared for the sometimes-gruesome tasks our world required of us. But then, it was Raven who had been the youngest of the Luca siblings, and while she might never have been exposed to the horrors of our world, she'd lived her own nightmares.

You're the reason for her nightmares, my mind taunted, *and you're the reason she and Gabe are in danger now.*

I tried to deny it as we crept up on yet another unsuspecting pair of Berlusconi men. I tried to rationalize it as I grabbed the dark-haired thug by the back of his head and jerked my knife across his throat.

But I knew.

Deep down, I'd known that they'd come for everything that was important to me one day. I could have protected them. All I'd had to do was keep my distance. No ties. No bonds. Nothing for them to take. But I'd failed.

I held on tight as the thug flailed while blood gurgled out of his mouth and his neck. The struggle was futile. After a moment, I laid him down quietly on the ground beneath one of the warehouse's broken windows.

I could see shadows creeping around cars and moving silently toward the building. Two hulking shadows came from my left, followed close behind by what could only have been the much smaller shadow of Greta. On my right and a little further back, I could see the familiar dark shape of Salvatore moving in tandem with Dante Luca.

Every step seemed to drag on forever, every second that ticked by was like an eon. The knot in my stomach grew and twisted up tighter. We were right here.

Raven and Gabe were just on the other side of the wall, but all I could do was wait. Wait for them to catch up, wait to infiltrate the building in tandem—all of us, all at once. There would be no second chance to get this right.

But it's taking too fucking *long.*

"Cardio ain't got nothing on this," Leo joked in a whisper that was barely louder than the light breeze.

Despite myself, I smiled. It was true. Movies might have made slitting throats look like easy work, but it was tiring. Even with a man's throat slit, he could put up one hell of a fight, even if not a long one. All three of us were dripping sweat. It mingled with blood spatter as it dripped down the sides of our faces.

Vito, Greta, and Marco disappeared around the left side of the building at the same time Salvatore and Dante vanished around the right. My insides sighed—it was time to move, time to act—but the knot in my stomach stayed twisted up tight.

There'd been one gunshot.

One execution.

One of the most important people in the world to me was gone.

All at once, the night lit up in blinding brightness. The shock wave hit me, knocking me back like a blow to the chest as shards of rubble flew in every direction.

All three of us fell.

And it looked like one of us wouldn't be getting back up.

Chapter Forty-Seven

Raven

The explosion lit up the interior of the warehouse, so bright I had to squeeze my eyes shut. The ground shook, making Tommaso's lifeless body quake on the floor as a deafening roar made me clamp my hands over my ears. But the sound of screaming men was so loud, it permeated my hands and the ringing in my ears. The light, the sounds, the putrid, charred smells—they overloaded my senses.

I couldn't think.

I couldn't move.

I felt like I was in the middle of a World War II movie.

"It seems our guests found my surprise," Diego said. He didn't look shell-shocked. He didn't look the least bit perturbed by the explosion that had ripped the far side of the building wide open and blown his men to pieces.

And then his words found their way into my brain, and my knees threatened to buckle.

This was the trap Gabe had been talking about.

The explosion, the flames, the heat.

There was no way Nico could have survived.

"No!" I screamed like I could scream the explosion out of existence, banish it, undo it.

321

The fire continued to crackle. Flames danced in some sick undulating ritual, growing taller with each passing second.

I couldn't breathe. I gasped, but it wouldn't come. I couldn't get enough oxygen into my lungs.

And then my wide tear-soaked eyes found Diego, and a coldness I'd never felt before slipped inside me.

It froze the core of me and turned the blood in my veins to ice. I'd never understood how Nico could do the things he'd done, how he'd been able to torture people, murder them.

But now I understood.

More than that, I felt it: The cold desire to tear a man apart piece by piece.

It might have looked like the only weapon I had was my bare hands, but in that moment, I didn't feel human. I was muscles, and teeth, and claws, and thanks to Vito, I had a wicked knowledge of how to use every part.

I lunged at him, baring my teeth like an animal, but the arm still wrapped around my waist held me back. A strong arm. An arm so much like his brother's, it threatened to thaw me right through. But I needed the cold. I needed it to keep me from feeling, from letting the horrible truth sink in. The truth that Nico—the man I loved— was gone.

"No," I cried, pulling against Gabe's hold, but he held on tight, and heat seeped back into my veins.

It was too late. The cold was gone.

"Stop, *bella,*" he said, holding me tighter. "Don't do anything stupid."

"That's good advice, Gabriel. Perhaps, you aren't as much of a loose cannon as your brother is... er, *was*," Diego said, glancing pointedly at the inferno with a disgusting smile.

Gabe shrugged. "I'm full of good advice. In fact, I've got some for you, Diego."

"Do you?" He cocked an eyebrow indulgently.

Gabe nodded, nudging my head to the left with his chin.

My heart skipped a beat and my lungs stuttered as I caught sight of shadows moving soundlessly along the walls.

"Run, *amico*. My brother doesn't die that easily."

Chapter Forty-Eight

Nico

Diego had his back turned, his shoulders squared in naïve confidence.

I was done creeping in the fucking shadows.

I could see Vito and all the others slipping in through windows all over the unexploded sections of the building. They'd take care of Berlusconi's men.

Diego Berlusconi was mine.

I strode forward, not bothering to soften the thud of my footsteps, daring anyone stupid enough to try to take a shot at me.

"Berlusconi!" I hollered as the man swung around at the sound of my steps.

Diego's eyes widened, but only momentarily. He raised the gun in his hand.

He was fast. But I was faster.

I shot him straight through the hand, making him drop the gun while he screamed bloody murder.

"Gabe's right," I said. "Better men than you have tried to kill me, and I've sent every one of them to hell."

I took aim for a second time and shot him in the knee.

He dropped to the ground amid fresh screams, landing awkwardly on his uninjured leg.

I holstered the gun but kept my eyes on him. I wasn't letting this slimy fucker out of my sight. The gun was out of bullets, so I reached behind to grab my knife.

"Nico," Raven cried.

The sound of her voice broke through the red haze that had clouded my vision since I'd left Onyx.

Everything I'd been trying to keep at bay flooded in all at once.

She was alive.

Gabe was alive.

The raw lump at the back of my throat grew, and a strange wetness stung my eyes.

Gabe let her go, and I caught her up and pulled her close, pressing her hard against the wounds from the explosion's debris. It stung, but I didn't care. I pulled her closer, but it didn't feel close enough. I wanted to pull her right into me so no one could hurt her ever again. If I held her any tighter, I'd hurt her, so I tried to focus on the feel of her chest rising and falling against mine, her breath against my neck, her warmth seeping into me—all things I'd feared I'd never feel again.

"I'm fine, by the way. Thanks for asking." Gabe shot me a cocky smile.

I swallowed hard, putting far more effort than should have been necessary into making sure my voice came out level and calm.

"I know you're fine, *stronzo*. Now, make yourself useful. Tie him up and make him quiet." I nodded to the piece of shit writhing on the floor.

The bloodlust I'd felt just a moment ago had given way to something so much more potent. I still wanted him dead, gone, never able to lay a finger on Raven—or Gabe—again, but I didn't particularly care how he got there.

"I thought you'd died," Raven whispered against my chest, digging her fingers into my shoulders. "The explosion…" Her voice cracked, and she pressed her face hard against me.

"Never," I lied.

Death would come for me eventually, but not today. I'd escaped it for now, but there were others who hadn't been so lucky. I had to tell her, but how was I supposed to do that?

I kept glancing over at the blazing ruin of the right wall, waiting to see two figures walk right through it, but no one came. The flames licked higher and higher, and there was no denying the charcoal and sulfurous odors of bodies burning. It was a repugnant smell that pasted itself inside the nostrils and mouth. It would remain there long after the burning was done.

Salvatore was gone, and though she wouldn't feel that loss as much as me, she would feel the loss of Dante. And while I'd left Leo tending to Dominic outside the building, it was entirely possible Raven had lost two members of her family today.

Two brothers.

If I'd kept her safe, they never would have been here.

"Raven, I…" I slammed my jaw shut. No part of me wanted to tell her, but she'd hate me all the more if I tried to keep it from her. "It's Dominic." I forced the words out.

She stiffened against me. "No," she croaked. "Where is he?"

She pulled back, looking around wildly for her brother, but finding only the blood-spattered faces of Greta, Vito, and the various Costa and Luca men around her.

"He's outside," I said, nodding back the way I'd come, but holding onto her for one more moment.

Just one more moment before whatever she'd felt for me got caught up in the flames around us and vanished with the smoke.

Chapter Forty-Nine

Raven

The early morning light had just begun to lighten the night's sky around the horizon, bathing the world outside the warehouse in muted shades of gray. Everything was gray aside from the fire, like it had sucked all the color of the world into itself.

A shirtless gray Leo was bent over a motionless form on the ground, ripping strips of fabric from his shirt and tying them around the motionless form's extremities like bandages.

I could feel my pulse pounding in my neck as I crossed the distance between us. It felt like I'd been plucked from my body and dropped into this strange gray world where nothing made sense. Not the bloody wounds that wept from Leo's scarred, bare back. And certainly not the body on the ground that looked far too much like Dom. It wasn't real. *This* wasn't real. It couldn't be.

"Leo," I whispered, dropping down next to him. I could see the tears in his eyes.

"I'm sorry, Sofia," he said, the first words my brother had said to me in more than a decade. "I…"

My breath caught in my throat, but at the same time, Dom's chest rose and then fell, and my breath came out in a strangled whoosh.

He's still alive.

"Stop," I said as Leo moved to pull out a thick piece of glass that had lodged in Dom's arm.

As a nurse in training, I'd learned about triage and emergency care, but for the first time, it wasn't techniques and skills drawn from a textbook. It was a certainty that powered my muscles and flowed through my veins as I grabbed a torn strip of Leo's shirt and bound up Dom's arm. I glanced over him in a quick assessment, watching for the reassuring rise and fall of his chest as I went.

He was covered in a lot of blood, but it didn't seem like all of it was his. Like Nico and Leo, he was covered in a lot of other people's blood.

I shuddered, thinking how that had happened.

There were no other major bleeds that I could see. I checked his pulse, counting out the strong and steady beats against my fingertips. My own heart seemed to flutter in my chest. He was alive. He was going to be all right.

I lifted his eyelids, checking his pupils, which contracted with the light just like they should. I checked his head for contusions, and right away, I found one at the back of his skull that probably accounted for his unconsciousness. The swollen lump was sticky with blood, but it wasn't bleeding profusely.

His eyelids fluttered open, but the gray that stared back at me wasn't muted. It wasn't part of the strange gray world that made no sense.

Dom's eyes, open and alive.

I sagged with relief and dropped my head on his chest, but instead of lying still like a good patient, he groaned, patted my head with his less-injured arm, and struggled to sit up.

"Don't move, Dom," I said.

He sat back against the wall and flashed me a pathetically weak grin.

"Stubborn fool," I muttered under my breath as he pulled me against him in a one-armed hug.

"That's kind of the pot calling the kettle black, is it not?" he whispered against my brow.

I laughed, grabbing hold of Leo's hand and tugging him close.

"It's been a while, *sorellina*," Leo said with a grin, then planted a kiss on my forehead. But there was something in the tone of his voice that made my throat tighten painfully.

"Where's Dante?" I asked in a strangled whisper.

If Dom and Leo were here, then Dante would have been too. And yet, there was a prickle of apprehension at the back of my neck as I sat up and looked around, searching for my missing brother. My brother, whom I'd yet to see. I'd wasted so much time with my stupid anger.

I found Greta and Vito easily—though I couldn't imagine how Vito had gotten from California to New York so quickly. There were plenty of faces I didn't recognize too.

But no Dante.

Leo grabbed my hand, but he kept his gaze averted like he couldn't quite meet my eyes. "I'm so sorry, Sofia."

"Damn right, you're sorry," a raspy voice called as two figures came around the burning corner of the building. Two smoking figures, both of them rather singed around the edges and leaning on one another for support.

A sob escaped my throat, and I could feel the collective sigh around me as the two men ambled forward. I recognized the man with Dante—he was a Costa man.

Lucas and Costas, they'd come together.

They were working together because of me and Gabe.

When Dante reached us, he pulled me up and drew me against him. He'd either never had a jacket on, or he'd removed it at some point, and the shirt beneath was charred in various places.

He smelled like a fireplace, but I could only find two concerning injuries on him—second-degree burns on his calf and his upper arm that, while nasty-looking, would be all right with proper medical attention.

I'd only just finished making my up-close assessment when a pair of smaller hands grabbed me from behind and yanked me into an enormous hug.

Greta inadvertently pressed down on the bullet wound in my arm, reminding me that I'd been shot—a flesh wound, fortunately. I resisted the urge to squeal and hugged her back.

"Don't you ever do that to me again," Greta barked, but the stern effect was lost when her voice cracked and she jostled us both with a wracking sob.

"I won't," I whispered, not bothering to mention it hadn't exactly been my intention to do it the first time.

Instead of dragging me away, Vito got his arms around me from behind, wrapping them right around Greta and dropping his head down on mine. He didn't speak, leaving me free to wonder again how he'd gotten here so quickly. He'd been spying on me the whole time, hadn't he? I decided it didn't matter at the moment and turned my head to plant a kiss on his cheek.

Now that it seemed all my family would be okay, I turned to find the one man I wanted to see most.

The man I would always want to see most.

Where was he?

Amid all the familiar and unfamiliar faces, I couldn't find him.

I'd only just managed to take a step back when the sound of a gunshot tore through me and the strange gray world threatened to turn black.

Chapter Fifty

Raven

I was running.

My feet moved, one in front of the other, but I couldn't feel them.

Nothing existed but for the loud crack that kept playing over and over again in my head.

I stuttered to a stop outside the open warehouse door and saw Gabe standing over Diego's body. Blood seeped from a single bullet hole in the center of Diego's forehead as Gabe dropped the gun from his hand and turned away.

Tears sprung to my eyes. Nico was fine. *But where is he?*

I whipped my head around, searching for him. It was only because the gray world had spewed back some of its color that I spotted him. He was so far away, I could only make out the general tall, broad shape of him, but it was him.

Ignoring the voices all around me, I darted after him, pounding along the gravel as fast as my legs would carry me.

Something was wrong—it had to be.

Why else would he have walked away?

My lungs had begun to burn by the time I caught up to him. I bent to catch my breath as he spun to face me.

He was bleeding. I'd been so relieved to see him alive before that I hadn't noticed it, but he'd suffered no small number of injuries rescuing me. Gashes and narrow puncture wounds dotted his body. Blood dripped in a slow but steady stream down his fingers from a wound I couldn't see.

"You're hurt," I said stupidly. Now that I'd caught up to him, I had no idea what to say. "Thank you" didn't really seem to cut it.

"I'll be fine, Raven. Go," he said, nodding back toward the others.

"No." I shook my head.

He cocked an eyebrow, but his expression was otherwise blank.

An image of Cesare flashed through my head, and I bit back the sob that tremored up my chest. Cesare was dead because of me.

"I'm sorry," I said, trying to keep my voice from cracking but failing miserably.

His stone expression cracked just a little. "You don't have to be sorry, Raven. I understand."

I tilted my head to the right. "What are you talking about?"

He heaved what I thought was an agitated sigh, but then I remembered what Gabe had said to me about reading between the lines, and I looked harder.

I could see it. The blank expression he used like a smoke screen. He tried to keep what he felt hidden behind it. But it was there in the hard-set of his jaw, in the uncertainty buried beneath the dangerous glint in his eyes, and in the slight creases at the edges of them that bespoke of more than physical pain.

He shifted his weight and drew himself up straighter. "I couldn't protect you, Raven. I understand your wanting to leave."

"Me?" Maybe he'd taken a hard bump to the back of the head too. "You do realize that *you're* the one walking away, right?"

He licked his lips then pressed them together, but he couldn't fool me anymore.

The tension that had been knotting my stomach changed. I'd had so much adrenaline coursing through my veins, and my emotions had been all over the place. Now, all of it was suddenly settling in a singular feeling in the core of me, low in my abdomen, setting me on fire.

I couldn't help but follow the contraction of his throat muscles as he swallowed or notice the hard planes of his chest where the top buttons of his shirt had come undone.

I wanted to see more, feel more. *Do* more.

"Raven?" he said, his brow furrowed.

"I want you, Nico," I said, the words spilling from my lips. I had no desire to hold them back. I felt strong. Alive. More than ever.

I lunged at him, slamming into his chest and reaching for his lips with my own. I felt feral. I was muscles, and teeth, and claws, just like earlier, but I didn't want to use them to tear a man apart. I wanted to use them to hold him close, to mark him in the same way he'd marked me.

His lips parted for me, and his hands moved to my hips and drew me closer. I dug my fingers into his shoulders as I swept my tongue across his teeth then slid along his tongue the way he'd done to me.

He groaned against my lips but then pulled away, leaving me gasping for breath.

"It's just the adrenaline, Raven. It isn't real. You don't actually want this."

"I know it's the adrenaline. I know I shouldn't want this, not now, not after all that's happened. But I do, Nico. I don't just want sex. I want you. I will always want you." I took a deep breath and steeled myself for what I was about to admit next. "I love you."

His eyes widened and his breath caught in his throat.

"You don't mean that," he said, though his hands gripped my hips harder, sparking up my adrenaline-fried mind.

"I do mean that."

I glanced around for somewhere more private than the open stretch of gravel road. There was an abandoned old shed twenty yards away with its door hanging wide open.

I grabbed his hand and tried to tug him along, but apparently, Nico was as immovable as a boulder when he wanted to be. He stood still, staring at me, then slowly pulled me back toward him.

I could see it in his eyes before he opened his mouth.

"I love you too," he said.

His words rippled throughout me, leaving behind the most exquisite warmth in every fiber of my body.

I flashed him a knowing grin. "I know you do."

He laughed, and then he kissed me.

"And what else do you know?" he asked when he leaned away a moment later.

I leaned up on my tiptoes until my lips brushed against the shell of his ear. "I know I want you inside me," I said, feeling a thrill rush through me at my own words.

He groaned then dipped his head down to leave a trail of kisses along the back of my neck. "But I want to make you scream, Raven, and I don't think you want your brothers breaking down the door when I do."

Every word sent a little jolt of electricity through my body, making me pulse and throb. It irked me that he was probably right, though. The way I was feeling, there was no chance I'd be able to keep quiet. I sagged against him, but he chuckled.

"Don't worry. I'll make sure the wait is worth your while."

He kissed me once more, long and thorough. A kiss that was full of every sinful promise a man could make.

Chapter Fifty-One

Nico

"I don't think Tommaso planned to betray us, at least not when he started working at Onyx," Gabe said in quiet undertones as we stood outside Dante Luca's hospital room.

Raven, Dominic, and Leo were gathered around him while he glared at the nurse who was taking his vitals.

It felt odd to be standing so close to a bunch of Lucas, but not nearly as strange as it would have yesterday.

Gabe had given me the rundown of all that Berlusconi and Tommaso had said, and I was inclined to agree with him. I hated to admit it, but it was probably a good thing that Tommaso had died at Berlusconi's hand.

I wasn't sure how I would have felt about having to kill him.

I heard a set of footsteps behind me; it was unlike the usual chaotic fashion of doctors and nurses.

I didn't need to turn to see who had arrived.

I've been waiting for him since we arrived here.

I'd filled Raven in on what my mother had told me on our drive over here. I hadn't wanted to tell her—I didn't want her to know that I was the reason our mothers had gone to great lengths to keep her from me—but instead of anger or resentment, she'd looked at *peace.*

"Our mothers love us very much," she had said after a painstakingly long moment of silence.

"All of your family loves you, Raven," I had responded, knowing there was still one reunion left to come.

The footsteps stopped directly behind me, and I turned around.

His face was etched in deep lines, some of them from age and others, I was sure, from grief. He was as good as the rest of us at keeping his emotions close to the vest, so there was no way I could have anticipated it when he put his arms around me and patted my back. It was a brief embrace, over just as quickly as it had begun.

"*Grazie,* Nico," Vincent Luca said as he drew back. His expression was blank, but there were tears in his eyes. "You saved my daughter. I will never forget that."

I nodded, at a loss for words.

"I know your father is a… difficult man, Nico. But your grandfather, he would be proud of you."

"*Grazie, Signor* Luca."

Vincent nodded, and I stepped aside.

Vincent walked through the open door of the hospital room. He moved quietly, as if he didn't want to be noticed just yet.

I found myself holding my breath, waiting for the moment she would turn around.

Vincent stood there for just a minute before his presence caught the eye of his daughter.

She froze mid-sentence, staring at him for just a second before she flew across the room.

"*Papà!*" she cried, flying right into his open arms.

The man looked happier than perhaps I'd ever seen a man look. I could guarantee Lorenzo would never look at one of his children that way, but it wasn't jealousy I felt—far from it.

It brought me more happiness than I could ever have imagined to know Raven was so loved, that there were so many people who I knew would go to the ends of the earth for her.

She looked up at me as her father held her tight. "I love you," she mouthed silently, and my heart did some weird flip-flop thing that wasn't entirely unpleasant.

"The perfect venue for a family reunion, right?" Leo joked, elbowing me. He'd sidled up next to me, giving Vincent and Raven some space.

I smiled.

The hospital would be a perfect venue for a Costa family reunion—nice and close to emergency care when fists started to fly.

"I was wondering if you wouldn't mind helping me with something—for Sofia, er… Raven?" Leo asked.

"Sure thing."

For Raven, there wasn't anything I wouldn't do, but damn, didn't I sound like an agreeable son of a bitch?

***

This was not what I'd had in mind when Leo asked for my help.

This hadn't even crossed my mind.

"Not much of a dog person?" Leo guessed, grinning at me from the passenger seat of my Porsche.

I shrugged. "I don't know, actually. Never had one."

340

In truth, I couldn't remember being within ten yards of a dog in my life. When Leo had asked for my help, I'd imagined he'd wanted to get Raven flowers or maybe one of those giant teddy bears with a sappy-ass message scrawled across its chest, and just needed a ride. Or perhaps, if he was a man more like me, he'd wanted to go back for Berlusconi to lay the motherfucker's head at her feet—I'd thought about it, but I didn't think Raven would share the sentiment.

So I had absolutely no idea what to do with the furry four-legged creature that currently paced back and forth across my back seat, no doubt poking holes in the leather with every step.

"He was the first and only pet my father ever bought. And he bought him for Sofia. You should have seen her with the mutt. She was so enthralled. I kept waiting to see the little guy walk on water or something. So far, he only swims." Leo shrugged. "But he'll grow on you. Trust me. Dominic used to have that same look on his face around Bullet that you've got, *amico*."

At the mention of his name, the dog yipped and hopped into the front seat. He walked across Leo's lap, then crossed the middle console and wriggled onto my thighs beneath the steering wheel.

He looked up at me with his enormous puppy dog eyes as I swerved into the hospital's parking lot.

I had to admit, I didn't totally hate it. The mutt was kind of cute.

As I shifted the car into park, Bullet hopped out of my lap, traipsed across Leo, then was back on my legs in a flash.

"It looks like Bullet's decided whose company he prefers," Leo joked, giving the dog a mock glare while he handed me the dog's leash.

I fastened the leash through the loop on Bullet's collar. The moment I opened the car door, he bounded out, then ran in circles on the pavement until I'd followed him out.

Two steps toward the hospital door, Leo stopped. "I don't think dogs are allowed in there. I'll go get—"

"Raven's going to be happy about *this*?" I asked, nodding to the dog.

"Damn right. You and I are getting major brownie points today, *amico.*"

I had no idea what Leo was talking about, but it was hard to deny that the dog's enthusiasm was rather infectious. Glancing at the yipping four-legged mutt, the smallest grin quirked my mouth upward.

Hospital rules be damned, I clenched my jaw, gave Bullet's leash a gentle tug, and set out toward the hospital doors, staring down every person I passed.

I quickened my pace at the thought of Raven's cheeks turning pink, my most favorite color now.

Chapter Fifty-Two

Raven

"You'd better not lie to me ever again. Do you understand me?" I said, waggling my finger at the two as they nodded in unison.

The two sat on the hotel room sofa, neither of them speaking, heads bowed.

Seeing them side by side now, I couldn't believe I hadn't noticed it before. It wasn't like they were identical twins, but the familial resemblance was there. Something in the shape of their faces and eyes, and the stubborn jut of their chins.

"Good," I said, dropping my finger. "Now, hug me, tell me to have a good time, and promise me there will be absolutely no spying going on this evening."

Greta's head shot up first, surprise marring her pretty features.

"I'm not mad, Greta," I told her honestly. "I've wasted too much time being angry, and I'm done with it. I love you, *both of you*, and I understand why you did what you did."

Greta smiled and hopped to her feet, Vito trailing behind her.

"Just don't do it again," I said, waggling my finger one last time.

Vito hugged me so tight, sturdy arms encircling me, that any qualms I had about letting them off the hook vanished.

Greta dove into the hug. She'd barely had time to wrap her arms around me as the knock at the door sounded.

I recalled the last time I opened the hotel room door with a nervous twinge, but luckily, I wasn't alone. Vito and Greta were here, my clandestine bodyguards. With that, my heart fluttered back to its normal pace.

I stepped back and looked up at them expectantly. "Well?"

Two blank faces stared back at me.

"Are you going to say anything to me?" I said, fisting my hands on my hips.

Greta smiled. "Have a good time, Raven."

She snuck in one last hug before standing back to look me over from head to toe. The dress had arrived shortly after I'd gotten back from the hospital, courtesy of Nico Costa, according to the courier.

To be honest, I felt a little ridiculous in the long, black strapless dress with a slit that went all the way up my thigh.

Greta nodded approvingly. "Don't do anything I'd do." She waggled her brows at me, and I laughed despite the heat that climbed up my cheeks.

"You remember everything I taught you, right, *passerotta?*" Vito said with a stern voice.

I nodded indulgently.

"If you need anything, you call me."

"I promise I will, *zietto,*" I said, then hugged him quick and hopped up on my toes to kiss his stubbled cheek.

Then I hightailed it across the room. I felt a bit like a teenage girl getting ready for her prom date.

It wasn't often I was rendered speechless, but the sight that greeted me when I opened the door left me grappling for words.

Nico, dressed all in black, in a suit that fit his broad frame perfectly; he looked like he'd just walked off a runway. The only bit of color on him was his vivid green eyes, and they glinted at me with a light that sent decadent shivers down my spine.

I could feel Greta and Vito staring as Nico leaned down and kissed me. It wasn't a long kiss, but by the way he lingered, his lips just barely touching mine, it felt like one of those kisses that was filled with a lot of erotic promises.

"You look... *delicious*," he whispered as he leaned away.

Once upon a time I'd been terrified that Nico Costa would eat me alive. Now, I kind of hoped he'd hurry up and do it.

I opened my mouth, but I could feel the eyes of our audience on my back.

"Let's go," I whispered instead, but the wicked smile on his face said he'd read my thoughts loud and clear.

I had no idea where we were going. Some fancy gala, if I had to guess. I would have been happy shacking up in a McDonald's with Nico, but I was looking forward to some private time.

The life-affirming adrenaline that had been coursing through my veins hadn't fizzled out entirely.

With Nico around, I wasn't sure it ever would.

Nico drove us right out of the city and along the route that led us to the familiar woodland fairy tale. When he pulled into the long, winding drive to his home, I was thrown for a loop.

"You'll see," he said, getting out of the car before I could probe him with questions.

He came around to open my door and led me up the front steps without a word.

The moment I stepped inside, I froze.

The interior was covered in blacks, golds, and vivid reds. The colors blanketed the floor and hung from tapestries on the walls. Bloodred roses and a gold candelabra stood on the dining table, its flames casting a warm glow across the main floor. There was even a bloodred fainting couch in the place where his sage green sofa had once been, and more roses on the now-black coffee table in front of it.

Holy crap.

The décor, the dress, even the classical music playing quietly from the speakers on the wall—Nico had set the stage for the most erotic fantasy I could imagine.

"How did you…?"

He shrugged. "It's amazing what you can accomplish with a few well-placed phone calls."

I couldn't imagine the number of people it would have taken to pull this off, and I knew how he felt about that.

I turned to him and leaned up, pressing my body against his as he lowered his lips to mine. The kiss was languid on the surface, but beneath it, I could feel the sparks and the exquisite tension that mounted with each passing second.

"It's perfect," I said when he leaned away.

He smiled, and his heated gaze traveled over me from head to toe. "I agree."

Without another word, he took my hand in his and led me through the decadent lair to the dining table where he poured two glasses of red wine.

I took a sip, but already every part of me seemed hyperaware. The cool rim of the glass against my lips; the bead of condensation that slipped from the glass and spilled over my fingers, the explosion of flamboyant tartness on my tongue, the lingering sweetness on my lips.

I licked it off, and Nico groaned. The sound rippled through me, making my nipples tighten and my breath come faster.

He placed his own wineglass down and moved behind me while I took another fortifying sip.

"You look like you were made to be devoured," he whispered against my ear.

The blood in my veins set off at a fast pace as his lips and teeth caressed my ear. I felt very much like Bella Swan when his mouth moved lower, kissing and nipping down my neck.

I couldn't move.

I could barely breathe.

When his hands took hold of my hips and drew me back against him, I thought I might just combust. The heat of his body, the hard planes, the thick erection pressed against my lower back.

His fingers found the zipper at the back of my dress as he suckled his way back up my neck. He inched the zipper down slowly, keeping his body pressed close to mine until he reached the bottom and leaned back, letting the dress pool at my feet.

I closed my eyes and reached out with my senses, searching for the feel of his heated gaze on me. I'd dressed for this—lacy black bra and thong, and thigh-high stockings—imagining him looking at me just like this.

"Fuck me," he breathed as my skin tingled everywhere his gaze touched—the lacy black bra that cupped my breasts, the thong that sheathed my hot core, its thin garter slitted between my wet folds, the thigh-high stockings that hugged my moist inner thighs.

"Yes, please," I whispered back.

The fire burning in me was ablaze. Suddenly, it felt like the temperature had been turned up. I felt empty, and I needed to be filled. I needed *him* buried inside me.

He chuckled, his breath brushing across the dampened flesh he'd been kissing. "In a hurry?"

I nodded, shivering in anticipation.

"Well, I'm not." He nipped my earlobe then stepped back.

Well, his massive erection suggested otherwise.

But I knew there was no point in arguing with Nico Costa. He was a man who was used to getting his way.

With a flick of his fingers, the clasp of my bra gave way, and the lacy fabric joined the dress at my feet. The cool air made my hard nipples tighten even more while my breasts felt heavier, aching for attention.

"Turn around," he said.

I obeyed, anticipating the feel of his hands on me, but knowing he wouldn't touch me yet, not until he'd looked his fill.

For a man who was used to getting what he wanted, whenever he wanted it, he had an amazing amount of self-control.

"You're the most beautiful woman I've ever seen, Raven," he said when his gaze had traveled to my toes and back.

He took his time then, kneeling down in front of me and slipping off my thong and stockings so slowly.

I wasn't sure who he was trying to drive insane more—*him or me?*

With my clothes fully discarded, he stood up in front of me, his hands on my hips, and he pushed me backward until I bumped into the dining table. He leaned forward, lowering me until my back rested on the table.

"Hands above your head," he instructed, leaning up enough to take in the view.

I complied while he hovered over me, still fully dressed. The contrast of my pale skin against his sinfully black suit made me feel utterly exposed.

He reached for something on the right of me.

He held it up in front of my lips, just barely touching them as he traced them with the soft petals of the bloodred rose he now held in his hand by its long stem.

The petals were cool and soft, like silk but with more substance to them. They didn't quite tickle as he grazed the rose down my neck, then down the center of me to my navel. He branched out as he glided the flower head back up, circling one nipple and then the other. The sensation wasn't like the warm, firm touch of his fingers, nor was it like his lips encircling me. Yet the soft, cool touch added fuel to the fire burning low in my abdomen.

I whimpered as he left my nipple, back to the center of me, but lower this time, so close to where I needed to be touched most. He smiled wickedly as he stopped just shy of my clit and slipped sideways instead, brushing the rose to my hip and then down my inner thigh.

He worked his way back up slowly, his gaze shifting back and forth between my face and the rose's path. My breath came faster with every inch he climbed, waiting, hoping, and yet, I expected him to keep up this torment.

When the rose touched my pussy, slipping across my slick lips, my hips jolted. I moaned as the petals grazed my clit. He kept the rose in place, the soft, cool blade pressed against my swollen flesh. My hips writhed, almost of their own volition, as if craving for the friction I desperately needed. Then he moved the rose away, gliding back through my slit over and over again.

"Nico," I breathed.

He grinned wickedly as he lifted the rose. I could see my own wetness glistening on the petals as he brought the flower to his lips and licked lightly at the petals.

My breath hitched. My entire body was on fire.

He dropped the rose on the table after a minute and stood up.

I watched in sparked-up fascination as his fingers worked at the buttons on his shirt, unfastening them so slowly, I was quite certain he was trying to drive me *insane.*

My greedy eyes took in every inch of flesh he exposed, following the ever-widening V down the smooth planes of his pecs until finally the fabric draped away, revealing eight-pack abs and the hard jut of his exquisitely tapered hips.

He leaned over me, capturing my lips before blazing a hot trail downward. He kissed, licked, suckled, and nipped as he went, tasting every part of me from my neck to my mound. He hovered there, and I could feel his warm breath like a light caress on my clit. My heart pounded and my whole body shook.

"Nico, please," I begged.

"Please, what?" he asked, his eyes flicking up to meet mine.

"Please lick me. I need to feel your mouth on my pussy." I could feel the heat in my cheeks.

He winked at me. "Anything you want, Raven."

His tongue flicked across my clit. The sensation shocked right through me, making me cry out as my hips jolted beneath him. He put his hands on my hips, holding me still as his tongue lapped at me a second time. I could feel it building already, the coil winding up tight inside me.

Another stroke of his tongue, and then more. Moans tumbled from my lips, and when he suckled my clit into his mouth, my body tried to buck clear off the table.

His lips and tongue drove me higher. It could have been seconds or minutes when I neared the edge of the precipice.

I was so close.

Right *there*.

Then he pulled away.

"No!" I cried, reaching for him, trying to pull him back with my hands on his firm, bare shoulders. The man was immovable.

"Hands over your head, Raven," he said, so close to my needy flesh that every word vibrated against me.

Reluctantly, I obeyed.

He turned his attention to my slit, slowly dragging his tongue between my wet lips over and over again, keeping me teetering on the edge, but never plummeting over.

Sweat beaded on my brow. I was no longer breathing. I was panting, like I was in the middle of a 10K marathon. I tried to press myself more firmly against him, but his grip on my hips held me captive. I tried to wrap my legs around him to pull him closer, but he didn't budge an inch.

His tongue dipped inside me, slowly, languidly exploring me. It seemed there was more than one kind of torture he was an expert at inflicting.

"Nico, please, I'm going to die if you keep this up."

"Never," he said confidently, gliding his tongue up to my clit.

The world exploded in a kaleidoscope of sensation that burst out all the way to my fingertips.

Like the tiny glittering pieces, I seemed to float back down onto the table. So caught up in the aftershocks of an earth-shattering orgasm, I felt disconnected from reality. Floating. Existing in a haze of bliss.

Until I felt the hard, thick head of Nico's cock at my entrance. Instantly, fresh heat blazed to life inside me. One hand at the base of his cock, he guided himself in slowly. My pussy pulsed, clenching, trying to draw him in.

I could see the muscles twitching in his jaw, but he wouldn't be hurried. He stretched and filled me one slow inch at a time. When there wasn't a molecule of space left inside me, he stilled, his gaze locked with mine.

"I love you, Raven," he said, jaw still clenched tight as he drew back until only the tip of him remained inside me.

He drove back in with one hard thrust, his gaze never leaving mine.

"I love you too, Nico," I said as he withdrew and plunged again.

I couldn't look away. Mesmerized, I could see every side of him in his emerald gaze, from the kindhearted man to the lethal killer to the man who'd risked his own life to save mine. He could have died today. At one point, I thought he had.

"I want to touch you," I whispered, my throat clogged with the fear I'd felt and the relief that had come after. Even more than the chiseled planes of his body, I needed to feel his heart beating and his lungs doing their work. I needed to feel him *alive*.

He nodded, and I reached for him, sliding my hands down his pecs. His heartbeat thumped steadily against my fingers, and his chest rose and fell in the same fast rhythm as mine.

As if he'd restrained himself for as long as he could, Nico lunged for me then, picking up his pace as he devoured my lips.

He propped himself with one hand beside my head, and the other hand moved, sliding down my neck, palming my breasts and catching my nipples between his fingers. Just as his lips had done, he touched me everywhere, and everywhere he touched ignited, feeding the fire that was blazing in my core.

I felt out of control, my body racing headlong for the precipice. No matter how much I wanted to wait for him, I couldn't slow it down.

"Nico," I screamed, begging him to jump with me as the first shocks of my orgasm shot through every fiber of my being.

He stilled deep inside me with a groan that sounded like it had been ripped from his chest as his cock pulsed through spurt after spurt of his own release.

With our gazes locked, we fastened the moment in time, freezing it and capturing it before it slipped between our fingers. We remained motionless for a long while.

Nico was the first to move. He pulled me up, but he stayed inside me. He wrapped an arm around me to keep me upright, while the other hand moved across my forehead, down my cheek, and across my lips.

"Marry me," he whispered.

My breath caught in my throat.

For the first time, he wore no mask. There was no smoke screen clouding what was going on behind it. His love, his happiness, his fears, even his pain was laid bare for me.

I didn't think a greater gift had ever been offered in all of time.

"Yes, Nico," I said without a quiver of uncertainty in my voice.

This was what I wanted.

This was what I was certain I'd want for the rest of my life.

Epilogue

Nico

A warm autumn breeze blew, rustling through the leaves of the towering oaks. Still early in the season, the canopy above us was vibrant green. Only the occasional bit of red and orange hinted that the summer season was coming to an end. It would have been more fitting, I thought, if the trees were bare and a biting wind was whipping ice pellets in my face. That was always the way I'd imagined this day.

"Into your hands, O Lord, we commend the soul of your servant," the short, stocky priest prayed, his arms lifted and his face turned up to the sky.

Padre Benzi stood alone at the head of the gleaming mahogany casket. Maybe that was for the best. Better for one devout man to draw His attention rather than the tainted souls of the men and women gathered in the cemetery. Not that the man in the casket had much hope for a heavenly afterlife.

I'd found him three days ago in his office, sitting behind his desk, his hands clasped over his abdomen. So much the same, but his eyes were different. Not cold, not narrowed with suspicion or widened in anger. They were vacant. Empty. Whatever had occupied his body—spirit or soul or the random firing of neurons—was gone.

355

I'd stood there waiting for relief to fill my chest, for bubbles of laughter to climb up my throat. I stared and I waited to feel something. Anything.

I felt nothing.

Lorenzo Costa was dead, and I felt nothing.

Raven stood next to me now, holding my hand. She squeezed lightly as the priest concluded his prayer and my father's casket was lowered into the ground.

I looked around at the black-clad men and women who'd come to pay their respects. Costas, Lucas, Lucianos; they were all here, standing stoically, every eye dry. We were going through the motions, but no one mourned the loss of Lorenzo Costa. No one would miss him.

"He was a fine leader," Enzo Luciano said, clasping my hand firmly as the interment concluded.

"He was a well-respected man, Nico," Amadeo said, standing next to his father.

One by one, they made their rounds, expressed their condolences for the loss of a strong man. Not a man who had been loved, not a man who would be remembered.

Vincent Luca approached last. He hugged Raven and then me, patting my back. Like the last time, I had no idea what to make of it. My own father had never hugged me once, never mind twice—not that I was suddenly starved for fatherly affection. It was just strange, in a not entirely unpleasant way.

"I am sorry for what will never be, son," he said as he drew back, "but you are welcome in my home."

"*For what will never be...*" The man was intuitive and honest; my respect for Raven's father grew even more. And to be welcomed to his home was a gift I was not too self-absorbed to recognize. The future of the Costas and the Lucas had become entwined, and he and I would be responsible for what came of it. *"Grazie, Signor* Luca. I appreciate your generosity."

He smiled. "Not generosity, son. I do not talk of business today, but rather family. *Famiglia,* Nico." He clapped me on the back once more, kissed his daughter's cheek, then strode across the rich green grass toward the parking lot.

And then only six of us remained. The only six people on this earth who really knew Lorenzo Costa; my mother, brothers, and I through our experiences with him, and Raven, through what I'd told her.

"He is at rest now," my mother said as a lone teardrop trickled down her pale cheek, her eyes had a faraway look to them.

I thought perhaps she mourned for what Lorenzo could have been more than for what he was. *"I am sorry for what will never be,"* *Signor* Luca had said, encapsulating in those few words everything that had been lost here.

Gabe nodded, but Caio and Sandro stood staring down at Lorenzo's casket. Neither of my youngest brothers had cried, but I didn't think it was due to the hatred Gabe and I had felt for the man. They looked shell-shocked, their faces blank, their eyes a little wider than usual. Lorenzo had been larger than life to Sandro and Caio, not the scum of the earth Gabe and I had known him to be.

Looking at them now, something hot and uncomfortable churned in my gut. *There's nothing but a monster sealed in that mahogany box,* part of me wanted to shout at them, but I couldn't force the words out. Maybe it was better to let them believe that our father was worthy of their mourning.

Perhaps I even envied them a little for it. I was still waiting, waiting to feel something. Maybe I wasn't as different from Lorenzo as I'd begun to hope.

"Gabe, take *Mamma* to the house. I'll be along shortly."

Gabe stared for a moment, then nodded. *"Dio sia con te, Papà,"* he said to the wooden box, then crossed himself, forehead, chest, left shoulder, then right. It seemed a little religious for Costa blood, but whatever helped him sleep at night.

My mother turned to me. "It's okay, Nico," she said as another tear slipped down her cheek. She wrapped her arms around me, but I got the feeling she was not seeking my support, but rather offering hers.

I'd never realized the depth of my mother's strength before, but I could feel it now in the sturdiness of her slender arms.

I hugged her back, wondering what she'd meant. *Was it okay that Lorenzo was dead? Was it okay that I felt nothing?* I didn't ask.

She let go after a while and took Gabe's arm.

"You too," I said to Sandro and Caio, and they fell into step behind Gabe.

I watched them go until they'd disappeared into the back of the black limo in the parking lot, then I looked back down at the casket.

Maybe now that they were gone, it would come to me.

"Nico, did you want a moment?" Raven offered gently, squeezing my hand tighter.

I shook my head. I wanted a moment away from them—from everyone else—but not her. I pulled her close, feeling the small, strong lines of her body against me.

"I don't feel anything," I confessed, still staring at the mahogany box.

"And that scares you?"

I nodded reluctantly, hating the admission. "Lorenzo was a cold, unfeeling bastard who wouldn't have shed a tear at my funeral, and here I am, dry-eyed at his. I need to feel something, Raven, so that I know I'm not like him."

She drew herself up on her toes until we were nearly eye to eye. "Kiss me," she said, closing most of the distance between us.

"I like your thinking, but that wasn't the kind of feeling I meant." I closed the remaining distance fast.

"Smart-ass," she muttered against my lips, then drew back just a little. "Kiss me, and think about what you feel, Nico. Tell me honestly if your father could ever have loved someone the way you love me."

I obeyed—which was a clear sign in itself that this woman had a hold on me unlike any other. But she was right. Touching her, kissing her did all the usual crazy shit to my body, but it was more than that; more than just physical.

There wasn't anything I wouldn't do for the woman in my arms. I'd die for her, I'd kill for her, and maybe most importantly, I'd live for her. Lorenzo Costa had lived for his empire. Now, that empire was mine, and I wouldn't make the same mistake.

"I know it's easy for me to say because I didn't really know your father, but I'm grateful to him, Nico. No matter how you look at it, there would have been no you without him, and that means there would have been no us. Regardless of his reasons, you're here because of him, and I'll be eternally grateful for that."

I nodded and pulled her so close I could feel her heart beating against my chest.

We were both quiet for a long time. I needed to leave. As the new head of the Costa family, my absence at the reception in the family home would not go unnoticed. But all I could do was hold Raven tight and stare at Lorenzo's casket.

It was Raven who leaned away eventually, just enough to look up at me. "Do you think maybe something happened to him that made him the way he was?"

"I know something did. He told me." Another father-son moment with Lorenzo I'd never forget, standing in my stone-walled hell when I was sixteen while the blood of one of Lorenzo's capos meandered toward the drain.

"No matter how devout a man appears to be, he cannot be trusted, Nico. Not men like him," Lorenzo had said, wrinkling his nose as he motioned to the dead man on the floor. *"Not even men of your own blood. Do you understand me?"*

Raven was silent, waiting.

"It was his younger brother," I said, remembering the paranoia that had climbed up my spine that day. "His only brother tried to kill him when they were teenagers. Lorenzo said there'd always been something off about Nico—that was his name," I explained with a dry grin. He'd named me after his murderous brother so that he'd never forget, never be tempted to get too close. "He said he'd looked out for the kid all his life, and then he woke up one night to a knife piercing his gut and his brother standing over him." I shrugged while Raven cringed. "Does that excuse what he became, do you think?"

She was silent for a long time, chewing on her bottom lip, but eventually, she shook her head. "No. Maybe it explains it, but I don't think it excuses it."

"But you're right," I said, lacing my fingers with hers. "Without him, I wouldn't exist; I would never have found you."

She smiled gently, but then her smile grew. "Actually, if you recall, I believe I was the one who found you."

"Really?" I scoffed. "You may have walked into Onyx, Raven, but I still remember the look in your eyes; right from the start, I was the one hunting you."

"Hunting, was it?" She chuckled, the sound inducing a warm feeling in my heart. "All right, we'll call it a draw. We found each other."

"I can live with that."

* * *

THANK YOU FOR READING: MAFIA KINGS:
CORRUPTED BOOK 2: CORRUPTED TEMPTATION

DON'T MISS THE FREE SIZZLING BONUS CHAPTER

EXCLUSIVE FREE BONUS CHAPTER

"Hit me," he said.

"What?" I asked, eyebrows furrowed together.

"Hit me, Raven."

"No."

He shook his head. "Not an option. If you won't let me keep you here under surveillance twenty-four seven, then you're going to train with me until you could pass as a Charlie's Angel. Now, hit me."

"Surveillance, huh?" I said, pressing my body against him. "I didn't know you were into that."

He laughed. "When it comes to you, Raven, I'm into everything." He tipped my head back and kissed along my jaw, sending delicious shivers down my spine.

Can't get enough of Raven and Nico? Download the free bonus scene for one more steamy chapter!

Download the FREE bonus chapter here -
https://geni.us/corruptedtbonus

What's Next?

Wow, I hope you enjoyed *Corrupted Temptation!* Your support means the world to me.

The next book in the Mafia Kings: Corrupted Series is Corrupted Protector.

Calling all Kittens! Come join the fun:

If you're thirsty for more discussions with other readers of the series, join my exclusive readers' group, Kiana's Kittens.

Join my private readers' group here - facebook.com/groups/KianasKittens

CAN YOU DO ME A HUGE FAVOR?

Would you be willing to leave me a review?

I'd be over the moon because just one positive review on Amazon is like buying the book a hundred times! Reader support is the lifeblood for Indie authors. It provides us the feedback we need to give readers what they want in future stories!

Your positive review would mean the world to me. You can post your review on Amazon or Goodreads. I'd be forever grateful, thank you from the bottom of my heart!